THE STAR CU

CLAIM THE VOID

KATE SHEERAN SWED

JOIN THE LIST!

Join my newsletter list to get "Highly Irregular," an exclusive *Parse Galaxy* story! You'll also get access to my VIP library, which has lots of other free stuff to read.

Sign up here: https://katesheeranswed.com/highly-irregular/

PRONUNCIATION GUIDE

- Echao - eck-AY-oh
- Echains - eck-AY-ins
- Pheon - fay-on

- Drachao - drah-KAY-oh
- Drachains - drah-KAY-ins

CHAPTER 1

IF THERE WAS one truth Damian Riddle held sacred, it was that the seediest places in the galaxy could be one and the same with the most beautiful ones.

Take the Dragon's Luck Orbiting Casino, as an example.

On approach, the monstrosity of a space station twinkled like a multicolored star. Damian always thought the fat, disk-like shape looked a bit too much like the coins his father expected patrons to start losing as soon as they'd disembarked from their private taxis and luxury cruisers, and even public shuttles like the one he was currently riding.

He stood by the viewport with the rest of the crowd, less because he wanted to see the casino than because he'd draw attention if he stayed in his seat when the rest of the passengers felt the need to press their hands to the glass in wondering admiration. The light of the nearby trade Current, which the shuttle had recently exited, bathed the entire station in a turquoise glow, increasing the carefully constructed impression of other-worldliness.

Damian leaned one shoulder against the frame, watching the other passengers idly and wishing he hadn't left his duster behind on his last job. It was chilly on the shuttle and, to put it somewhat mildly, he hadn't been feeling his best lately. Mostly, though, he felt wrong without the weight of the jacket around his shoulders, and the helpful ability to raise the collar and hide his face in shadow.

Though in this crowd, the duster would probably call attention rather than deflect it, and he definitely wanted to slip in and out of the hellhole of a casino without being seen. This crowd was packed with little kids calling out the colors as the casino shifted from purple to blue to pink, while their parents traded excited glances over their heads. This crowd had couples and giggling groups of friends. This crowd was moonbeams and candy shops, while Damian was leather and blood.

Of course, he wasn't the only one who'd come here alone. The families and couples and gaggles of friends, they'd probably all been saving for a Center System year to afford this trip. The hotel, the food, the shows—and, of course, the gambling. If they wanted to hand their hard-earned tokens to his father, they could go right ahead.

They weren't the ones that worried him.

The ones that worried him wore shabby suits, shirts with frayed button holes, and dresses with patches where the sequins had worn off. They haunted the edges of the crowd as Damian did, watching the casino draw nearer with hunger burning in their eyes, the kind that said they were here for that one lucky round at a card table, that single life-changing throw of the dice.

Once, Damian would have tried to dissuade them. Today, he forced himself to look away. He was just here to retrieve his spaceship. And his jacket. Nothing more.

The shuttle took its time docking, no doubt a calculated move to increase the crowd's anticipation. Damian's father was many things, but a poor businessman was not one of them; he would have tested every landing scenario multiple times.

By the time the transport doors huffed open, Damian was working hard to keep his hands relaxed. He stuck near the center of the crowd, shadowing a tall, grandfatherly looking fellow and doing what he could to mask his own noticeable height.

Sneaking into the den of iniquity owned by one's father? Not the easiest feat. But if there was one thing Damian thrived on, it was the pursuit of the impossible.

At the moment, he wasn't quite feeling up to 'impossible.' With that never-ending headache rapping at his temples and the constant prickles in his chest, was hoping to settle for 'that was suspiciously easy.'

Which, so far, it had been.

Flashing banners named this level the 'Winners Welcome Deck.' Feather-capped drones bobbed through the crowd like deranged tropical birds, swooping to drop strings of beads around visitors' necks and plop drinks into willing hands. Damian ducked to avoid a particularly aggressive glass of champagne, stooping his shoulders as he shuffled toward the nearest side stairwell. The casino did its best to obscure these exit points behind strings of lights and flashy holo-figure directories—Dad wanted everyone to pass through his preferred entrance funnel—but they also needed additional doors in case of security issues or emergencies. And Damian knew exactly where to find them.

He skirted behind a curtain of purple hanging lights, shoving aside a blinking pineapple, and exited into the stairwell, letting out a breath of relief. Crowds were terrible.

His father wouldn't have hidden Damian's ship up here near the guest docks. But though Damian didn't quite know this place as well as some of the others in which he'd spent the various shards of his childhood—by the time his father established this place, he'd been old enough to be more interested in the wearers of sequined gowns than in finding secret passages—he knew it well enough.

He hurried down the stairs, leaving the excited chatter of the crowd in the distance, until he found the entrance to Level X.

Level X. So dramatic. Might as well post a neon sign: 'Evil Doings Here.'

Subtlety. An art lost on so many. Damian pushed the door open, shivering at the breath of cold air that rushed at his face. Or maybe it was just that he was still a bit under the weather. Hard to say.

At least it was unlikely that Level X had any cameras. His father would not want to record the shady activities that went on down here. Damian pushed ahead, walking more quickly now. Most of the berths were shut fast, as if this were merely a storage level. Nothing to see here. No treasure. No card games. Certainly no crimes, not at all. Just boring corrugated metal doors.

Damian knew exactly where his father would be hiding the *Quandary*. And no doubt good old Dad, aka Archimedes Sol, knew that *Damian* knew. But Damian knew that Archie knew that *he* knew, so they were pretty much even on that score.

He'd slip in undetected, steal his ship back, and get the hell out of here, with Archie none the wiser.

Damian made his way to the end of the hall, where a single black door waited amid an ocean of silver. His stepsister, Ivy, had shown him how to bypass the control panels down here without being noticed, so all he had to do was jimmy the—

Before he could slice any wires or activate any magnets, the door whipped open with a deafening rumble.

"It's about short-circuiting time."

The bot that squatted before him had no arms to place on her hips—and no hips to place them on—but that didn't stop her from looking like she might stick out one of her stumpy utility claws and rip his off so she could use them to demonstrate her disapproval. She wouldn't, not Lex, though she definitely *could*.

"Hey, Lex." Hiding his surprise, Damian ducked inside the

berth, pulling the door down behind him. Not that it mattered if Lex picked up on his reaction to her sudden appearance; it was more habit than anything. "Almost took my head off there."

"Don't you 'hey Lex' me," the bot said. "We've been worried about you, young man."

Damian suspected that Lex had been a nanny module before she'd been repurposed. She was shaped like a stocky cone, and her middle was always stuffed with tools and supplies. Bandages, mostly. Tissues. The occasional peppermint candy.

Behind Lex, the *Quandary* waited. Damian let himself exhale his relief at the sight of her, safe and whole.

The ship's design was one he'd obsessed over for years; shining black and fat through the middle, she had four claw-like landing props that gave the impression of an overlarge crab. In flight, the claws could retrieve lost items or salvage, and each was equipped with a pair of hidden plasma cannons. Very useful.

The Dragon's Luck employed expensive atmo shields on all its docks so that clientele wouldn't have to wait for the bays to pressurize before pouring out to have their fun. This berth was no different; the shine of the stars glinted outside, highlighting the *Quandary*'s every curve. He could even make out the pebble-like glow of a Torrent System planet out there. Scope, most likely. Prettier from space than it was on the ground, that was for sure.

In and out. No problem.

Damian headed up the gangplank, at the top of which a second bot was spinning in anxious circles. For some reason, its makers had fashioned it to look like a rodent, with skittering feet and a long tail. It also had the disposition of one. He didn't have much excuse for keeping it around, except that it'd been an impulse buy. It was a tolerable engineering assistant, too.

"We waited and waited and waited!" the bot trilled. Its voice was half squeak, half clatter.

Damian stepped over it, taking care not to tread on its tail. "Meet anyone interesting, Mojo?"

"No! I was much too afraid to leave the ship!"

Probably for the best.

Quandary's gangplank led to a single living-and-piloting area that gave the illusion of absolutely nothing to hide. Trap doors in the floor provided access to engineering, and there was no reason for any visitor, whether Fleet or Trade Federation or criminal cartel, to suspect the presence of hidden smuggling hatches below *that*.

Damian's cot was situated to the right, his collection of mechanical clocks untouched on the circular shelf he'd installed to display them above the room like a crown. He'd been gone too long; the clocks sat silent, clearly in need of winding. He flexed his hands, resisting the urge to count them, to make sure none had gone missing, as he breathed a deep lungful of cedar and new carpet and the pine-scented oil he used to keep the seats from squeaking.

His own ship, finally. After months of pin-balling around the galaxy, he was home.

Mojo skittered around his feet, so close that Damian feared the bot might try to race up his leg. Again. "Are you back for good?" Mojo asked. "Are you? Are you?"

"Nah," Damian said. "Just here for my jacket."

Mojo let out a sob, and Lex extended an arm to place the quivering bot on her head. "He's joking," she soothed.

Damian dropped into the pilot's seat. Every minute he lingered here was a minute his father might realize he'd come. Avoiding cameras was all well and good, but no doubt there'd been security goons lurking around up there. Who could say what old Archimedes would do if he learned his son had come to call? Another murder attempt, perhaps.

Or worse, he'd offer Damian a job.

"Where's Bruce?" he asked.

"Why?" Mojo sounded petulant now. "Bruce is mean."

Damian ran his hand along the dash, reveling in the smooth depressions of the controls. "I need him to help me reprogram the trade Currents."

There was a brief silence. "That's not a thing, dear," Lex said.

"It's true," Mojo added. Damian wasn't looking at the bots, but judging by the enthusiastic amount of clicking and clacking, he suspected Mojo might be jumping up and down on Lex's head. "The parameters of the trade Currents are confined to this sector. In 7787, the Dhoman Science Group tried to investigate the possibility of extending the Current network, but the results were—"

"A disastrous failure, I know." Damian initiated the startup sequence. "But they didn't have me."

"Did you hit your head, dear?" Lex asked. "I took the liberty of replenishing the nano-healer supply. Perhaps—"

"Where is Bruce?" Damian lifted his fingers from the controls and swiveled his chair around, giving the bots his best disapproving eyebrow. He liked bots for company; they were typically less complicated than humans. Sometimes, though, it took a firm hand.

Bruce might be sulking in the smuggling compartments, or in the cabinet where Damian kept his jacket; he did that, sometimes. Not that Damian would blame his third bot for needing a break from Lex and Mojo. But if that were the case, they'd simply point him out, and he'd emerge grumpy but curious about Damian's assignment.

The bots weren't wrong. The mysterious Currents that wound through the Parse Galaxy, allowing physics-defying travel speeds, had not as yet been reprogrammed. Not by anyone.

Damian, however, knew a fair number of facts about them that no one else did.

"Also!" Mojo squeaked, "Why won't the ship start?!"

Damian swiveled back around, hoping the bot wasn't just making a bid for a subject change.

But no, bots didn't do that. Usually. Mojo was right; the dashboard remained dark. The startup sequence had paused.

"Investigate please, Mojo," Damian said.

Mojo was already scurrying down from Lex's head. It opened the engineering hatch and disappeared inside, reappearing after a few seconds. "Reactor's disconnected," it said.

Cursing himself for skipping diagnostics, Damian pushed up out of the chair with more energy than he felt. He wanted to get underway, to work on this experiment. Before it was too late.

But his father would not have left the *Quandary* sitting here without a failsafe. Not in a thousand years.

Too cozy, indeed. Damian stepped down the gangplank, then used one of *Quandary*'s under-hull handles to ease himself beneath the ship. He popped open the exterior control panel and dug his hands into the rainbow of wires. With no time bomb ticking down in his face, he'd happily spend a week fussing with wires and cords, merely for the fun of it. And the pretty colors.

Today, he needed to hurry.

Not least because the reactor wasn't disconnected at all. It was being jammed. Damian's fingers closed around the telltale box, its smooth, milk-white opalescence giving away its purpose. His father loved beautiful tech. With a quick pull, Damian wrenched the offending box out of the control panel.

"Should be good to go now," he said.

Pain shot through his wrist, sudden and bright, and he looked down to see a set of beautifully manicured nails digging into his shirt. Sharp enough to pierce the fabric, they curled painfully into his skin, drawing little wells of blood around the claw-like tips. Lovely.

The wounds that laced up his arms had long-since healed,

but they remained tender. As a general rule, he tried not to expose them to sharp objects.

He also kept them hidden beneath long sleeves whenever he could. Few people knew they existed at all.

Sharp red nails. Fingers curved with feminine grace. Knowledge of his scars. And a whiff of smoky-sweet perfume. Only one person it could be, unfortunately.

Damian swung out from under the ship before she could pull him, the jammer box clenched in his fist. So much for getting in and out without detection.

"Damian," his latest stepmother said. "You didn't tell us you'd be stopping by."

CHAPTER 2

WHEN DAMIAN HAD last laid eyes upon Heloise Hall, the woman had been standing over him with a knife, gleefully and bloodily peeling his embedded inlay tech out of his arms. After which she'd intended to murder him, with the full blessing of his father.

Yes, he'd robbed her. A little bit. But she'd deserved it.

Thank goodness for foiled plans and excellent stepsisters. From a different stepmother, of course. No spawn of Heloise's could ever be counted as an ally.

Back then, Heloise had favored backless evening gowns and slits for miles. Now, she wore a tailored black suit that hugged her curves as tightly as the gowns once had. Her heels brought her near his height, if not quite equal to it. She'd bound half her golden hair into a crown of braids, while the rest flowed across her shoulders in pristine curls.

Heloise Hall was a beautiful woman. She also led one of the most secretive and dangerous criminal cartels in the galaxy. While the rest of the cartels stumbled around like drunken chickens, pecking and scratching each other for scraps of feed, Heloise's Catch Clan strolled by with a machete and casually lopped off their heads. They were ruthless, efficient, and not remotely prone to distraction.

"Hey, Hella," Damian said, tipping her his third-best grin. Heloise didn't deserve the best one. She didn't deserve this one, either, but he wasn't in the mood for extreme nuance, not with her nails about to carve new wounds into his flesh. She enjoyed drawing blood, Heloise. "Just passing through. No need to intrude on your marital bliss. Tell me, did Archie propose before you tried to kill his only son, or after? My timeline's never straight there."

Heloise dug her nails deeper into his wrist. "Funny thing about your ship." Her voice was like liquid honey mixed with flash-pepper seeds. Smooth and warm, with a promise of heat on the finish. "It refuses to leave without you."

"It's loyal like that."

A smile from Heloise was a harbinger of evil to come, a debt paid in bloody tokens. She gave him one now, and he raised his eyebrows. Like it didn't scare him one bit.

"Your bot, however," Heloise said. "That was more portable. Interesting thing. Irascible."

Damian's throat went dry, and he narrowly prevented himself from swallowing hard. She'd notice that. She'd notice any sign of weakness, any reaction. He just kept his own smile on his face, locking his fear down in his chest. He was accustomed to that, even those he counted among his non-enemies.

Damian didn't do friends.

Heloise had taken Bruce. And without Bruce, Damian had no chance of reprogramming the Currents. No chance of finding his way to a cure for the alien disease that ailed him. No chance at all.

If Heloise knew that, she'd probably throw a celebration gala. Damian Riddle, dead at long last. Her only regret would be that she hadn't managed it with her own hands.

"Why not take the full set?" he asked, keeping his voice casual. "There's another pair of bots in there for the taking, you know."

Heloise rolled her eyes. "The other two are worse than toys. You made alterations to the third yourself. That makes it... special." She tilted her head. "But you are not looking well, Damian. Where have you been all these months?"

"Assisting a crew even more dangerous than yours," he said. "You would not believe the depths of their depravity, truly. Best not to think about it. And I look fine, thank you. I'm trying a new beauty regimen. Cella blossoms and apple seeds. Rejuvenating. You ought to try it. You're looking a little peaked yourself."

She stepped closer, fingers still locked on his arm, and let her gaze drop to his neck. He had the sudden urge to hunch his shoulders, to bury himself deeper into the shirt and hide the evidence of his infirmity. Why hadn't he thrown his duster on before coming out here?

"I've heard rumors," she said. "I wonder if they're true?"

She reached for the top button of his shirt, intention glittering in her eyes. Damian twisted his wrist, breaking her grip, and shoved her back toward the door. She stumbled, though she righted herself with impressive quickness, considering the height of those heels.

Damian threw the jammer on the floor, shattering the delicate case of moonstone. He'd need to have Mojo sweep the ship for additional devices.

Assuming they managed to escape.

If it were just Heloise, it'd be the work of a moment. She was strong, and she was fast—smart, too—but even as sick as he was, Damian could take her.

Unfortunately, it was never just Heloise.

Three of her ever-present bodyguards peeled away from the wall where they'd been lingering in the shadows and headed for

Damian. The closest one was a brick of a man, with beetle-black hair and shoulders the size of a hov-train car.

"Carter," Damian said as he ducked out of the path of the man's fist. Carter was big, but he was also slow. A good thing, too, considering that the other two men were still skirting around to either side of the fight, as if they each intended to take one of Damian's arms and pluck it off. "Haven't seen you in a minute. Reilly started at the academy yet?"

Carter's expression darkened, and he took another swing.

"Guess she opted for poetry instead," Damian said. He dodged a third swing, feinting right as if to attempt a punch of his own. As Carter lunged, Damian crouched and swiveled, somersaulting straight into the big man's legs.

Not graceful, perhaps, but it did the job. Carter went down flailing, his head smacking into the floor with a loud *thuck!*

Damian rolled to his feet as the remaining guards closed in on him from either side, their features mostly obscured by the blur of the fight, the gleam of the yellow-tinted lights above. Damian caught a flash of light against a bald head on one of them, and an ill-considered chain around the neck of the other.

He made a grab for the chain, hoping it was strong, and used it to jerk its owner forward. Surprised, the man cartwheeled his arms, trying uselessly to grab hold of Damian. But Damian's reach was long, and it wasn't much trouble to slam the necklace-wearer straight into baldy's shining skull. Another satisfying *thuck!* and the men lay on the floor, unmoving.

Heloise strode toward him, her face impassive. As if he hadn't just taken out her bodyguards. As if she were entering a spa for the day, and expected superior treatment.

Assuming the spas she visited allowed hand cannons. Because she was also brandishing one of those, the barrel staring him down like a black hole. Damian raised his hands, still breathing hard from the fight. Harder than he should be.

"Archimedes will want to see you," she said. "And I plan to deliver."

Mojo came zooming down the gangplank and popped out onto the floor. "Starter sequence initialized!" it said. "You can come back in and—"

The bot skirted under Heloise's feet, and she stumbled, losing her balance and cracking her knee on the floor. The hand cannon went flying.

"Oh!" Mojo cried. "I'm sorry! I'm sorry!"

Damian wasn't. He scooped up the bot and dashed for the gangplank, punching the door closed on his way into the ship. He couldn't resist peering out at Heloise through the narrowing crack. "Worse than toys, did you say?"

Heloise drew a pistol and aimed at his face. Damian ducked, but it didn't matter; the door slammed shut, and her shot ricocheted harmlessly off the hull.

Damian headed for the pilot's seat, heart hammering hard against his ribs. He'd never been opposed to a good brawl, and usually would have taken grim pleasure in fighting twice as many opponents. Though that would take a fair bit more trickery to win, and likely would have ended with him in a holding cell or worse.

But he would have taken pleasure in it. That was the key point.

Today, the fight left him feeling like a peeled torkfruit. Wrung out. Exposed. His hands were trembling, and a bitter taste lingered on the back of his tongue. This wasn't how it was supposed to go. At all.

Hands on the controls, Damian pushed the *Quandary* out of the bay and away from the Dragon's Luck, making for the blue-green flow of the Current. The bots were unusually quiet, and he glanced over his shoulder to make sure they were both still with him.

They were.

"Nice work, Mojo," he said.

Mojo jumped—its wheels actually came off the ground—and began to spin in a circle. "I hope she's okay. I didn't mean to trip her."

"I said *nice* work," Damian replied. "Tripping her was a good thing."

"Then why do I feel so bad?"

"Because you need to work on your pirate skills." Damian urged the ship along faster, though no other vessels had taken off from the casino to pursue them. He wondered what Archimedes would say when Heloise revealed that he'd been there, and that he'd stolen his ship back.

Perhaps his father had only been holding the *Quandary* because of Heloise's wishes. Perhaps he didn't care one way or the other. It'd been one thing to know that his father had been aware of the damn woman's murder attempt—the first one—and another to learn the man had married her.

One did not marry a woman who'd tried to kill their son. It wasn't done.

Didn't matter. With luck, Damian would never have to return to this cursed place. He had his ship. He had his bots, most of them.

He had his plans, too.

"Bruce will be at the Catch Clan's hold," he said. Their main seat of business was out in the Fringe, on a planet called Bromar. It was part of a binary system, one of the busier spots in the Fringe, with a couple of inhabitable surfaces and a handful of stations. "We'll need to retrieve him."

Mojo didn't stop spinning. "They'll know you're coming."

Damian eased the ship into the Current, steeling himself for the wash of headache-inducing sound he'd grown accustomed to when traversing the things. But nothing happened; the Current remained silent.

He didn't know if that was a good sign or a bad one.

"They'll expect me," he agreed, setting the controls on auto. He let himself relax against the headrest. "But I need Bruce."

"To help you slingshot the Currents." Lex sounded decidedly uncertain. "Are you sure you're okay?"

It was a fair question. He might as well be saying he planned to bend the laws of physics, or break them altogether. There were no known ways to adjust the flow of the Currents. The exits could be reprogrammed, but otherwise, the technology was mostly a mystery.

Or at least, it had been.

"No." Damian made the admission with his eyes still shut, the watery light of the Current flickering behind his eyelids. "I think I may be dying, actually. Also, funny story. I'm part alien."

There was a brief silence, during which Damian wondered idly if he might need to adjust Lex's processors.

"Nothing's ever simple with you, is it?" she asked finally.

Damian rolled his shoulders. The ship was warm, the seat more comfortable than any he'd visited lately. His arm throbbed where Heloise's claws had pierced it, and the skin on his neck was prickling with pins and needles. "That would just be boring," he said.

And then, with the blissfully familiar background sounds and smells of home, he fell asleep.

CHAPTER 3

THE KEY TO A GOOD ARTICLE, a good human interest story, was always in the details.

Shannon Forest collected details like a weaver collected thread, tucking them away to add color to a story, a feed post, or a gossip column. Details were the bite of chocolate in a handful of nuts and dried torkfruit. Details were flutes trilling in the background of a rock song, a single ruby gemstone in a sea of sand.

Details, whether good, bad, or ugly, told the reader everything.

Unfortunately, most of the details on Bromar were ugly ones. She'd been staying in a town called Gamerin, which on any other planet would have been dubbed a seaside town; but Bromar's seas were the color of rust, and they made the entire town smell of ancient metal. The water wasn't potable or swimmable. Any building that touched it ended up with stained foundations.

Why they'd placed a town here at all, she didn't know.

Gamerin had other details, though none that particularly recommended it. Cracked cobblestones, where cobblestones existed at all. Spiral signs splashed on certain street corners to warn people away from Catch Clan territory. Rusted out gravity anchors and spiderwebs in doorways and smells of old ale, burned oil, and that ever-present metallic tinge that the seas pumped into the air.

Shannon wanted to find kittens tucked safe in the hood of a criminal's sweater. She wanted to unearth secret gardens and meet assassins with big dreams, or—she *was* growing desperate— at least a stamp collection. She wanted to find more to the story.

If the 'more' she sought was here at all, it was buried. Which was why she needed to get on the inside.

Shannon slipped between two squat, mud-gray apartments buildings and padded down the shallow steps that led to Masters Pub. The door let out a long squeak when she pushed it open, as if she'd woken it from a deep sleep.

Phil Masters sat snoozing at the end of the bar, his head propped against one hand. Despite her noisy entrance, he didn't rouse until she gave him a businesslike tap on the shoulder. At which point he snorted and jerked his head up, a default spark of fear igniting in his eyes before he registered her identity.

"Oh," he said, propping his head back in his hand with a yawn. "It's just you."

With jowls to rival a bulldog's and a scraggly beard of short white whiskers, Masters had a permanently disreputable look about him. His jacket was wrinkled, his thin hair waving around his scalp in little wisps, and a cloud of liquor smells hung around him like a fog.

Still, of all the proprietors she'd met in Gamerin, he was the most lucid. And the least likely to kick her out on her ass.

Also, he'd been willing to make a deal.

Shannon opened her fliptab, where she'd left the information he requested open on the screen, and shoved it in front of his face, giving him a moment to focus his bloodshot eyes. "I got what you wanted," she said.

Masters squinted at the screen. "That's hardly a closeup—"

Shannon swiped to the next photo, and the next. "There are fifty. Your business partner's definitely embezzling and using the money to invest in Fox Clan's new ships. Best show these to your Catch Clan friends before they find out and assume you're involved, too."

Masters rubbed a hand over his face. "Leave the scheming to me, girl. What's your price?"

Girl. She was almost thirty. Shannon let the comment go, leaning an elbow on the counter and weighing the pros and cons of reaching across the bar to pour herself a drink. It would be a power move, for sure. And she could use a drink right now. On the con side, she was as likely to lose her balance and *fall* over the bar, thus negating the power move. Also, she'd seen Masters watering down the gin with her own eyes.

She stayed put. "I want you to get me in to the party tonight."

Masters chuckled, eyes lighting with a hint of challenge. "What party?"

"I know Catch Clan's having its annual gala tonight, and I want in."

He leaned forward, straining for a bottle of amber liquid that might once have been whiskey, depending on how much water he'd added to it. He poured himself a finger. "How the Fringe do you know that, girl?"

She'd been hiding out here for several weeks now, during which time the vendor traffic on the main street had peaked at ten hov carts per hour. For the last three days, it'd been steadily running at double that. The market shelves had been picked over this morning, too, if not completely bare—the Catch Clan would get the majority of their deliveries privately—but in the end, it was the wine that told the story. All the mid-to-high-range wine was gone. Gift-range wine, no doubt swiped up by guests with images to uphold.

She'd purchased a bottle herself, at that. One of the last.

She didn't say any of this to Masters. Instead, she plucked his drink out of his hand and swallowed the whiskey, wincing at the watery bite of the liquid. He didn't even save the decent stuff for himself. "You want the pictures or not?"

Masters watched her finish his drink. "Listen, girl," he said, "you don't want to go to the cartel. They're gonna recognize you in a second. Probably already know you're in town."

Shannon winced. Ever since she'd accidentally released that article out of a war-occupied space station—the only article to leak through the occupation—going undercover had been... complicated.

She was just a little bit famous at the moment.

"The party's my best shot." She held up a hand to staunch further protest, though Masters hadn't opened his mouth. "See these heels? I don't do heels like this when there's no party to go with them."

He barked a wet laugh, then wiped his mouth with the back of his hand. "You should," she said. "You're short."

She raised her eyebrows at him, and he sighed. "Fine," he said. "I'll take you. But at least go in disguise, will you?"

———

Shannon had been present at more than a few celebrity festivals, balls, parties, mixers, and premieres. With few exceptions, her job had been to line up along the sidewalk beside the other reporters with a microphone in her hand and a camera hooked to her shoulder, and to shout through the crowd, hoping someone important would bestow a catchy comment on her. Or, better yet, a juicy one.

And yes, being short made that job much harder.

For a few events, she'd managed to sneak all the way into the party, hiding with the caterers or bribing an usher to kick out someone's grandmother.

Somehow, the Catch Clan's annual party was simultaneously like these events and very, very different.

There was no press here, of course, and no sign of law enforcement. Plenty of Catch Clan guards, recognizable by their muscles and the watchful way they scanned the crowd for signs of danger. Some of them shadowed close to one particular clan member or another—Shannon caught sight of Ian Moore, the Clan's second officer, as she and Masters approached—but many simply watched the crowd, sidling into it and through it, eyes dropping to pockets and chests and thighs as though they could sense the presence of firearms. Perhaps they could.

There were drinks in abundance, even outside the multi-story apartment building where the party was to take place. There was ice clinking and heels alternately clicking and scuffing on the uneven ground. There were guests laughing, a few of them, though the sound was uniformly restrained, as if they were attending a funeral rather than a gala.

The music that pumped through the windows, loud enough to vibrate her molars, suggested the dance floor would be more like a club than a ballroom. There were no cameras, no autographs, and very few smiles.

There was, however, a bouncer. Masters approached the woman with clear trepidation, wiping his hands on his pants every few steps. Shannon wanted to smack him on the head and tell him to chill. The bouncer was already watching them, her penciled-in eyebrow quirked just high enough to suggest that not enough weird stuff had happened yet tonight, and she was ready to take it on.

That could be a very good thing, or a very bad one.

Shannon had let her black hair down around her shoulders,

where she usually secured it in a loose bun. Loose strands kept brushing against the back of her neck, and she had to resist the urge to mess with them. Masters had wanted her to go in disguise, but short of showing up in costume at a party that clearly was not a masquerade, there wasn't much she could do. Aside from the atmosphere-challenging height of her heels and the metric ton of shimmery powder she'd slathered onto her cheeks and arms. It would have to be enough.

She felt stuffed into the dress she'd chosen, which featured a short, puffy skirt and a tight top that wound around one shoulder, leaving the other bare. She'd have preferred something simpler, but she couldn't very well show up slacks and a leather jacket. Not if she hoped to infiltrate this gang.

Masters sidled up to the bouncer and gave her a nod. He was sweating profusely now, his jowls bouncing. "Mellie," he said. "How's the party so far?"

The penciled-in eyebrow ticked up a little higher. "I wouldn't know, Phil. I'm out here." She gave Shannon a look, as if sizing her up. "And so are you."

Shannon smiled brightly, taking the opportunity to snap a first impression. Mellie said 'I'm out here' like it was a joke, like it didn't matter, but there was the slightest twist to her lips that said she regretted the fact that she was working tonight instead of enjoying the party. She had on bright pink lipstick, and there were sparkles dabbed in her black braids, like she hoped to let them out of the tight crown she'd arranged them in and do some dancing herself.

"Ah," Masters said. "This is my niece. Katlyn. Didn't know she'd be in town. Was hoping to show her the party."

"Are *you* even on the list, Phil?"

"Ah, yes." Masters scrubbed a hand over his head, sending what was left of his hair into a riot of staticky spikes. "Yes, I am."

Mellie paused, eyes flicking back and forth like she was checking something on her eye screen. Shannon had never liked eye screens; they obscured the world, and therefore its details. She had one, but she rarely turned it on. The software probably needed an update, or ten.

"You're right," Mellie said, refocusing her eyes on Masters. "To my unending surprise. But you didn't clear a plus-one. Sorry, kid."

Shannon would have bet all the tokens she had left that she and Mellie were close to the same age. She might even have a few years on the bouncer. But she just smiled, batting her eyelashes.

Mellie shifted on her feet, glancing over her shoulder and into the party, and Shannon took a second to size her up. If Shannon was disguised in shimmer and tulle, the bouncer was disguised in shoulder pads and heel lifts. She was trying to make herself look bigger, more formidable, but her figure was actually fairly slight. Strong, sure. But on the petite side, for a bouncer.

Shannon leaned in, engaging her best conspiratorial smile. "Uncle Phil said they hired Torrent System dancers to come in."

She felt Masters startle and turn to blink at her in surprise. He didn't know about the dancers. *Keep it together, Phil,* she thought.

"Don't believe everything he says," Mellie replied. "Dancers, yes. Torrent... I wouldn't bet on it."

She glanced over her shoulder again, though, licking her lips. As Shannon watched, she lifted herself gently onto the balls of her feet and then back down. Probably didn't even realize she was doing it.

If Mellie wasn't a former dancer herself, Shannon would eat her own camera.

"Uncle Phil could watch the door for a sec," Shannon offered. "If you want to watch the performance. He's trusted, right?"

Mellie turned back, the eager spark in her eyes making her look younger. "Just for a minute," she said.

Shannon clasped her hands together and gave a little jump—the best one she could manage in these heels—trying to look like the kind of clueless niece who'd beg to get in to a Catch Clan party. "Thank you!" she said as Mellie opened the door, then hurried into the party on light steps. Shannon half expected the bouncer to turn a pirouette on her way in.

Masters shot Shannon a warning look, but she just waved as the door shut him outside, leaving her in the darkness of the entry hall.

Who threw a party with a pitch-black entry hall? Not very inviting. Maybe it was a test: make it inside without falling on your face, and you're one of us.

They must teach their thugs to see in the dark, she thought, feeling her way along the wall. Music vibrated through the stones, and every breath brought the thick aroma of cella blossom smoke, mixed with something darker and more acidic.

The passage curved, and pulsing fuchsia lights reflected along the walls, beckoning her forward. Before she stepped out of the shadows, Shannon shed her tulle skirt, transforming the dress into a sleek black number that hugged her body like a shield. After a brief moment of indecision, she decided to leave her hair hanging loose. She was here to infiltrate, not to interview. Not yet.

Smoothing her skirt one last time, Shannon strode out of the shadows and into the party. It was time to get to work.

CHAPTER 4

THE FLEET RECORDS, Damian knew, listed a scant four hundred and seventy-seven habitable surfaces in the Parse Galaxy. They counted a fair number of stations, orbiting platforms, and interstellar mines, though ironically, they left out the Fleet ships themselves—upon which plenty of soldiers made their entire existence. They counted belt asteroids that were contained to certain systems, but they skipped interstellar ones.

They missed a lot, the Fleet.

Despite having joined up himself for a full three years for the sake of stealing an itsy bitsy bit of technology—that'd been a good heist—Damian didn't claim to understand their logic. At this point, his count of habitable surfaces was nearing double their estimate. The number of nooks and crannies defied imagination, from teensy science colonies to single-fugitive outposts. There were supposedly uninhabitable moons where he'd dwelled without a helmet for weeks at a time. There were stolen domes that'd been popped onto the most inhospitable rocks, and people who dug like moles to live unbothered at the center of remote asteroids.

Perhaps he simply took on a broader definition when it came to the term 'inhabited.'

Or perhaps the Fleet didn't know which rocks to turn over.

Take Bromar, as an example. Take Gamerin, its primary city —and the primary seat of Catch Clan's misdeeds. Damian would wager the Fleet simply chose not to turn over this particular rock. It was always possible that they opted to pretend they didn't know about it while keeping a sharp eye in the background. That *would* be like its Commander. Not a man to tip his hand, if he could avoid it.

Either way, Damian couldn't blame the Fleet for turning its righteous assistance on other, more deserving portions of the Galaxy. He respected the Fleet, ish—though no amount of torture would ever force that admission from his lips—but the less deserving spots needed a protector, too. Or at least a rat to bite the asses of the more treacherous bosses from time to time.

He made his way down *Quandary*'s gangplank to the tune of shouting and scuffling feet. Passing hov carts slammed regularly against the uneven cobblestones, most of them too broken to stay aloft for long, while mismatched drones buzzed about on no particular path. As he left the outrageously expensive berth where he'd docked the *Quandary*, a pair of button drones came within a hair of smashing into one another.

After the cacophony that'd lived inside his head for the last few weeks, it was simultaneously overwhelming and comforting to be among so many real sounds, rather than psychic murmurings from a technology no one understood.

"I should accompany you on your infiltration." Lex rolled along beside him as he entered the melee, scanning the open-air passage with clear disapproval. As if she expected danger to pop out from behind one of the many bent door frames.

Since he didn't know how they'd gotten bent in the first

place, he supposed it was a reasonable theory. "You have Bruce's signal?"

Lex made a chirping sound, which Damian had come to interpret as a yes. "He's in the Catch Clan's seat. On one of the upper levels, for some reason."

Yes, well, Catch Clan no doubt had plenty of hidey holes. Who could say where they'd stash a stolen bot?

Lex was still scanning, the yellow lights above her visual input band blinking worriedly.

"We've seen worse places," Damian reminded her. "I'll be fine."

"It's not the place I'm worried about," Lex said.

Ignoring her concern, Damian turned back, giving the *Quandary* a final look. He was reluctant to leave the ship again so soon, though it had nothing to do with his own wellbeing. It was more about the ship's questionable accommodations; the landing fees hadn't even procured him a fully functioning security barrier. He didn't want to lose the ship again.

Of course, most thieves would try the locked doors here on the ground and move on. A thief like Damian, though, would try for the open ceiling, where the shield didn't fully close.

Yes, it would take a climb, and a fifty-fifty chance of cracking his head open on the ship instead of landing inside it. But it was more than doable.

Luckily, most thieves were not like Damian. And besides, *Quandary* ran for him and him alone. That was the way it'd always been.

"Stay here," he said. "Be ready to leave in a hurry."

"I don't like it," Lex said.

"Neither do I."

At least he had his duster back. He let the jacket flow unhindered around his calves as he strode out into the port, nearly upsetting an overladen hov cart in the process. The driver shouted at him, but he ignored the man's ire and continued on, shouldering his way through the crowd.

Thick sepia fog clogged the air, no doubt dragged in from the bizarre seas that bubbled around Gamerin like an unappetizing stew. It made it difficult to see where he was going, but it would also obscure his presence here. Lex and Mojo had scanned the *Quandary* for tracking devices and found nothing, which was unsurprising, given that his father and Heloise had no doubt intended that jammer to stop him from leaving at all. Still, Damian liked a good backup plan, and Heloise was no fool. Catch Clan would be looking for him here.

And indeed, as he followed Gamerin's winding streets toward Catch Clan's not-so-secret headquarters, it became clear that they'd increased their security since his last foray onto this planet. The streets were thick with patrols, Catch Clan's spiral logos flashing on half the people who passed, lighting up arm bands and chest emblems and even the occasional belt buckle.

But as Damian proceeded through the streets, keeping an ear open to the surrounding chatter, it became clear that the increased security had nothing to do with him; it was because they were having a *party*.

Sometimes, luck truly did decide to fall on Damian's side. Suppressing a grin that would call attention more quickly than a weapon, he followed Lex's directions to the Catch Clan's seat.

If Damian knew anything at all, it was that the cartel had plenty of resources at its disposal. Despite that, the Catch Clan's block was just as seedy as the rest of the town. If anything, the presence of glittery dresses and feathered hats only made the place feel more ramshackle in comparison. The structures here were squat, three or four stories at most, and each one ended in a flat stump of a roof, as if the builders had forgotten to show up to complete their task. Pale lights flickered in a few of the upper floors, as if trying their best to be seen through the warped glass of the windows, and he felt more than heard the distant thrum of music beating nearby.

The people lined up to enter the party were decked out in their fake furs, fake diamonds, and fake smiles, clutching bottles of wine and other offerings. None of them looked particularly happy to be here—the bouncer included. The man was pale, with jowls for miles. Damian wouldn't have imagined that his rumpled suit lived up to Catch Clan dress code standards, either. Maybe he was new.

Filing that detail away for later, Damian strolled by on the far side of the street, passing a few unwise citizens who'd lined up to gawk. Parties meant increased security—there were broad-shouldered thugs hulking on every corner, their suits much crisper and more fashionable than the bouncer's—and shadows on the roof told him the place was guarded from above, too.

Parties also meant a certain amount of chaos. Also, and this was the key point, pirates got in any damn place they wanted.

Stifling the urge to tell those gawking citizens to go home, Damian continued down the block, nodding to the thug on the corner—whose non-response suggested he might be made of stone—and turned down the street as if heading away from the festivities. As any wise Gamerin resident would do.

Damian strode down the long block, taking his time, then rounded the end and started back toward the party. A decently prepped job would have involved city blueprints, and potentially a sewer entrance. Everyone loved a good sewer entrance. But Damian didn't have blueprints, and he certainly didn't have time to procure them; the party was now, the chaos was now, and Heloise would very likely have her manicured claws clenched tight around his ship by morning.

A grift, then. It would have to be. With the decision made, Damian headed back to the main road, walking quickly. There were fewer hov carts now; the first to pass was driven by a white-haired woman whose expression brooked no nonsense. Damian would sooner have crossed his fifteenth nanny—the woman had been more piranha than human—so he let her pass without interfering.

The next cart, though, was laden with something that clinked and clanked as it made its hobbling way along. Every few seconds, it drooped toward the ground, and the kid driving it—he was eighteen or nineteen at most—cringed and ducked as if afraid the contents would shatter.

Perfect.

Damian waited, counting the beats between drops—there was something wrong with the front right mechanism, which gave the cart's failure a beautifully predictable pattern. *Hover, hover, drop. Hover, hover, drop.*

When the cart came close, Damian strode straight off the curb on the second *hover*, screamed on the *drop*—he had an excellent scream, when he really went for it—and shoved his leg under the cart on the next *hover*.

The kid screeched—not as beautifully as Damian, but it was serviceable enough—and wrenched the cart to a halt.

"Are you all right, mister?" he asked. "I'm so sorry, this cart, it's a menace, and I—"

"No, I'm not all right." Damian felt only ten percent guilty at the way the color drained from the kid's face. "Get a medic before I bleed out! And hurry, will you?"

The kid raced off fast enough to tick Damian's guilt level to twelve percent. But it had to be done.

With any luck, he could return the cart in better condition than he'd stolen it.

As soon as the kid was gone, Damian pulled himself out from under the cart, then tugged it around the corner and back toward the party, steadying it with his hip on each *drop* until he was well out of sight. He paused, knelt beside the platform, and ran his hand under the hov controls until he found the offending module. Disconnected line, obviously. Too much weight. The kid had probably overloaded it so he could take fewer trips.

Damian connected the line, then peered under the cloth. The kid had been hauling vases.

Not helpful when he'd been hoping for wine. But not entirely *un*helpful, either. Could've been manure. Though that would've rendered the clanking rather confusing.

Damian unloaded half of the vases, then pulled the now-functioning hov cart back toward Catch Clan's seat, hoping the rumpled bouncer was still on duty at the door.

CHAPTER 5

DAMIAN ABANDONED the vases in the hall outside the party, congratulating himself for the fact that the muddy water he'd filled them with had resembled the worst of the swill they called wine around here. That might have been skill, of a kind, but the fact that the bouncer had let him in with barely a hesitation? That was luck. They must be running low on booze.

The man hadn't appeared to recognize him. He'd barely even looked. And tomorrow, he'd probably be in trouble.

Not Damian's problem. Only his solution. He made his way down the dark corridor, pausing when he reached the mouth of the party. The music thumped in his throat, beating at his eardrums as he made his way along the perimeter of the room in search of an exit passage.

The one he found was *also* full of people, some of them leaning against the walls with glassy looks in their eyes, others folded together into amorous pairings. The lights here faded between red and orange, giving the passage a menacing sort of glare. The people didn't seem to mind, though. Quite a gala, this.

After the passage, a staircase. Lex had said that Bruce was upstairs, so upstairs Damian would go.

He tried not to imagine the riot that would occur if a fire broke out in this building. The stairs were far too narrow for the number of guests, and made narrower by the fact that many of them stood in pairs and clusters upon it, blocking the way. At least these were talking, unlike their eerily silent fellows back in the red passage. Laughing a little too loud. Drinking a little too deeply. Kissing a little too—well. No judgments on that score.

A few of them merely leaned elbows on the rickety rails, staring down at the passage below. Waiting for someone, or perhaps considering a fall. But the passage was sheathed in darkness, leaving little to see. Just that reddish glow, like hot coals left behind after a blaze.

Damian passed them all, grateful for the comforting weight of his duster around his shoulders as he pushed by. They paid him no mind until he opened the door at the top, where the smell of roses and sugar candy wafted out of the room. Several of the guests did turn then, watching with open interest as he slipped inside.

Here, the thumping music of the party faded behind a crystal tinkle of bells, the darkness replaced by soft lights. The flowery-sweet aroma thickened around him like a fog.

Ah. The pleasure house, then. The most legitimate of Catch Clan's business engagements, though whether the place was legitimately run, he didn't know. Maybe he could look into it while he was here. Make sure everyone was happy with the arrangement.

With a clock ticking in his ears and those manicured nails closing around his ship. Sure.

He'd return, then. But he *would* return.

A bot thumped out of the corner, the soft carpets doing little to disguise the whirring thumps of its steps. "All of our hosts are currently visiting with other clients," the bot said. "If you care to picture that, which I certainly do not. But then, I had the misfortune of meeting them all when they arrived. You may picture them any way you would like. You can wait, or you can leave. I don't care."

Damian grinned. "Bruce. It's good to see you."

Bruce was closer to an android than a bot, though for some reason he'd always objected to the term. Maybe because while his skeletal structure was humanoid, he didn't have the skin coverings that defined android actors or most in the hospitality industry.

He stood taller than Damian by half a head, with five-fingered hands and a head like a wedge of cheese. Triangular in shape, it gave him a pointy jaw and a wide-flat skull. He was holding a bowl of hot washcloths.

"I do not know anyone named Bruce," he said. "I know only Herbert, the long-suffering pleasure-house greeter bot."

"You haven't been here that long."

"I have been here for twenty-one weeks, three days, and six hours. During which my previous owner completely abandoned me. The things I have seen. The things."

Damian reached forward to pat Bruce on the arm. "Sorry, buddy. I've been through it. When you hear the story, I think you'll—"

"Whine, whine." The bowl cracked under Bruce's grip, and he set it gently on a nearby chair. "Pirates do not whine. Pirates *act*."

"News to me," Damian said. "I can simultaneously whine and pirate quite effectively."

"And yet it has taken you twenty-one weeks, three days, and six hours—nearly seven—to locate me. No, I think I will remain Herbert." Had Bruce been capable of tears, Damian suspected he'd have shed one just for the drama of it. "Now, may I schedule you with a redhead this evening? I know your preference is for brunettes, but—"

Damian took Bruce by the arm. "No play tonight, my friend. Only rescues of very good friends."

"Oh, very well," Bruce said. "I suppose I could use the rest."

Damian decided not to inform Bruce of his Current-sling-shotting plans until later. He shrugged off his jacket, immediately missing its weight, and slung it over the bot's shoulders. "Try to look human, will you?"

"A disgusting prospect." Bruce shuddered.

"Just until we get outside."

Bruce didn't protest, so Damian decided to assume he was in agreement. They made their way down the stairs, where the music was thankfully loud enough to obscure the whir-thump rhythm of Bruce's descent. People were too far into their drinks, their drugs, and each other to notice, though Damian did feel an errant hand or two brush against his shoulders and upper arms as he passed.

He'd intended to sneak Bruce out the same way he'd come in. Skirt the shadows, dive through the corridor, duck past the abandoned not-wine vases and the nervous not-a-bouncer. Easy.

When they reentered the party room, however, a fresh set of guards had taken up a position at the head of the passage, and a second pair was walking the perimeter. The dance floor rippled uneasily, a telltale sign that a third pair—and perhaps even a fourth—patrolled through the dancers.

They knew he was here.

Damian changed direction and tugged Bruce toward the bar, plunging them into the center of the room. Keeping one hand locked around the bot's wrist and the other lifted to help hide his face, he moved them into the crowd.

"There is an exit at the far end of the room," Bruce said. "It is not being guarded. However, it is an emergency exit. Which means an alarm will likely sound if we go out that way."

Chaos. Damian liked it. He headed deeper into the room,

aiming for the doors. They were nearly past the bar; not far now. In a minute, they'd be breathing the sweet air of freedom. Or, since it was Gamerin, the slightly rancid air of freedom. Still preferable to being trapped here.

Damian emerged from the dance floor and stopped.

At the end of the bar, a woman sat with her legs crossed, her back straight as she perused the crowd before her. She had light brown skin, upon which she'd slathered a truly horrifying amount of shimmering lotion. Her hair fell around her shoulders in soft curls, ostensibly to disguise her identity, but it had the effect of drawing attention instead. At least, it drew *his* attention.

Her beauty, though obvious, wasn't the concern. Even without her reputation—which he well knew, along with everyone else in the galaxy—her posture, combined with her clear curiosity, might as well have thrown a blinking sign above her head, with arrows and shooting stars: REPORTER.

But she *did* have a reputation. She was famous. Catch Clan had to know she was here. Any minute now, they'd send someone to take care of her.

Maybe those bouncers weren't looking for him at all. Maybe they were looking for *her*.

Damian stopped, fingers still locked around Bruce's wrist.

"She doesn't belong here," Damian said.

"And neither do I," Bruce replied. "But you do not see me complaining."

Damian lifted an eyebrow, but Bruce didn't even have the decency to blink his eye modules. "Will it do any good to remind you that you are a pirate?" Bruce asked.

Damian let go of the bot. "Nope. Go wait by the door," he said. "I'm going to get her out of here."

CHAPTER 6

IN THE DARK, details faded to murk.

Shannon had spent the last hour pretending to sip her tork-fruit martini, when she'd have actually preferred an orange-blossom whiskey. A fact that was well known, because of her regular mention of the drinks—and yes, partially because of a sanctioned sponsorship—in her old gossip column. She'd been watching the shadows writhe on the dance floor, wondering if the beat of the music ever changed and whether she ought to begin to wander in search of more interesting rooms. There was a passage to the back that'd looked intriguing.

But her entire reason for being here hinged on making connections, not poking around for little stories. She wasn't here to unearth a crime; everyone knew there were crimes. She was here to unearth a story, a juicy one, complete with richly under-stood players and intricately understood plots. Details. Nuance. And sure, a crime or two.

She couldn't wait all night, though. Not when this might be her one chance.

Just when she was about to hop off the stool and take the plunge, a man leaned his elbows on the counter beside her.

"Orange-blossom whiskey for me," he told the bar-bot. "And another for the lady."

"No, thank you," she began, but he placed a firm hand on her wrist. Didn't grip it. Didn't pull. Merely set it there. The bar lights illuminated him enough to let her see the swath of reddish brown hair that fell across his forehead. His nose was just crooked enough to have been broken once or twice, and the dim light illuminated the indent of a scar below his right eye. The color of his eyes, and the exact contours of his jaw, were lost in the shadow.

More important than any of that, though, was the fact that this man knew her drink. He knew who she was.

"In all the time you've been sitting here," he said, "has anyone else offered to buy you a drink?"

They hadn't. It'd been in her mind, too, that she might show up all mysterious and elegant, and fall into conversation with someone dangerously knowledgeable, with access to the back passages, the leaders. The true Catch Clan.

A childish notion, perhaps. A dangerous one, for certain. But then, she hardly needed a meddling stranger to tell her that.

The man accepted the cocktails from the bar-bot, tossing one back and passing the second to her. "You're known, doll," he said. "Best accept that."

"I don't know what you're—"

"You might've been anonymous enough before the fall of Ve Station," he said, cutting her off. "But that war piece blew your face across the known galaxy. You need to cut loose. This story isn't for you."

"I'm not working on a—"

"Of course you're not," he interrupted. Again. "And I'm not deliriously handsome."

She ground her teeth, barely suppressing her irritation. If she smacked him across the face, they'd probably both get thrown out. Even if not, it would certainly draw more attention than she wished. "You're one of those things," she said.

He grinned, propping his head on his hand. Like this was a joke. Or worse, a date. "Thank you, doll."

So she didn't have a story yet. So what? Once she got one, her boss would have to let her back into the fold. The Ve Station story had scared him off, fool that he was.

There was always a story. Always a way to get back in, even when the bosses were too afraid to let you publish again. Always.

Shannon had a unique opportunity here, and she wasn't going to squander it. She refused.

So she decided to change tactics.

"Listen," she said, keeping her voice low as low as she dared. Which wasn't all that low, or he wouldn't have heard her, even as he leaned his ear a tick closer to her mouth. "I'm working under-cover. You caught me. Well done. Now please go away and let me do my job."

The man actually looked sympathetic for a half second, though he quickly masked it behind an eye roll. "Doll, you are the opposite of undercover. You're splayed out on *top* of the covers and covered in neon paint."

Shannon suppressed the urge to throw what was left of her martini in his face.

"Unless you are eager to perish, we should go."

The new voice spoke from behind her, making her jump, and she turned to see a shadowy figure in a long, beat-up jacket. She squinted, trying to make out the person's features, but the top of their head was lost in shadow.

The orange-blossom whiskey man straightened, snatching the drink he'd ordered for her off the bar. It was the same color as his hair. "If you're not going to, then I may as well."

He swallowed it in one shot, then tossed her a wink.

"I'm not going anywhere with you," Shannon said. "I can take care of myself."

"No doubt," the man said. "Unfortunately, I've got a beast of a conscience. I won't sleep for weeks if you don't escape with us."

"How sad for you."

The man gave his chin a jerk. "Bruce, if you will?"

"You always make me do the hard jobs," the voice behind her complained.

The man straightened. "Indeed, I'm cruel like that. Nonetheless, I see guards approaching, so if we'd like to prevent this nice lady from getting drawn and quartered? Hm?"

Shannon followed his head tilt toward the dance floor, where a pair of bouncers were working their way through the crowd. She could tell they were bouncers from the way people parted before them, and from the wide sweep of their shoulders. Too much to hope that one of them would be Mellie.

Or maybe it would be better if it *wasn't* Mellie. She was probably pissed right about now.

Before Shannon could decide, a pair of decidedly metal hands clasped her around the waist, hoisting her off her stool. She kicked, smashing the martini glass in the process, but the arms didn't even flinch as they lifted and then flipped her, belly first, to rest on top of sharp shoulder blades. If one could call them shoulders, or arms.

Bruce was an android. How had she not seen that?

The damn darkness, that was how. Also, the android's friend had distracted her.

"Why don't you have skin?" she asked, still flailing.

"Rude," the android replied.

The crowd parted like a tear as Bruce jogged toward the door. Shannon's view jostled and spun, but it wasn't hard to see the orange-blossom whiskey man as he made his way behind them, arms flung to the sides. She couldn't make out his face, but she could imagine the smile well enough. He was just the type to smile as he went down in flames.

The bouncers lunged for him. But the man was like mist; he sidestepped their blows, landing a few of his own in the process. One to a stomach that bent his attacker double, then a second to the same man's shoulder—which knocked him directly back into his oncoming friend. The crowd parted, allowing the guard to crash to the floor. In the back of the room, people were starting to head for the doors.

The orange-blossom man actually whirled around, like this was less a fight than it was a dance.

"Is he fighting to the beat?" Shannon muttered.

It was a rhetorical question, but Bruce's audio sensors must have picked up her words through the noise, because it said, "Oh, yes. He does that."

"Of course he does."

Hands closed around her ankle and pulled, upsetting her precarious balance on the android's shoulder. She went back to flailing, and her heel struck what might have been flesh. A cheek, maybe. The person fell away, but more hands replaced theirs.

"Hold on," Bruce said.

Like she had a choice. Still, she wrapped her arms tightly around its neck.

The android planted its feet on the floor, hunching just slightly, like a runner poised on the starting line. And then, without warning, it spun its torso.

Shannon's legs smashed into a face—definitely a face that time—and then another. A neck, a chest, another face. She couldn't see who was who or what was what; she could only hear the shouts that petered into grunts as her legs slammed into their pursuers, taking them out like dominos.

She craned her neck, trying to see who her legs were taking out, but the room spun around her like an out-of-control carousel.

One of her heels gave up and flew away, lost forever. She hoped whoever was in its path would be quick enough to duck so they wouldn't be impaled.

Unless they deserved to be impaled, in which case, she had no qualms.

Bruce stopped spinning so abruptly that she nearly went flying after the shoe. She hung on, swallowing against the bile that threatened to upend what little she'd had of her drink and the snack she'd eaten before coming here. She'd never done well on amusement park rides.

"I'm a woman, not a weapon," she said.

"Error," Bruce replied. "I do not see why those conditions should be mutually exclusive."

With the path clear, Bruce clicked its torso back into place and headed for the doors. Which, she had to admit, were much closer than they'd been before. Despite all the grabbing and spinning, Bruce had managed to make progress.

Stepping over the fallen Catch Clan members, Bruce shoved the door open and exited into the night. She thought she could make out the keening wail of an alarm, though it was difficult to tell behind the thump of the music and the shouting of the crowd.

The fog was thicker than it had been, giving the street a rusty orange pallor, and the Catch Clan's block soon faded to indistinct shadows as Bruce hauled her away down the street. Though the commotion from that quarter still bounced along the brick buildings, the echoes of it made all the more otherworldly by this strange mist.

Shannon couldn't help but notice that the streets had otherwise emptied of traffic.

And though she hated to admit it, she had to acknowledge that some of those Catch Clan thugs *had* come directly for her. Not for the orange-blossom man. Not for the android. For her. They'd known the entire time.

"I guess they really were after me," she said.

"Yes. The likelihood is an astonishing ninety-four percent. The likelihood of them being after Damian was only at eighty-three point seven five before he approached you."

That was still pretty high. No reason to feel guilty about his interference. He was the one who'd interfered, not her. She'd have handled herself just fine in there.

Still, she had to push back a wave of disappointment at the fact that the man—Damian, apparently—was not a rogue Catch Clan member at all. Some part of her had thought he might be her in, her story. Some part of her had almost hoped for it. As a matter of professional curiosity, obviously. He was weird; weirdos sold.

Shannon propped her elbow on the bot's chest and rested her head on her hand, resigned to go wherever it had decided to take her. It was cheaper than a cab, anyway. "Are you making things up?" she asked.

"Error. I do not, quote, make things up."

She was about to ask what had happened to Damian when the man himself came jogging out of an alley to the right, nearly startling her into a scream. Nearly. His hair was even messier than it'd been in the bar—when had the man last bothered to trim it?—and he was sporting a fresh cut across one cheek. It didn't look too deep, but she had to push down a twinge of sympathy.

"My jacket, please, Bruce," he said.

"Priorities," Bruce replied.

"Oh, yes. Apologies. You may release the reporter. So I can have my jacket back."

Bruce set her down, then shuddered, knocking the long coat off his narrow frame. Damian leapt forward to swipe the jacket before it could drop to the ground.

Feeling lopsided, Shannon ripped the laces from her remaining heel and tugged it off, trying not to think too hard about what sorts of age-old spills this street had seen. If Damian didn't want his jacket to fall, she certainly didn't want her bare feet on it. No other option, sadly.

"Thanks for nothing," she said. "You blew my cover, jackass."

Damian shrugged the jacket on over his shoulders. If it'd hung off the android like loose skin, it hugged him close around the chest, falling in long folds around his legs. "As previously discussed, you *had* no cover."

Maybe not. But that could have been a story in itself.

With no other recourse, Shannon threw her shoe at him. He ducked, batting it away, and it clattered uselessly to the street. He raised his hands, trying for that effortless smile again, but the weary lines around his eyes ruined the effect. That, and the way his hands kept curling slightly, as if he wanted to drag the jacket tighter around his body.

"Stay away from me," Shannon said. Then she turned on her heel—as best she could, anyway, with her bare foot against the rough cobblestones—and stalked off down the street.

"Not a problem," Damian called after her. "Have a good life. Which you'll have because of me. But I don't need the glory. Not even a thanks."

Shannon rolled her eyes and rounded a corner, mostly so he'd stop talking. Though from what she knew of him—which wasn't much, but still more than she cared to—the man would probably keep talking posthumously. She didn't care who he was; she only cared about getting as far away from him as possible.

She made it an entire block before she realized she had no idea where to go.

———

"Damian Riddle." Masters was cradling his head in his hands, pressing a cold pack to his right eye. It was puffy and bruised after the fight, though Shannon didn't know if he'd engaged in the brawl directly or if it'd simply made its way to him. "I should've known."

Masters Pub had been shut fast when she'd hobbled in this morning, her feet scratched and bleeding from the walk across the city on broken cobblestones. But Masters must have been watching for her—or for someone—because he'd cracked the door open before she could knock.

She was surprised he was willing to let her in at all. But she'd take it.

Masters uttered the name of the man who'd extricated her last night—just a few hours ago, really—like he was some sort of celebrity. Like Damian Riddle was supposed to mean something to her.

"I don't know who that is," Shannon said.

Masters dropped the cold pack to peer out the window, clearly expecting trouble. When none appeared, he replaced the pack, wincing. "He's got a comic book."

And that was supposed to explain things? When she just stared at him, Masters used his free hand to open his fliptab, then shoved it across the table for her to see.

She supposed the character on the screen might slightly resemble the orange-blossom man she'd met last night. The hair was right, and he did have the jacket. No scars, though, and no android sidekick. Bit too handsome, though she wasn't exactly unbiased in that regard.

She flicked through the story, trying to understand how some comic book fit with what had happened to her last night. The character flew a spaceship, for one—that seemed to be a major theme—and he did impossible stuff like towing asteroid shards away from evil kings and fighting supervillains. None of which looked anything like the cartel members they'd encountered last night.

"So what," she said, passing the fliptab back to Masters, "he's a hero or something?"

"No," Masters said. "I mean, sometimes. But, well, it's complicated. There are a few theories. Most of the fans feel—"

She held up a hand. "You know what? Never mind. I don't want to know."

Masters got up abruptly, hitching a thumb toward the window. Whatever he'd been waiting for, it was here. "Back door," he said. "Come on."

Shannon followed his thumb to where a pair of men were thumping down the steps toward the pub. They didn't look much like Catch Clan members—one of them had a yellow beret perched on his head—but if Masters thought they were, then they probably were.

She followed him through the kitchen, where the stove's knobs were rusty with disuse, and out a back door that led to a narrow alley, all too aware that she still had no shoes on. Masters hovered in the doorway, the cold pack still pressed to his cheek. "Do yourself a favor," he said. "Get off Bromar."

Yeah. She supposed she'd have to. Nodding her thanks, Shannon darted down the alley and away from the pub. She needed to get to the port and hop a ship—any ship.

Bare feet stinging on the cold cobblestones, she ran.

CHAPTER 7

"IT IS TRUE," Bruce said. "They would have killed her."

Damian scraped his heel on the nearest cobblestone in the futile hope of dislodging some of the mud that had accumulated on his boots during their hours-long trek through the city. The eerie orange fog had burned away, leaving them with only the quiet roar of the even oranger seas that seethed in the background. Far from the melodic rhythm that defined the best resort planets in the galaxy, these waves somehow sounded like a pot near boiling. Near it, but never actually hot enough to bubble. It left him feeling like he was perpetually waiting for an event that would never occur.

"Your perspective is inspiring," Damian said, giving his heel one last scrape before moving on. "Truly, I'm so glad I retrieved you. But in the interest of full disclosure, it's time for a performance review. Know what would've been helpful back there?"

"I helped to the full extent of my ability."

"Oh, clearly. Next time, though, feel free to chime in with your opinion while the angry woman is still yelling at us."

"I do not see how that would have helped."

"No, you wouldn't."

Damian had trained himself never to regret a rescue. Shannon Forest wasn't the first ungrateful recipient he'd encountered, and she wouldn't be the last. Besides, Catch Clan had most likely been aware of Damian's presence on Bromar, anyway, so it wasn't as if she'd cost him anything. Heloise would have prepared them for it. Why kidnap Bruce and employ him as a host in a pleasure house, if not to tempt Damian into retrieving him?

Still, they'd boggled the trap terribly. He might even owe Shannon for that; they'd probably been distracted by her audaciousness. Her presence might well have split their attention.

He could imagine Heloise back at the casino, clicking her fingernails together while she devised a plan involving Shannon's newly minted fame as an ace reporter. However accidentally garnered that fame might have been.

Damian gave the curb a kick, knocking a slab of it out of place. This city was in dire need of a renovation. Might be best if they just removed the people, razed it to the ground, and started over.

Though he wouldn't mind if Catch Clan were here when the razing part happened.

"You are cranky," Bruce said. "You need a snack."

"I'm not cranky. I don't do cranky."

Even with the opening notes of today's headache buzzing by his temple like an airshow. Even with the poison in his chest—which he'd managed to forget for an evening—renewing its burning trails across his skin. Even with his knuckles still smarting from the fight and his ears ringing from the music, and his eyes dry with weariness.

Definitely not cranky.

"That is incorrect," Bruce replied. "We have been collaborating for eleven-point-six years. I can recall eight hundred and forty-two situations to which the term applied during that period. Eight hundred and forty-three, counting today."

That seemed excessive. Damian turned onto the main street that housed the port, narrowly suppressing an exhale of relief when there were no guards loitering outside. Tired as he was, he made himself scan the recesses of the alleyways across from the port entrance, searching for drones or spies. He studied the sleepy food carts that lined the walk, but none of them had human operators. Any one of them might have cameras, but he couldn't do much about that.

"Cranky is subjective," he said.

"Once again, that is incorrect. Cranky is defined as ill temper, often brought on by fatigue or hunger. The term is frequently associated with toddlers. Synonyms include grouchy, sullen, petulant, peevish—"

"It's impossible to be cranky and debonair and the same time," Damian interrupted. "Therefore, it's impossible. I'm simply... out of sorts."

"Another synonym."

Fine. Maybe a little. But after their explosive exit from the Catch Clan's seat, he and Bruce had been forced to wind their way through Gamerin's streets for hours, ducking into alleyways or hopping onto fire escapes whenever someone passed. They'd seen corners of the city Damian would rather have left to his imagination; they'd sloshed their way through all manner of suspicious puddles that would leave his boots stained for weeks.

Didn't matter. They were back at the ship now. He had Bruce. If the Catch Clan had a trap waiting for them, they hadn't sprung it yet.

The almost-boiling feeling increased, raising the hair on the back of his neck, and he removed it to the back of his mind. Aware of it—he'd learned that instincts were best heeded rather than shoved aside—but not distracted by it. Hopefully.

The *Quandary* waited untouched in its berth when Damian returned. Solid. Reliable. A gem, hidden within a city that was made of muck and despair. When his shoulders loosened in relief at the sight of the ship, he realized that some part of him had expected it to be gone when he arrived.

But no. *Quandary* was his.

As soon as the doors shut behind him, Mojo came whirring down the gangplank, tail flicking back and forth behind it like a deranged pendulum.

"I won three games of hide and seek!" the bot said. "On the last one, it took Lex four hours and seventeen minutes to find me! Hi, Bruce! Damian saved you! Hurray!"

Four hours and seventeen minutes during which Lex had charged her batteries and paged through the gossip feeds, no doubt.

"Hello, small nuisance," Bruce said, stalking up the gangplank. He had to duck his head to get inside. "You have grown no uglier in my absence, so I suppose that is to your credit."

Mojo zipped around in a circle. "Lex says I shouldn't listen to a word you say. I *did* grow uglier! You can't say I didn't!"

"But no smarter," Bruce grumbled.

Damian beckoned to Mojo, and it followed him up the ramp and into the ship.

———

They left without trouble, which usually would have set Damian's teeth on edge. But when an hour passed without interference as they made their way toward the Current—which ran along the far edge of this particular System—Damian settled in to review his calculations for a third time. His pilot's chair was the most comfortable pilot's chair in the galaxy, bar none, and he'd have engaged the heating pads if he thought he had time to close his eyes for a few minutes.

The stinging in his chest said that he did not.

Bruce sat in the chair to the right and side of Damian's. There were no co-pilot seats on *Quandary*; there were only console chairs, each of them designed with bots in mind. Humans could sit there, but they rarely did. The control boards ran around three quarters of the circular space, an almost-full circle that cut off at the supply closet where he kept his jacket. And assorted other belongings. That was followed by his cot, the gangplank, the head, and, finally, the narrow counter that served as the galley. Smaller than the one in his recent accommodations, but it served him well.

Above it all, the circle of clocks watched down from the shelf above their heads. They still needed winding, and Damian thought of setting Mojo to the task. But he liked to do it himself. He liked the feeling of his fingers winding the gears, the way they clicked against his skin. He liked the feeling of making something work again, rather than tearing it down.

Lex sat in the corner, clacking a strand of purple yarn between two of her stumpy claws. He didn't know where she'd obtained the yarn or what she intended to make with it. Sometimes it was better not to ask.

"The calculations are correct, if the data you provided is accurate," Bruce said, watching as Damian ran the simulation again. "However—"

"It's accurate," Damian replied.

"*However*," Bruce repeated, "you may wish to call your Fleet Commander friend for help. His resources would—"

"Veto," Damian interrupted. "I work alone."

Bruce made a sniffing sound, though it came out more like a digital gurgle. "And I suppose I am nothing to you. Just a pile of chopped data chips."

Damian scanned the dashboard, looking for any sign of an error. The simulation showed perfection, but this was a delicate maneuver. It had to be exact. "You're welcome to leave."

Bruce did his almost-sniff again, but he didn't log a request to leave. One of these days, he probably would. He might not be human, but Damian never assumed anyone would stay for long. Even if the person in question was a bot.

Mojo scrambled up onto the dash, deftly avoiding the depressed buttons. "Cartel ships incoming," it said. "We've been detected! We're going to die!"

The pot finally reaching a boil. It was almost a relief. Damian leaned over the dash, steadying his hands. "We're three minutes out from the Current," he said, ignoring Mojo's panic. "Destination's entered. Bruce? Triple check?"

"Missiles incoming." Lex had stowed her yarn and was now focused on the weapons controls.

Damian urged the *Quandary* forward, reveling in the punch of speed that sang in his chest like a forgotten song. The Current drew nearer, like an infinitely large turquoise necklace that someone had draped across the galaxy, but elation replaced fear as he spiraled the ship out of the reach of the Catch Clan's missiles, causing them to meet behind *Quandary* in a glorious burst of fire that was nonetheless close enough to shake his shields.

Now he would get answers. He would get them before this illness wasted him, or he would die in the process of trying. Not in a bed, not with test needles sticking out of his arms and computers measuring his brain waves. In action.

"Bruce," Damian repeated, "triple check?"

"The numbers remain unchanged. I cannot predict whether your untested theory will succeed in rerouting the trade Currents or result in our untimely deaths."

The Current was close now, so very close.

"It's the Current or the Catch Clan," Damian said. "Pick your poison."

"Activate the slingshot," Bruce said. "In three, two—"

The Current closed around the ship, sending a burst of song crashing into his head. As soon as it began, it shifted, a new melody joining the throng with every beat that passed, until Damian wanted to bow his head and cover his ears.

It wouldn't do any good when the song was coming from inside his skull.

The change in the song did influence the outside world, however. The ship tipped sideways without his consent. As it did, the supply-closet doors crashed open, flinging a *person* straight out of them.

Faster than Damian could register it, Bruce was out of his chair, catching the stowaway before she could crack her head open on the dash.

It was Shannon Forest. Because of course it was.

The *Quandary* righted itself, the Current still singing in Damian's ears, the ship shuddering as Bruce set the reporter on her feet. "Unfortunately," Bruce said, "our calculations did not account for *her*."

CHAPTER 8

SHE SHOULD HAVE KNOWN it was his ship.

The protections had been shoddy, the security shield failing to reach the top of the berth, making it all too easy to climb the outer walls and drop in from above. That wasn't so uncommon; there were a dozen such berths in Gamerin's port. Enough to make Shannon to suspect that those who ran the port allowed these berths to remain half-functional on purpose, perhaps as part of their dues to the ruling cartel. On a non-gala night, the Catch Clan might have sent thieves to pick them over.

Tonight, three of the faulty berths had contained ships. The first had been a rusted-out hull, clearly dumped for scrap. Or maybe as a warning. It might've been there for a day, or for a year; either way, it wouldn't be going anywhere soon. She had, however, stolen a pair of discarded boots from the far corner. They were big on her, but better than going barefoot.

The second ship had been a freighter, and a hotbed of activity as the owners loaded crates of goods into the cargo hold. Stolen goods, if she could judge by the shifty glances of the look-outs, the heavy arms, and the urgency with which the captain rushed the crew to move faster.

The third ship, this ship, had been quiet. Clean to the point of sparkling, it'd looked like it might be headed somewhere that didn't suck. So she'd dropped from the ceiling, made her way up the open gangplank, and stuffed herself into the supply closet. Where she'd stayed for hours, long enough to make her muscles stiffen.

She'd been so relieved when the ship had taken off.

Now, Damian Riddle was staring at her with open shock, an expression she suspected did not cross his face very often. His tan cheeks were flushed, his lips parted, hands frozen in front of him like she'd surprised him into immobility. She'd found him annoying last night, if slightly—very slightly—intriguing as well.

Today, he looked dangerous.

"What the hell are you doing here?" he asked.

Shannon decided the best course of action would be to pretend. She was a reporter, wasn't she? An ace reporter would have come here on purpose, curious after last night's events. A reporter would be after the story.

It might not improve her standing, but at least it would allow her to maintain a shred of her dignity. Which was bruised, if not broken, after her tumble out of the supply closet.

Masters had shown her that comic, the drawings of this man as a... not a hero, Masters had said. A villain? Suddenly, she wished she'd allowed him to finish his lecture on fan theories.

Shannon leaned against the side of the ship, trying to look casual as she withdrew her fliptab from her pocket. Ready to take notes. The fan theories didn't matter; Damian Riddle's perspective mattered. And no man who appeared in a comic book would want to be drawn as a villain. She'd start with that.

"Tell me," she said. "When did you get started in the hero business?"

He blinked. "Excuse me?"

"Obviously, you're well known," she said. "I wanted to find out more."

"You ran away fast enough last night."

"You surprised me."

Damian stalked forward, maintaining his footing even as the ship gave another lurch. He ripped the fliptab out of her hand and set it on the dash. "I'm a pirate," he said. "I'm a criminal, and, relevant to this conversation, I'm a practiced con artist. I don't believe you."

She wasn't sure how to respond. She crossed her arms, giving him what she hoped was a look of forthright appraisal. She didn't know him. He'd saved her last night—or so he seemed to see it, anyway—but her appearance here was obviously far from welcome.

As she watched him, she couldn't help it. She started to pick out the details.

It was warm on the ship, for starters, yet Damian wore his jacket pulled tight around him, his shirt buttoned all the way to his throat, though it didn't entirely obscure the black tip of a tattoo that reached out from beneath his collar. His autumn-brown hair was long and unkempt, but carefully so; he'd run streaks of black dye through some of the strands, though an inch of root was showing. He wore a large ring on his right hand, the seal turned toward his palm so that she couldn't make out its image.

And then there was the ship itself. Spotless, yes, but with an air of... abandonment, almost. She wasn't sure what gave her that impression until her gaze landed on the shelf that ran above the room. A circular shelf, one that might hold a toy hov-train if they were in a children's store. Only this shelf was stuffed with clocks.

Each one was different; some were made of untreated wood, while others had been meticulously painted. Some looked like molded plastic, while one in the back had clear sides to display the interlocking gears within. They were shaped like planets and homes, like spaceships and sailboats, like owls and fish and, in the back, the laughing jaw of a Bronian hyena.

The one thing they held in common? They were silent.

Goosebumps prickled her skin, for no good reason. Perhaps Damian simply liked the look at the clocks, or used them to smuggle stolen goods. Perhaps he didn't keep them wound.

Somehow, though, she knew that he did.

The android from last night, Bruce, made a chirping noise that might have been an approximation of a throat clearing. "I believe," he said, "that the captain is awaiting your response."

What, to his claim of pirating and conning, and generally not believing her story? What was she supposed to say? *Oh, yes, you've got me, guess I'll be going now?*

Damian shot Bruce an eyebrow-raised glance that might have been surprise, though whether because the bot appeared to be backing him up or because it had referred to him as a captain, Shannon wasn't sure.

"Those were delicate calculations," he said, gesturing toward the dash. "I've never done them before. There was no room for error."

Shannon forced herself to meet his gaze, even as embarrassed anger spiked through her gut. "If you've never done them before, how do you know there's no room for error?"

"She has got you there." Bruce reseated himself in the chair next to the supply closet. It'd been a poor hiding spot, but she hadn't wanted to risk poking around for something better. Now that she was out here, she could see panels in the floor that would have led to much better places. Oh, well. Next time.

Because knowing Shannon's life these days, there probably *would* be a next time.

The viewport stretched nearly in a full circle, allowing the flickering light of the Current to wash across the deck, where they reflected distorted rainbows in the mercury-gray surfaces of the chairs and control panels. Everything was black or gray—everything except the clocks—even the narrow cot against the far wall. It looked more like a bed in a field hospital than a place where a person could actually rest.

"Weird aesthetic you've got here," she commented. "What's with the clocks?"

Damian glanced out of the viewport, the Current reflecting oddly against his cheek. As if, when it touched his skin, it somehow began to crawl. A trick of the light, surely.

Like most people in the Parse Galaxy, Shannon had traveled the Currents plenty of times. She'd never paid much attention to them, really; they just *were*. Now, though, she couldn't help feeling that the colors had changed. Just slightly. The blues had deepened, winding strands of purple into the mix. Her fingers itched to retrieve her fliptab so she could snap pictures of the change.

When Damian turned back to her, she thought she caught a spark of silvery purple gleaming in his eyes. She swallowed. Another trick of the light. So many to go around.

"Fine," Shannon said. "I'm sorry. You wanted to save me, right? Well, you did. A second time."

"Again," Bruce said. "She has got you there."

Damian drew in a deep breath, then let it out slowly. Trying to rein in his reactions, clearly.

"Just drop me off at the nearest station," Shannon said. "I'll be on my way."

Provided that the nearest station was in an Outer System, or, better, a Middle one. The possibility of getting shoved off this ship and onto a random Fringe station was more frightening than the prospect of remaining on Bromar. There were plenty of places in the galaxy that were way worse than Bromar. Even with the Catch Clan after her.

Damian shook his head. "Not an option."

Shannon swallowed, wishing her throat hadn't gone so very dry. "Why does it sound like you're kidnapping me right now?"

"He doesn't mean that to be as threatening as it sounds." A cone-shaped bot who sat in the third crew seat spoke with almost a motherly tone; even the Current's reflected light looked a bit less frightening against the light gray materials that made up her siding. "He literally *can't* drop you off at the nearest station. There are none."

She sounded regretful. But she had to be crazy; there were always stations within quick reach of the Currents. Always.

"Looks like you kidnapped yourself, doll," Damian said.

Shannon opened her mouth to demand that he exit the Current as soon as civilization presented itself—*any* civilization— but the ship lurched, and she cried out instead, reaching for the nearest handhold, which happened to be the back of Lex's chair.

On the other side of the viewport, the Current went dark.

Shannon knew the telltale swoop-and-lurch of a usual Current exit. It was like that every time, comfortingly normal. Even as a little kid, she could remember dozing in the back of a shuttle and feeling that swoop-and-lurch that promised she'd soon be home.

She swallowed the memory, as unwelcome as the wad of bile in her throat, and focused on what was. Not what should be.

But the only details that surfaced were the ones that told her what should be.

There should be stars in the viewport; there should be the blue-green light of the Current behind them, even if it no longer surrounded them.

Also, and this was a key point, they should not have *stopped*.

Movement was relative; Shannon had traveled extensively, enough to know that relative distance could make it feel as if a ship had stopped even when it was traveling at its fastest. She didn't trust her own eyes, or even her guts, when it came to velocity.

But she also knew how to interpret dashboard readings. And they said, in no uncertain terms, that the ship really had stopped.

It was impossible.

A rodent-sized bot shot out from beneath the console, making Shannon jump. "We're pancakes!" it wailed. "Flapjacks! Crepes! *Waffles!*"

"There, there," the motherly bot said. "We're fine."

"But we *should* be pancakes!" the rodent cried. "Physics is broken!"

"The ugly one has got a point," Bruce put in. "It is disconcerting."

Damian leaned one hand on the dash, peering out of the viewport. "We didn't land."

"And yet," Bruce said, "we are landed. Impossible."

"Yes, well, I *am* me." Damian straightened, picking up his swagger like a dropped coin, and tipped Shannon a smile. He could swagger all he wanted; it did nothing to hide the relief that relaxed that corners of his eyes. "It's our lucky day, reporter. The calculations worked."

Shannon had been too busy arguing with him, and defending her trespassing, to ask what calculations he meant. Not a great oversight. Not a great oversight at all.

In what world could a color-changing Current, a whiplash exit, and an impossible not-landing make for a *lucky* day?

Damian was already moving toward the gangplank. "Lex, how's the air?"

"Rated for human breathability," said the cone-shaped bot. "You don't need a helmet."

"Excellent."

Shannon retrieved her fliptab from the dash and shoved it into her pocket. Wherever they'd landed, she might need it.

Lex swung down from her chair and rolled over to Shannon. "You might want to bring a sweater, dear. Atmosphere's a bit chilly."

Shannon blinked at the bot, confused. "I... don't have a sweater?"

She was still wearing the party dress from last night, though it was now paired with the work boots she'd stolen. She suddenly felt more than a little ridiculous, with one shoulder exposed. And uncomfortable. Very uncomfortable. She'd kill for a pair of sweatpants right now.

The bot opened her front panel. "Pink or green?"

"Um," Shannon said. "Green?"

Lex let out a pleased chime and extended a lumpy ball of yarn in Shannon's direction. In certain lights, it might have been interpreted as a sweater. "Thank you," Shannon said.

Lex chirped again. "Don't let him scare you, dear," she said. "He's going through some things."

Shannon started to say he didn't scare her, then hesitated. She wasn't entirely sure what to think of him, actually. She nodded, then followed Damian toward the descending gangplank.

She'd thought he might try to bar her from leaving the ship, but he seemed to have forgotten her entirely as he stepped down the gangplank. Shannon followed, pausing at the bottom of the ramp. Damian had walked right out onto the platform, his footsteps sending wet echoes through the space as he moved, but she found herself hesitating at the bottom.

Dim lights strobed out of the ceiling, flickering in vertical bands along the walls as if the effort it took to light the place were something monumental. The ceiling looked closed, with only a small circle of a skylight in the circle, but it must have opened at some point. Because strange though their landing might have been, they *had* landed. And that required an open ceiling.

Details. Shannon honed her focus, trying to look past the obvious.

Water on the floor, an inch high, with silvery-gray markings shining below it. Damian, turning a slow circle in the center. She pushed back a hysterical image of the floor opening beneath his feet, the water whipping into a whirlpool to suck him into an abyss.

The ground stayed firm.

Shannon dragged her gaze along the walls, where dim lights framed a set of rectangular consoles. Each one had a diagonally tilted panel above it, like a slice of umbrella. The panels formed a strange circle, enclosing the ship. On the floor, the water reflected the technology like a mirror, except where ripples from Damian's footsteps pulsed through the images. She wanted to tell him to stop walking, but the words clogged in her throat. Where the hell had he brought them?

"Is this the Fringe?" she asked. Her voice rung out into the space.

Damian turned, his jacket drifting around his calves, and met her eyes. "No, ace reporter," he said. "We're not in the known Parse Galaxy. Not anymore."

Shannon clutched her fliptab, fear and hunger at war in her gut. This? This was a way better story than the cartel. And she was going to crack it.

CHAPTER 9

DAMIAN WASN'T sure when it had become normal for him to think thoughts like, *Huh, this place makes my blood tingle*. But he was thinking it now, and it wasn't as weird as it should have been. His blood did feel like it was tingling, like a limb awakening after being left in an awkward position overnight.

But tingling in a waking limb happened because of poor circulation, and his blood *was* the circulation, which made the sensation more than mildly alarming.

He filed the thought away for now, taking a moment to enjoy the expressions of surprise and excitement that crossed Shannon Forest's face as she absorbed his announcement. They were no longer in the known Parse Galaxy. They'd flung themselves beyond it and into the heart of an alien civilization.

The way she was staring at him, struck silent by the new information—a temporary condition, from what he knew of her so far—he was fairly certain she believed it. He wouldn't have blamed her for freaking out, either, but he'd be damned if the woman didn't look... eager. Shocked, yes, but hungry too. Not like the desperate gamblers on their way to Dragon's Luck had been hungry, though. This was ambition, and he liked it.

Unfortunately, he couldn't stand here and enjoy Shannon's reaction forever. The landing pad was far too quiet for his liking. He'd intended to arrive here the normal way, with no attempt at secrecy. He'd expected to be coaxing reluctant space traffic controllers into allowing the *Quandary* to land, to be communicating in gestures, and, possibly, to be carted off to a prison before the situation was properly explained.

He'd expected, to be frank, something along the lines of little green people. And he could say that, because he was one of them. Kind of.

This landing pad was far too quiet. It *was* a civilization, certainly. No question about that. But what civilization had a silent space port? None that he had ever seen.

They might have landed in the wrong spot after all. They might have landed in the correct sector only to find it abandoned. There might be no one here at all. And if that was the case, the mystery of his illness would never be solved.

This was a last-ditch effort, the trick to end all tricks. This was the do-or-literally-die moment. He'd rather face down an army of multi-tentacled aliens with cannons locked to every sucker than wither away in the silence of an abandoned world.

And, despite all his efforts to the contrary, he'd accidentally brought someone else along to die with him.

It was a lot of fear to pack into one moment. Always an overachiever, his brain managed it anyway.

Shannon was still gawking at their surroundings as if she planned to start hammering the walls with questions. She still had on her dress from last night, though she'd covered it with a knotty lime-green sweater that fell all the way to her knees. Longer than the dress. She was wearing ratty work boots, too, which rose high enough to nearly meet the sweater.

"I don't see an exit," Damian said. Plenty of door-shaped consoles, but they couldn't be actual doors. They were covered in buttons and appeared to be welded shut. From what he could tell.

Shannon pointed up. "There's a ceiling, though."

A ceiling that must have opened to let them land, even if they hadn't seen it happen. It was made up of interlocking panels, and though they were twisted shut, he could make out a glint of gray daylight through an eyelet in the middle.

He'd seen entrance tunnels on underground and domed worlds. He'd seen tractor beams that yanked ships out of orbit, unwilling to allow guests even an ounce of control over their destinations. He'd seen escort drones, barren wastelands, and landing pads that pushed visiting ships through a city like individual train cars.

There was nothing like that here. The ceiling had to be the entrance, unless the redirected Current could deliver ships through walls now. Unlikely.

"The ceiling it is," Damian said.

From the *Quandary*'s roof, which Damian regretted treading upon with his dirty boots, they were able to scramble onto the slanted caps of the tech modules that surrounded the ships. They looked delicate, but they didn't so much as shudder when Damian pulled himself up. He squinted at the ceiling, now just a few feet above his head. There *was* an opening there, and gray daylight *did* filter inside, though in its current position, it wasn't in any way large enough for his ship to have passed through.

Large enough for a person, though.

Shannon scrambled onto the panel beside his. "Now what?" she asked.

Damian could easily stand on his tiptoes, grab the edge of the ceiling, and hoist himself out into the air of the alien planet. Alone. Shannon, though, was a fair bit shorter.

He probably ought to leave her here. It was probably safer, and it would definitely be more private.

Somehow, he didn't think she'd go for that. And somehow, he suspected that he could tie her up and leave her in the supply closet—though that would most assuredly go against the few principles he did have—and she'd still find a way to escape and dig into his business. For the moment, he was stuck with her.

"I'll give you a boost," he said.

She opened her mouth as if to protest, then gave the roof a glare, like she found the distance personally offensive. "Fine."

Resting a hand on his shoulder, she stepped onto his offered arm and allowed him to boost her up toward the hole. She grabbed the edge and practically kicked him in the face as she wiggled her way up and out. She reappeared a moment later, stretching a hand as if to help him up. Cute.

"Seal her up," Damian called down, and *Quandary*'s gang-plank retracted as one of the bots—probably Lex—closed it from inside the ship. "No stowaways this time," he added, though he wasn't sure if the bots could hear.

Ignoring Shannon's proffered hand, Damian jumped, clasping the edge of the ceiling and swinging himself up. His arms shook as he trusted them with his full weight, and he very nearly lost his grip before managing to tip his body in the right direction to flop, most indelicately, out of the opening.

Shannon scrambled out of the way as he landed on his stomach. "Thanks, doll," he said, though the words sounded strained. "I'm good."

She shook her head, like she knew exactly how 'good' he was, then straightened.

The first thing Damian noticed was the air. It smelled fresh, crisp. Like fruit, sweet without being cloying. Like an undertone. It was a relief after Bromar's oppressive musk, yet unlike anything he'd breathed before. The sky was a dull gray color, as if a storm might be moving in, but he couldn't tell if it was permanently like that, or if it was merely the time of day. Twilight perhaps, or dawn.

The second thing he noticed, though it should have been the first—there was blood pounding in his eyes, and his chest stung in sympathy with the rhythm of some far-off tune, so he supposed he might be forgiven—was the parade.

It made its way along the wide thoroughfare below, the street stuffed with whirling dancers. They wore long robes dyed in startlingly vibrant shades of red, orange, blue, and green. From here, it gave the impression of a street splashed with moving paint. The dancers looked humanoid enough—a relief, since he certainly shared DNA with them—and they escorted what looked like a parade float, the kind a champion zeeball team might bring out to celebrate a major win. Layers upon layers of those same vibrant cloths dripped over the sides of the float.

The dancers might be escorting the float, but the things that escorted the dancers... those were more difficult to put a name to. They resembled crystal balls, the kind a two-bit fortune teller might whip out to enhance the drama of a reading, and there were hundreds of them. They were clear-sided and shining, even in the gray-tinged light, and they closed a perimeter around the dancers. Above them, too. Everywhere he looked, there were crystal balls, clearly fashioned out of glass or plastic, or some other clear material that this part of the galaxy had invented.

He cringed each time one of them dipped closer to the ground, expecting it to shatter. None did.

"Bubbles," Shannon breathed.

Yes, that was a better descriptor than crystal balls, even if the things didn't quite act like bubbles. The light breeze didn't determine their course, and they didn't undulate the way bubbles might.

Whatever they were, the bubble things were everywhere. They kept pace with the parade float, they bobbed around and over the dancers, and when he scanned the rooftops—most of them were shorter than the one on which he and Shannon currently stood—he could make out the shining reflections of more bubbles.

Also, they hovered around the heads of the crowd.

It took a moment for Damian to absorb the fact that there *was* a crowd. Because despite the dancing, the vibrant colors, and the thrumming beat of the music, the people who lined the streets and crowded the balconies on the other side of the thoroughfare and poked their heads out of windows... they were utterly silent.

He was too far away to make out their expressions. He couldn't see if they were smiling, or crying, or if there was any indication at all that someone might have forced them to be here. But he knew the sounds of a crowd; even the quietest one contained a certain roar. Hundreds of people packed into one place made rustles, whispers, coughs. They dropped things. They bumped into each other. They shuffled their feet.

Not these people. Aliens. Whatever they were. Their reverent silence was like a direct opposition to the joy of the whirling dance below. The difference might've been jarring; instead, it was captivating. Like complementary melodic lines, a soprano weaving airily above a contrabass.

Shannon had her fliptab out, the bulky sleeves of the green sweater slipping around her elbows as she snapped pictures of the scene. "Did you know this was here?" she asked.

Not precisely this. "You don't even know where 'here' is, doll."

"Don't sidestep the question. What are you after?"

Damian was beginning to feel rather exposed, standing here on the roof like this. Eventually, someone was going to notice them. Should they ditch their clothing and try to fit in? Or would the shape of their ears or the color of their tongues give them away as soon as they tried? His blood buzzed in his veins, washing a lightheaded sensation through his skull. It would be unfortunate to come all this way just to faint and fall off a roof.

Shannon was staring at him, eyebrows drawn together in obvious annoyance as she waited for him to answer her question. He thought he could probably push that a little further.

"Haven't yet found the galaxy's best brothel," he said. "I live in hope, however."

She didn't even roll her eyes. "Are we even still *in* the galaxy?"

Did it matter? They were in a land far, far away. Unless the Current blazed nearby, in all its mysteriously fast-moving glory, they wouldn't be traveling anywhere soon.

Across the galaxy. Across the universe. It was all the same, really.

Before he could piece together an appropriately flippant response, a movement on the roof beside theirs caught his eye. A trio of figures stood upon it, watching him. Their long robes marked them as participants in the parade, which continued to process by them on the thoroughfare below. Up close, they looked like humans. No pointy ears or weird eyebrows. He couldn't see their tongues, so those still might be sporting stripes or polka dots. He didn't know whether to hope for that or dread it.

"Ah," he said. "Spotted."

The figure in the center of the group nodded, and a swarm of bubbles drifted out of the ether, quickly forming a bridge from one roof to the other.

Damian raised his hands in what he hoped was a universal indication that he wasn't armed. Or at least, that he wasn't currently *holding* any of the arms at his disposal. Shannon shot him a glance, then did the same. Though it would have been more effective if she'd have dropped her fliptab first.

The aliens, who'd made it halfway across their bridge,

paused. Damian wasn't much for vertigo—couldn't be, when you were known for leaping out of moving hov-trains and such—but he thought the clear material of that bridge would challenge that notion.

The aliens exchanged a glance, then turned back to face Damian and Shannon. As one, they raised *their* hands.

Damian couldn't help it. He laughed.

"Cultural miscommunication," he said, dropping his hands to his sides. "What's that phrase they like to use in the vids? Ah. We come in peace."

The aliens exchanged another glance. And then the one in the center dropped his hand, calling one of the bubbles—not a bridge bubble, thankfully—to hover in front of him. He held it for a moment in the center of his palm.

Damian had shut off his eye screen for the Bromar infiltration. Now, it flickered to life without his permission. And judging by the way Shannon started in surprise, hers was doing the same.

A moment later, the lead alien stepped forward, pushing back his hood. A cap of gray hair hugged his skull, like moss on a rock. His cheeks were cragged with wrinkles, his eyes watery behind light colored lashes. "My name is Ahnien," he said. "Your translators ought to be functioning now."

Shannon narrowed her eyes, and Damian could just imagine the barrage of questions about to stream out of the reporter's mouth. Enough to cause a diplomatic incident. How did they know the Parse Galaxy languages? They'd visited, of course. How they could access eye screens? Well, they'd invented the Currents, so it was entirely believable that their tech would be advanced enough to crash through the best he and Shannon had ever known.

Shannon couldn't possibly know any of that. But Damian wasn't interested in rehashing what he knew, so he stepped in front of her, earning himself a smack on the shoulder.

"Thank you," he said, ignoring her. "The translators are working."

Ahnien sighed. "Good. Well. We'd best call a council meeting."

One of the others stepped forward. They were bigger than Ahnien, but Damian couldn't make out much about their features; the crimson hood was still raised, their hands tucked within the sleeves. "On a funeral day, Champion?"

Shannon looked down at the thoroughfare. "That's a *funeral?*"

Strange funeral, with all the colors and the dancing. But then, there had been the silent reverence of the crowd. And Damian could see the benefit of celebrating those who'd gone before, rather than wasting time on tears.

Ahnien grimaced. "Can't be helped," he said. "Come."

CHAPTER 10

ZAHLIA HAD BEEN a fool to count on the funeral, to assume it would give her a chance to slip away unnoticed. The chaos and crowds promised ample opportunity, with everyone participating in the ceremony. Even the infirm had their beds carried to the streets. No one missed a funeral.

It was a fair guess. But she had assumed, and she had not arranged a backup plan.

And her husband had decided to be... clingy. Requiring her presence. And grumpier than usual, too, which was saying something.

"Not enough dancers," Sileux grumbled as they looked down over the parade. "Not enough by half. The children, they should be learning the dances. Where are they?"

They stood together on the lower balcony of their boulevard home. Zahlia preferred their canal-side residence, but this one came with a convenient viewing spot that allowed them to view the procession without shouldering through the throngs. She could smell the spiced honey of the warm funerary drinks being passed about below, and the music hummed between her ribs like an embrace.

It was not that she *wanted* to miss the funeral. Merely that her mission demanded it.

"Peace, husband," she said. "I'll bring you some ash-ka."

And then conveniently forget to return. She was a distractible woman, by his own description. Luckily, he was no less so; he'd forget her absence in ten heartbeats. Possibly less.

"No," he said. "We ought to fast, as in the days of old."

She tsked. "Hardly celebratory."

"You are young," he said. "You do not remember."

Sileux was old, but he was not *that* old. He could only have heard of the fasting days from an elderly grandparent, if he'd even ever met someone who'd participated in it. Zahlia suspected he'd read about it in one of his books, and nothing more.

She held her tongue, however. No sense in picking a fight. She rested a hand on the balcony rail, an intricate mold of gold-speckled concrete, and allowed her gaze to drift, to follow the spheres along their spiraling paths. The air was thick with them today. It seemed that every one of them had come to pay their respects.

The temple across the way peaked in a shallow dome, its odd shape standing out amid the sharp angles of the rest of the city. The other structures that lined the boulevard were made of crisp stone, with shallow balconies extending a short way above the street below. Only the temple had curves.

The building was eye-catching under any circumstances. Today, though, her gaze landed upon it and held. She grasped the rail, hardly believing what her eyes were telling her.

"Husband," she said. "There are people on top of the temple."

Strange people they were, too. The taller one wore a long coat, blasphemously drab for a funeral day. The smaller figure, at least, wore a frock of bright green, though it was surprisingly short.

"Don't be ridiculous," Sileux bit back. "There can't be... dear souls, there *are* people there."

What an overwhelming shock, she thought.

She and Sileux were not the first to notice the visitors; Ahnien was already moving across a bone bridge to meet them, with two of his hangers-on by his sides. His lips were moving, and Zahlia found herself leaning forward, as if there were any hope of hearing his words from this distance.

"Champion Ahnien will call a council meeting," she said.

Sileux's ragged eyebrows shot up, as if she'd suggested they dump water on the passing procession, or take to batting at spheres with a measuring stick. "Not on a funeral day," he said.

No sooner had the words left his mouth than a sphere expanded into the space before him, Ahnien's message beaming out with clear instructions. Emergency council meeting.

Zahlia enjoyed gloating; it was, after all, among the only pleasant pastimes she had left. In a massive effort of self sacrifice, however, she schooled her face to smoothness as her husband cursed, looking out upon the dwindling procession once more before hurrying away, his cerulean robes billowing around his feet.

She listened while he gathered his things, the rustle and clatter of books and paper. The door shut, and she waited until he'd returned to retrieve a forgotten item—he did that eight times out of every ten times leaving the house—and the rooms had grown silent, leaving only the fading music of the parade and the honey-tinged aromas.

Soon, the streets would empty. The music would cease. The sky would darken, leaving the spheres to sparkle their own dance of mourning and celebration.

Now, however, was the perfect moment. Everyone was moving. Especially the council members.

Perhaps Command had found some way to distract Ahnien

into calling a council meeting. She cringed, considering the possibility; she did not need his assistance to complete her mission.

Little used though this home was, Zahlia had taken the time to hide a sphere of her own in her chambers. She withdrew it now, removing the black-sided sphere from the panel she'd built into the floor beneath her hammock. Keeping a sphere to oneself was forbidden. But then, many things were forbidden. It did not signify.

The sphere was already activated.

"Did you place the ear?" the voice that came through the sphere was tired, and she wished she could see the face that accompanied it. Best not to risk such a power draw. It might call attention.

"Your shift ought to be over, Ches," she said.

A soft laugh. "And here I thought you preferred me to Command."

She did. She truly did. "You shouldn't sacrifice your rest," she said.

"Zahlia. Is the ear placed?"

"Not yet." She hesitated, running a thumb along the smooth surface of the sphere. It was hard and smooth, as soft as water— but not pliable in the least. "There are strangers here. Did Command send them?"

"No." His answer was immediate. "What kind of strangers?"

What kind, indeed? She didn't know. "From away. They appeared on top of the temple. Ahnien called a council meeting."

A brief silence. She wondered if he was checking to make sure that Command truly hadn't sent them, or if he was simply surprised beyond the ability to respond. Though whether by the appearance of the strangers, or the news of a council meeting on a funeral day, she did not know. "Strangers," he said. "It's impossible."

"And yet I observed them myself." She paused. "Should I investigate?"

Another silence. She imagined him running a nervous hand through the star-kissed locks of his hair. She imagined him gazing into the sphere, wishing he could see her face. "Your mission remains. It is too important to set aside."

She knew that it was. Zahlia assented and ended the connection before Command could decide to come and berate her personally.

No better time would occur, not when Ahnien himself had called this meeting. Not when the city was celebrating, all work set aside in honor of the dead. All work but hers.

Robed in black, Zahlia took to the streets and made her way through the shadows to Champion Ahnien's home. She would place the ear where he would never detect it, giving Command a direct link to his plans.

But the leadership had not forbidden her from learning more about the visitors. So once she'd finished her task, she would locate them. And she would learn what she could.

CHAPTER 11

SHANNON DIDN'T KNOW what to expect from these people, if they were people at all. They certainly looked like people, and they spoke like people, though she wished she could have heard more of their own language before this Ahnien person had engaged the translator technology.

The gray-haired man and his posse led them away from the domed building and along the main boulevard, where the crowd was beginning to dissipate, and Shannon tried, rather fruitlessly, to take in every detail.

Which proved impossible, because there were so many. *Too* many. The frosted-glass look of the paving stones beneath her feet. The tinkling melody of the music, still present. The smells of honey and fruit that sweetened the back of her tongue with every breath. The gem-colored robes and the ornate balconies and the bubbles. Everywhere, the bubbles.

There were far too many details to absorb.

Damian walked along beside her, whistling. Infernal man.

Ahnien led them to a nearby building, an understated one compared with the bright colors of the clothing and even the other structures, many of which were painted in eye-searing shades of yellow, blue, and purple.

This one, however, was made up of pale gray stones. The doors—which seemed to be made from the same clear material that formed the paving stones, and perhaps the bubbles—opened before them, ushering the party into a large, empty space. Shallow steps rose to either side, leading to a mezzanine balcony lined with closed doors. Offices?

"Now *this* looks like a government building," Damian said, breathing deeply. "I can practically smell the paperwork."

Shannon elbowed him in the ribs, but he just grinned. At least he hadn't mentioned brothels again.

Several people were already waiting for them in the center of the room. They all wore green robes like Ahnien's, and they nodded respectfully as he entered. They all appeared, at first glance, to be men.

And they all looked quite human, too.

"How did they know to come here?" she whispered.

"It's simple, doll," Damian replied. He didn't bother to whisper. "The nice man spoke to his pretty bubble toy, and it called his friends over to play."

Shannon elbowed him again, but this time he caught her arm, holding it gently. "Violence isn't necessary, my darling. Words will do."

If he didn't stop with the pet endearments, she was going to brand one across his forehead.

One of the council members stepped forward, offering them a short bow. It might have been Shannon's imagination, but she thought he was angling himself slightly more in Shannon's direction than in Damian's. He was nearly Damian's height, with jet black hair and a jawline that would make a model cry. When he straightened, meeting her gaze, she saw that his eyes were crystal blue. When he smiled, a jolt of electricity curled through her ribcage.

"I do not see why we couldn't have allowed our guests a few minutes to rest," he said.

"Oh, we don't need to rest," Damian said. "Our trip took approximately three point four minutes. We're ready to council. And be counseled."

Shannon hadn't intended to travel to another galaxy, or another part of the galaxy, or anywhere beyond the systems and planets she knew. But now that she had, she felt certain she'd done so with the most embarrassing possible companion. What was the foolish man thinking?

"My name is Borona," the handsome man said, tossing a bemused smile in Damian's direction as a seventh council member—at least, judging by the green robes—came bustling through the doors. The newcomer had long scraggly gray hair, and his arms were laden with books and papers. More books, and more papers, than Shannon had ever seen together at one time. Nearly everything in the Parse Galaxy was digital.

The newcomer dropped his papers, which were immediately caught by one of the orbs. She hadn't even realized it was there; they did seem to pop out of nowhere. "*Champion* Borona," he said. "It is most unusual to interrupt a funeral day for a council meeting. Most unusual."

He pounded at the stack of papers and books, scattering a few pages to the floor. The orb zoomed to retrieve them.

"Come now, Sileux," Ahnien said. "The passed will understand. Please, sit."

Sileux pointed a gnarled index finger at him, and then at Borona. "Penance will need to be paid."

Borona's smile turned wry. "Indeed? You seem most willing."

Sileux sputtered, but Shannon was watching Borona, who looked away as if finished with the conversation. When he caught

Shannon watching him, he lifted his eyebrows in amused acknowledgement. An apology for his fellow council member, perhaps. "Please, sit," he said, echoing Ahnien's request.

Damian, who was still holding on to her elbow—no doubt afraid of another jab—said, "Where we come from, there is a marvelous invention. We call them chairs. They stand about thus high from the floor, and one can settle one's posterior comfortably within them."

Borona blinked at him, as if uncertain of how to respond. "Is he always like this?"

"I haven't known him all that long," Shannon said. "But I think so."

Damian bowed.

Champion Sileux made a sound of disgust, then bent his knees. And kept going, lowering himself toward the floor, as if he planned to collapse and begin flailing his arms in a tantrum. Judging by his behavior so far, that probably would have been in character. Instead, one of the bubbles caught him, materializing around his body as if its molecules simply knew what he wanted and reorganized themselves as such.

"Even more marvelous." Damian released Shannon's arm and let himself drop toward the floor. She hoped rather than expected that the movement would end with him sprawled out on the salmon-pink stones. Instead, a settee shaped like a wave caught him mid-fall, and he landed in a perfect lounge.

Somewhat more delicately, Shannon moved to sit. The air produced a stool, setting her at a height slightly above the rest of the council. She'd take it.

They were arranged in a haphazard sort of circle, each chair as different as the person who sat upon it. Ahnien's was ornate, with wide arms and a back decorated with what looked like grapes. Borona's was simpler, though the seat was cushioned; Sileux's, of course, was a study in austerity, as unyielding as stone. It had a back, but no arms, and it forced the man into what had to be a painfully rigid posture, his books and papers floating on the sphere beside him.

"A council meeting on a funeral day—" Sileux began.

"Is regrettable," Ahnien finished. "I agree, and I apologize. If penance is to be made, it will be mine."

Sileux folded his arms over his chest with a humph of agreement, but he said no more.

"Our visitors arrived from another sector of the galaxy," Ahnien said. "And it was crucial I inform the council of their arrival."

On the settee, Damian snored. He'd been the one to bend logic to travel here. Why was he acting like he didn't give a damn? Impossible man.

If he wasn't going to collect information, then Shannon most certainly would.

"So we *are* in the same galaxy," she said. Her fingers itched to withdraw her fliptab, to record this conversation, but she forced herself to stay focused. She'd have to take in what information she could, particularly since it seemed Damian wasn't going to be of any help.

"Most likely," Ahnien said. "However, we have no idea how you got here."

They all looked at her, expectant. Like they expected her to pull out a whiteboard and start explaining the physics of landing without landing. As if she knew anything about that.

When she glanced at Damian, he met her gaze with a wink. Completely unhelpful. An orb floated above his head, and he raised a hand to poke at it, sending the thing soaring up toward the ceiling in a controlled spiral. "We have absolutely no idea," he said.

The council's attention shifted to him so suddenly, their heads moving simultaneously as they looked at him, that

Shannon had to stifle a laugh. Had they honestly thought she was the mastermind here?

Damian poked at another bubble. "I set the Parse Galaxy's trade Currents to resonate with the underlying layer of stasis-field technology, which allowed me to calculate the exact location of distant resonant fields, and pop—" He flicked the bubble with his finger, sending it rocketing up to join the others. "—we sling-shotted across the galaxy and onto your fair planet. The name of which, I'm just now realizing, we don't know."

The council members were looking at him like he was out of his mind, which was actually a rather fair assessment. Shannon thought that very well might be the case. He'd programmed the trade Currents to do *what*? Resonate with the underlying *stasis* fields? She wasn't a scientist, but a ten-year-old could have told him that made no sense.

"This is the planet Pheon," Borona said slowly. "In the star system Echao."

"That won't do. I'll never remember that." Damian rolled his wrist, like he was preparing to flick another bubble across the room. Having learned their lesson, though, they were now giving him a wide berth. "I'm going to call the planet... Finn. The system can be Echo. Or Karl. I like Karl."

"Pheon," Shannon repeated, ignoring him. "And the city?"

"Dear heavens, don't add a *city*," Damian said.

There were hundreds of planets in the Parse Galaxy, and Shannon would have wagered that Damian Riddle could name most of them. More, perhaps, than the average galactic citizen even knew about. Why was he acting like a fool?

"We simply call the surface Pheon." Ahnien was watching Damian with a strange look on his face, like he wasn't sure whether to call a doctor or a prison warden. Or perhaps assign the man as court jester.

"Well," Borona said, holding Shannon's gaze with his

arresting blue-eyed one. "I don't have any answers. But I do know where we ought to start."

"No," Sileux said. "Don't say it."

"We'll introduce them to the people," Borona said. "We'll throw them a party."

Sileux threw his head back, grimacing in agony. As if Borona had suggested they ought to plunge knives into their own guts.

"You seem distressed," Damian said. "Does party mean something different here? Are our translators glitching?"

"A party is a start," Ahnien said slowly. Shannon didn't see how a party was a start, or why a council meeting had to be called to plan one. Though she supposed there were politics at work that she didn't understand. Ahnien had been the one to discover them, to greet them. Perhaps there were protocols involved. Rules, spoken or un. And expectations.

She wanted to know them all.

"If there is to be a *party*," Sileux said, articulating the word like something rotten, "it must be in penance for interrupting today's funeral. A memorial party. A celebration of the passed. A—"

"I do not see why it cannot serve both purposes," Ahnien replied.

Sileux sputtered. "That is almost worse."

"Almost," Borona murmured, "but not quite."

Ahnien rose, robes billowing around him as he did. "Yes. Tomorrow will suffice. But first, we must allow our guests to rest. Come."

Damian rolled off the settee, pushing off it with one hand and straightening with a sigh as the seat evaporated. "I hope your beds are as comfortable as your magic chairs."

Ahnien stood, gesturing toward the door. "I will show you to the guest house."

Damian fell in beside her as she followed Ahnien toward the

door. He yawned, stretching his arms as he walked. Laying it on a little thick, in her opinion. But then, she wasn't sure this man ever did things by half measures. Go big or pretend to sleep; that appeared to be his motto.

"I thought you weren't tired," Shannon said. "The trip only took three-point-four minutes, right?"

"A good memory is unforgivable." He was striding after Ahnien, the stiff fabric of his jacket a stark contrast to the softly billowing material of the robes. "I'm weary beyond belief."

"Yet not weary enough to shut up."

"That day will never arrive, I'm afraid. Come along, little reporter. I've got a feeling there's much to see."

CHAPTER 12

DAMIAN HAD SPENT a significant amount of time figuring out what it would take to zip him across the galaxy to an alien planet. He'd burrowed through dusty old library shelves. He'd fought off angry people so he could steal those books from the dusty old library shelves. And, worst of all, he'd spent months *reading* the books from the dusty old library shelves—the horror—only to find that they contained nothing of value.

He'd turned his considerable powers toward getting here, for the purpose of saving his own life. And now that he was here, he had no idea what to do.

It was a new sensation.

The whole place was a touch too sparkly, a touch too... welcoming. Damian didn't trust welcoming, and though he could appreciate a bit of sparkle, he didn't entirely trust *this* sparkle. It was difficult to see beyond it, impossible to make out the true core of this place.

He'd have put significantly more trust in an honest bit of dirt.

Ahnien escorted them away from the boulevard and into a section of the alien city where the streets were a touch narrower. Still covered in those crystalline paving stones, however; Damian would have bent to crack a sample off of one, had Ahnien not been watching them so closely. The council member didn't seem to fear them, which made him either very foolish or very experienced in matters of intergalactic affairs. Damian hoped it was the former, though he supposed the very fact of his own alien blood pointed to the whole intergalactic affairs thing.

Either way, it was disconcerting that Ahnien and the others appeared to have viewed the arrival as an inevitable event. *Champion* Ahnien, that was. It appeared to be some kind of honorific, a title. Somehow, Damian didn't think the people had voted this man into power. Or any of the rest of them, either. But what were they champions *of?*

With thoughts like these tumbling around in his brain, who could appreciate the sights and smells of an alien city?

Well. Shannon, for one. She had her fliptab raised and was taking pictures of the ground, the buildings, the bubbles, and even Ahnien. For all her concern over Damian's behavior back in the council room, the reporter was perfectly willing to record without asking.

Ahnien didn't seem to mind. He led them a few blocks away from the main thoroughfare, a task one of those bubble things probably could have performed on his behalf—Damian could swear the ones in the council chambers had been trying to spy on him, swooping in his face like that—and into an unremarkable building, where he deposited them into separate guest rooms with a final sweeping bow.

He'd never admit it, but Damian did feel a certain responsibility for Shannon's wellbeing. In a certain light, he could see how it might appear to be *somewhat* his fault that she'd ended up here. He wished Bruce were here so he could stuff the two of them in a room to watch each other. Probably should've brought the bot off the ship.

Even so, he didn't regret the separate accommodations. She

shouldn't have stowed away on his ship, though she couldn't possibly have guessed the consequences of doing so, but she could still rely on him to get her out of here. Eventually.

For now, Damian needed to focus on his own problems.

The door closed behind Ahnien, leaving Damian alone in the alien hotel room. A brief inspection told him that, shockingly, the door was shut fast. No knobs, no locks. No way out.

He could have slept. He *wanted* to sleep. But the first obstacle to that desire was the fact that this room wasn't equipped with a bed. There was only a hammock, which hung unappealingly from the ceiling. He never liked this idea of tangling himself in a cloth so he could sleep suspended from the ground. It would be too difficult to a maneuver an escape, in the event of an attack.

The second obstacle to sleep was the fountain they'd stuck into the middle of the space. It reminded him of the Interplanetary Dwellers station where he'd spent a not-unpleasant shard of his childhood. And a bit of time recently, too. The trickle of water was supposed to be peaceful, but he'd always found it unconducive to slumber.

Otherwise, the room was clean and pleasant, but spare. No bots, no clocks, and, worst of all, no cookies.

"Well, what did you expect?" he said out loud. "A welcome basket?"

Resisting the urge to give the hammock a try in spite of his aversion to sleeping while dangling, Damian walked a full circuit of the room. He prodded the window at the far end of the room, but it was shut as tightly as the door.

He experienced a brief spike of hope when he discovered a sliding panel beside the hammock, though it turned out to be the door to a small bathroom. As grateful as he was to find this planet came with a version of a toilet, it wasn't precisely what he'd hoped for.

The ceiling panels in the bathroom, however, were deliciously accessible.

When Damian dropped out of the ceiling and into the hall outside his room, Shannon was already there waiting for him. She leaned against the wall with her legs crossed in front of her, paging through the photos she'd taken on her fliptab. She'd replaced the work boots with a pair of soft black slippers, the dress with leggings and an eye-searingly orange blouse. Damian wondered if a change of clothing had been provided for him as well.

Shannon was still wearing Lex's horrible green sweater. Which only increased the eye-searing-ness of her outfit.

Resolving not to ask how she'd managed to get out of her room faster than he had, Damian started down the hall as if he'd been expecting to find her there. "I wonder," he said, "how anyone procreates on this planet. What with all the hammocks."

She pushed away from the wall, clearly determined to follow him. "Are you serious?"

"Entirely. Now, if you'll excuse me, I have places to be."

The halls of this place were as spare as the room had been, though they were at least painted in light blue tones. Understated, thank goodness. His eyes were getting tired.

In a typical Parse Galaxy hotel, there'd be noise leaking out of the various rooms. Music. Laughter. Drama vids turned up so loud that you'd be forced to pound on your neighbor's door at three in the morning if you ever hoped to fall asleep. But the halls of this hotel, or guest house, or whatever it was supposed to be—a welcome prison, perhaps—were silent. Perhaps they had sound-proof paneling.

Or perhaps no one else was here.

Shannon was practically jogging to keep up with him as he made his way down the 'calming' hallway. He regretted the absence of her clattering boots. They'd have slowed her down. "Where are we?" she asked. "What are we after?"

"*We* are not after anything."

"All right," she said, "what are *you* after?"

The woman was extremely bad at taking hints. Perhaps, given her history as a nosy gossip columnist, she was simply well versed in ignoring them.

He gave her his best grin. "I told you. Best brothel in the galaxy."

"What if they don't have brothels?"

"Doll, everyone has brothels. They're a universal constant. I don't know how these particular people manage it, what with the hammock obsession, but I admit I'm intrigued. Now, once again, if you'll excuse me. I'm not partial to an audience."

He supposed he should have guessed that she wasn't the type of person who'd be shocked into storming off. Even if she did buy his story, which she probably didn't.

She followed him out into the street, which was as silent as the hotel halls they'd just left. Lights burned in a few windows, but it was much too quiet. No clinks or clanks of restaurant noise. No late-evening cooking smells. No one peering down from balconies or sitting on a roof to gaze up at the sliver of moon that looked as if it'd been stuck there as a party decoration. Though, on further inspection, he could see that many of the upper windows were propped open, their colorful curtains dancing in and out on the ghost of a breeze.

It might be due to the fact that they'd arrived on a funeral day. Or it might be that this city had a curfew. He slowed his steps, trying to glean information from the quiet streets. But he didn't know this place, didn't know its people. He couldn't say what any of it meant.

Golden light washed the street in a ubiquitous glow, and he frowned at the paving stones, trying to understand whether it was emanating from them, or if they were reflecting it from some-where else. But there were no street lights, only the occasional glimmer of an orb passing overhead.

The light didn't matter. He hadn't come here to look at weird light. He needed to find a genetics laboratory, or perhaps a medical center. Or, barring that, a library of some kind. Sileux had been carrying paper books, though there was no guarantee that the eye screen translator would allow Damian to read what he found.

He needed to find a place, a resource, that would teach him how to heal himself. He could start on the main thoroughfare and work his way along from there. It seemed as good a place to begin as any, even if he doubted he'd be lucky enough to find an inter-active directory bubble to assist him in his search.

But his reactions were still sluggish, the prickle in his veins still pulsing at his chest and throat. And he'd paused for a beat too long. Long enough for Shannon to reach over, to place a hand on his arm. He'd forgotten she was there.

"I'm good at finding shit," she said. "I could help you."

No one could help him. No one but a good alien doctor, or even a semi-competent one. Or, preferably, their notes. Damian was a do-it-yourself type. That was all.

Assuming they had doctors here at all. Assuming his ailment wasn't peculiar to his precise blend of blood. The people here might be just as confused as the physicians and scientists in the Parse Galaxy.

No. He had to figure this out for himself. Damian reached down and plucked Shannon's arm off of his.

"No one can help me, doll," he said. It was the closest he was willing to come to the truth. "Go back to your hammock."

And with that, Damian strode away, melting into the first shadow he encountered and leaving her alone.

———

...and time broke. Or maybe it just skipped.

Damian lifted his foot to take a step, to fall deeper into the shadows, to slink further away from Shannon Forest and her shrewd stare—

—and then he was back on the main thoroughfare, with dawn prodding at the sky. The suddenness of the change made him stumble, and an orb zoomed to his side, steadying him by propping itself beneath his elbow. He batted it away, looking around in confusion.

Moments ago, the streets had been silent. Now, doors were opening here and there along the avenue, the alien planet's residents getting ready for the day. The smell of baking bread joined the fruity sweetness. The city was awake.

Damian's hands were shaking, his breath coming in shallow gasps. And oh, lovely, the headache was back. For a brief moment, he allowed himself to lean on the orb—it still hovered patiently by his side—as he tried to pull himself together.

"Short night," he said.

The orb, apparently convinced of his ability to remain upright—more so than Damian—bobbed up to look him in the eye. Though it didn't have eyes of its own. "The time between sundown and sunup at this time of year is ten hours and thirty-seven minutes," it said.

He supposed he shouldn't be surprised to find that it could speak. The orb things must be bots, of a kind. The voice was a smooth, alto tone, and it didn't use as much inflection as his own bots did. Though his bots were a special case, in more ways than one.

Damian ran his tongue along his bottom lip. His mouth felt dry. His eyes, too. Like he hadn't blinked since sundown. "But your hours are short?" he asked hopefully.

"Pheon's days last twenty-seven hours. Therefore, the length of an individual hour falls in the average range of inhabited planets of its size and proximity to the system star."

There was still a lot of room for interpretation, but Damian decided to take that as a 'no, our hours are not short.'

The orb started to bob away, and Damian stifled the urge to call after it to ask for directions back to the guest house. He didn't need its help. He'd find it on his own.

And he did. After three wrong turns and an unfortunate encounter with a chicken, he recognized the red awning of the guest house and made his way gratefully inside.

Any lingering hope he might've had of a short Pheon night—one that would explain the skip between night and morning, if not the skip from the alley to the boulevard—was dowsed when he met Shannon on her way out, fliptab poised to record. She was dressed in a fresh set of leggings and a flowing pink shirt, and she'd finally ditched the monstrosity of a sweater. She looked well rested, and she smelled like some kind of herbal soap, which meant she'd had time to shower. Or however they cleaned themselves here. Perhaps that was the purpose of the in-room fountains.

When she saw him, she rolled her eyes. "Just getting in?"

He tossed her a wink, though he really wasn't feeling it. "The night life here is wild, if you know where to find it."

She narrowed her eyes, studying him closely enough to make him want to back away. He held his ground, but only out of principle. The woman was halfway to terrifying. "Looks like you did more fighting than loving," she said, nodding at his hands.

He didn't dare look at them. But now that she said it, his knuckles did feel sore. He balled his hands into fists and gave her the most nonchalant shrug he could muster. "I don't kiss and tell, love. And I don't punch and tell, either. Now if you'll excuse me, there's a hammock waiting for me."

With that, he turned and swept into the building.

He didn't open his hands until he was safely in the confines of his own room, with the door shut fast behind him. They were still shaking from the time skip or time break or portal passage, or whatever the hell had happened to him back in that alleyway, but that was only to be expected.

What was worse, much worse, was that Shannon was right: his palms were covered in blood.

CHAPTER 13

DESPITE WHAT DAMIAN CLAIMED, Shannon's first night on Pheon left her with no evidence that the place enjoyed a thriving nightlife. He might consider himself to be a creature of the dark, but Shannon had her own knack for discovering secret veins of activity. She'd done it on Bromar. She'd done it on Ve Station.

So now there were aliens. Was it really all that different? After Damian had vanished, ostensibly in search of sex, she'd wandered the streets for a few hours, looking for the telltale signs of the hidden nightlife he'd been so certain he'd find. In the Parse Galaxy, she'd keep an eye out for misplaced cobblestones, an errant splash of color, or a flower displayed on an otherwise stark windowsill.

Here, there were no such signs. Not that she expected them to be the same, just... she thought she might be able to notice something that was out of place. Even though, as she'd reminded herself as she'd made her way back to the guest house, it'd taken her months to learn even one sign back home. It would take time.

She hoped she'd have some.

Last night was last night. Tonight, there was a party, and Shannon stepped out of the guest house and into an entirely different world. There'd been a crimson gown waiting in the closet when she'd returned from exploring the city's canals—it hadn't been there yesterday, when she'd rummaged through it for leggings and a fresh shirt—and it brushed her legs in pleasant swishes of fabric as she moved into the streets, feeling as though she'd wandered into a fairy story from her childhood.

Last night, the city had been silent. Tonight, it *sang*. Orbs filled the sky, sparkling like nearby stars. A high concentration of them hovered above the boulevard, the rest spiraling away from that center like fireflies released from a jar. Hundreds of them. Thousands. Every person she passed was swathed in glimmering cloth, and string music played joyfully in the background, always giving the impression that its makers were just around the corner. No matter how far she walked, though, she never encountered them.

She paused, trying to pinpoint the source of the music as an orb descended to hover in front of her, its sides gleaming silver as if it, too, had dressed for the celebration. Its smooth alto voice offered to escort her to the party, and she nodded, though it seemed that the entire city *was* the party.

But when the orb led her to the roof of the council building where they'd had their meeting yesterday, it became clear that this was indeed the heart of it. The concentration of orbs she'd noticed hung above this place, lending their radiance to the gathering of council members and other important citizens like an oversized and ever-moving chandelier.

"Enjoy the celebration," Shannon's guide-bubble said. And then it zoomed away, back in the direction of the guest house. Not assigned here, apparently. How did that work? Who directed them? She'd have to ask about that. Maybe find a way to get a tour of the control center. If there *was* a control center.

Shannon turned a slow circle, accepting a drink from a passing orb more so she'd have something to do with her hands than because she particularly wanted it. This must be one of the taller buildings in the city; from here, the network of canals she'd explored earlier reflected the light of the orbs, giving the whole place an otherworldly sparkle.

She would need to see the view from up here during the day. For now, she turned back toward the party, scanning for a familiar face. She didn't quite realize she was searching for Damian until her eyes landed on him, tucked away in the corner with a drink like hers propped between two fingers. If they'd given him clothes to wear, he hadn't opted to do so; that duster jacket might as well be fused to his body.

He was standing with a pretty woman, her hair shining like strands of gold. As Shannon watched, he bent close to her ear— very close—to whisper something that made her raise a hand to her mouth, laughing.

Shannon rolled her eyes. Typical.

"You are not enjoying the party."

Shannon turned as a woman spoke beside her. She hadn't heard anyone approach. But then, she'd been distracted. By the party, the music, the lights. Nothing more.

"Neither is my husband," the woman continued, nodding to where Champion Sileux stood with a pair of men she recognized from the council meeting, though neither of them had spoken in the brief meeting. Shannon supposed the woman might be referring to any of them, but Sileux alone looked unhappy. His lips were pursed, his eyes narrowed to match, as if he wanted everyone in the room to know that he objected to the party. Or perhaps to everything; disapproval did seem to be his default.

Shannon looked back at the woman, trying to picture the two of them together. This woman was young, perhaps near Shannon's age. Her blonde hair spilled over her shoulders in waves, and there was a dusting of sparkles across her cheeks and lips.

"Champion Sileux is *your* husband?" Shannon asked.

The woman raised an eyebrow. "Is it so difficult to imagine?"

"No," Shannon said quickly. "I'm sorry. I just—I hadn't—"

The woman smiled, raising a hand to cut her off. "Please, do not apologize. You are from away, after all."

There was a question in that statement, though Shannon could not precisely make out what it was. "We are," she confirmed. "I am, that is. Damian is... who knows?"

The woman looked across the party, watching as Damian twisted a strand of his new friend's golden hair around a finger. She was gazing up at him like he was some kind of hero. He'd probably shown her one of those comic books.

"He is not with you, then?" the woman asked. Something about her tone made it feel like she was being careful with her words. Shannon couldn't imagine why, though she supposed she would have done well to take more care with her own surprise at Zahlia's marriage.

It wasn't any of her business. But then, she'd made a career of broadcasting things that were none of her business, or anyone's. Curiosity was her natural state.

"He's with me in that we shared a taxi here," Shannon said, forcing herself to look away from Damian. He could do what he wanted; it was nothing to her. She didn't even know him. "That's it."

The woman nodded. "My name is Zahlia."

"Shannon."

"Yes." Like her name was common knowledge by now. Well, perhaps it was. Did they have news feeds here? How did they get their information?

"Your husband," Shannon said. "He seems to think we shouldn't be celebrating now. Because of the funeral?"

Zahlia smiled. "If Sileux had his way, we would celebrate each death for a month. The shopkeeper who departed this life had a good, long one." She offered Shannon her arm. "Come, Shannon. Allow me to show you around my city."

Forbidding herself to glance back at Damian, Shannon nodded. "I'd be delighted."

———

"None of us witnessed your ship's arrival," Zahlia said. "What is it like?"

Zahlia had led Shannon away from the center of the party, along a gentle downhill slope of the main boulevard where the crowds were thinner. Even without the city's ever-present light, the orbs provided more than enough illumination.

Shannon was well acquainted with the art of interrogation. Enough, certainly, to recognize someone else's attempts at it. Even if that person was an alien, one who hid her interest behind a thin veil of casually polite interest. She could almost taste the woman's fascination.

"It's not my ship." Shannon couldn't think of a reason not to answer the question; she didn't know much, in any case. "I was on it for... an hour, maybe two. And most of that was spent stuffed in a cabinet."

Zahlia's thin brows ticked closer to together. "This Damian Riddle, he kidnapped you?"

Shannon wondered whether Zahlia's Champion of a husband would throw Damian in jail for a night or two if Shannon called him a kidnapper. Unjust, perhaps, though it would serve him right for disappearing on her last night if nothing else.

As much as Shannon would love to throw him under the hov-train right now, she didn't know what these people might do to him if they thought he was a criminal. Which he was, as far as she knew, but they didn't know it. They might feed him to an alien pet or something.

Shannon sighed. The truth, then. "I kidnapped myself, unfortunately."

Zahlia's expression didn't lighten. "I'm not sure my translator is working correctly. How does one kidnap oneself?"

"By choosing the wrong ship to stow away on."

"I think your culture might be a strange one, Shannon Forest."

Shannon just shrugged. Maybe so.

They'd been heading steadily away from the party, the sounds blurring and combining until they were nothing but a thin layer of background noise. Along with that ever-present thrum of string music, of course. A thread of woodsmoke wound through the air, and she wondered if someone might be holding a bonfire.

She'd expected Zahlia to lead her toward a busier part of the city, that a tour might consist of shops or marketplaces. Or, sure, a bonfire—why not? But the section of the city that spread out below them was too quiet. And darker, too, with only a few trailing orbs left in the sky. Most of them were concentrated back over the city.

"Your husband seems nice," Shannon said, trying to shake the sensation that Zahlia was leading her into danger. The smell of smoke was stronger now.

It wasn't a lie, exactly, even if it wasn't a complete truth either. Sileux seemed... curmudgeonly. Set in his ways. Not unlike plenty of politician types she'd encountered in the Parse Galaxy. That didn't mean he wasn't nice, though.

"My husband." Shannon recognized the telltale huff-and-headshake of a person holding the truth on the tip of their tongue. Zahlia pressed her lips together, as if to hold it in, before opening her mouth to speak again. "My husband was an epidemiologist during the war. He is a brilliant man, highly respected."

No doubt her words were as true as Shannon's had been.

"A war?" Shannon asked. "What—"

The question dried on her tongue as they crested a hill to look down on the lower-lying areas of the city, where an entire city block was engulfed in flame.

Shannon gasped, clapping a hand over her mouth as Zahlia let out a cry and began running toward the fire, much faster than Shannon would have imagined she was able, especially in that dress. But as Shannon ran after her, hurrying to catch up, it was obvious that the dress was sliced into flowing pants.

"We should send for help," Shannon called after her, but if the other woman heard, she gave no sign. She kept running, and it took all of Shannon's breath to keep up with her as a wave of heat smashed out of the burning block. Every instinct screamed for her to turn around, to run as fast as she could away from the heat and the raging flames.

Zahlia had no such hesitations. She barreled forward like a woman gone mad, hair streaming behind her as she dove toward the nearest building. She couldn't possibly be considering going in there.

One of the buildings exploded, sending wood and bricks rocketing into the street, and Shannon ducked as she ran, little good though that would do if one of the burning beams came straight for her. What the hell was inside these buildings to make them explode like that? The smoke had a chemical tinge to it, the fire lit with sparks of green and purple, but it might have been her imagination. They weren't solid details, not reliable. Not with the heat pushing at her from every direction.

An alarm sounded in the distance, like grinding chimes, and she glanced behind to see bubbles converging on the place from above. Would they fight the fires somehow? They'd formed a bridge earlier. Maybe they could make hoses, too.

Zahlia didn't even slow. She darted through the gaping door

of the building that had just exploded. Shannon cursed, slowing outside with her arm across her forehead, coughing as she peered between the doors. The room was thick with smoke.

Shannon cursed again, then ducked inside.

Sweat poured down her cheeks as she pushed deeper into the room, searching through the smoke for Zahlia. The far wall had gone up in flames, and a quick look at the ceiling said the beams up there would not last long. Shannon dropped to a crouch, but it only helped slightly with the smoke. The air was too thick with it; in a minute, she'd have to choose between saving Zahlia and saving herself.

A heartbeat, and then another.

On the third, she ran straight into Zahlia.

"It has to be here," the other woman said. She was standing, and Shannon forced herself to rise as one of the beams above gave a loud warning groan.

Shannon grabbed Zahlia's arm and pulled her back. "Whatever it is," she shouted, "it's not here."

Her throat was burning, her eyes stinging with tears. The whole place was about to fall down around them.

Zahlia coughed, eyes widening, then dropped into a crouch, yanking Shannon with her. "What are you doing here?"

As if Shannon were the one who'd run into trouble without looking back.

All right, she kind of had. But only to help someone else. She gripped the other woman's sleeve and pulled her toward the door. If Zahlia wanted to blame her, she could go right ahead.

Right after Shannon saved her life.

CHAPTER 14

"IF YOU DIDN'T SET the fire," Command said, "then who did?"

Zahlia didn't know. Her lungs were burning, and her dress was badly singed, yet she'd refused Shannon Forest's urging to see a physician. A medical sphere had administered pain medication. That was all she needed.

She was home now, shut in the safety of her own chambers. Sileux thought she was resting after the exertions of the party; he had not seen her return from the fire. He didn't know she'd been there.

Command did, however. There was no Ches to warm her ears with kind words today, or to ask whether she was well after she'd gone diving into the flames. Command certainly didn't bother to ask. She could be lying in a hospital bed near death, for all he knew.

He would likely prefer it that way.

"I do not know who set the fire," she replied.

It had been her mission. Hers. And someone else had beaten her to it. Last night, she'd been certain that person had been sent by Command. Judging by the barely restrained fury in his voice, that wasn't the case.

And she hadn't managed to retrieve any samples, either. A complete and utter failure.

"It spread further than it was meant to," Command said. "Much further." The sound of his voice made her want to punch a hand into her black sphere and grab him by the neck.

If it were possible, she might consider it.

"As I told you, I was not the one who set the fire," Zahlia said.

"And therefore carry no blame for its size?" Command's tone was incredulous. "It was *your* mission. We're trying to stress them, not starve them. Not yet."

Half a dozen grain houses had burned before the water spheres managed to contain the blazes. The person who'd set the fires must have done something to delay their arrival. But who would be operating without Command's knowledge?

"Did you retrieve the samples?" Command asked.

It was not just the aftereffects of breathing ash and smoke that made Zahlia's chest tighten. She'd known the question was coming. She would have asked it herself, of any operative. She would, in fact, have asked it much more forcefully. So why should it alarm her?

"No." She forced the word out from between gritted teeth, knowing full well what his response would be.

"Pull yourself together," he said. "Or I'll be forced to replace you. Find out who else is acting behind the scenes, if you can. But your primary mission remains unchanged."

She might have stood in his place. She nearly had. Instead, she was exiled here, away from everyone she knew. Stuck living in these frilly chambers, where lace covered every surface and danger lurked around every corner. Forced to live a double life. Utterly alone.

Command would never replace her, though; no one else wanted this job. *She* didn't want it, but she endured it. Because it was necessary.

She might have thrown all these words right back at him. She might have seethed. But to do so would set her back weeks, if not years. So instead, she merely unlocked her teeth, holding her head upright even though he could not see her, and forcing calm into her tone. "I understand."

CHAPTER 15

DAMIAN'S HANDS WOKE HIM, not because they were bloody this time, but because they hurt like the devil.

Throbbing hands. That was a new one. Usually it was his head, especially after a party like that one, or those lovely black ribbons on his chest. He sat up, intending to swing his legs over the side of the bed.

Instead, he upset his hammock and flipped himself onto the floor. Hammocks. The *worst*.

"At least it is carpeted."

Damian looked up to see Bruce silhouetted in the window. Excellent. He did love having an audience for his every mistake. Particularly a sardonic audience.

"Mmph." He rolled over, wincing, and pulled himself up to sit. Now his head did hurt. "What are you doing here?"

Bruce turned away from the window, his leg joints whirring softly as he moved. "The ship became tedious. I decided I should assist you. Which is tedious, too, but not quite as tedious as watching Lex and Mojo play checkers seventy-five thousand times. What happened to your hands?"

They were becoming something of a giveaway, these hands.

Damian opened them to find a layer of red blisters covering his palms. "No wonder I feel like I've been fried in oil."

He got gingerly to his feet and stalked over to the fountain, dipping his hands into the running water. It was cold, at first unbearably so; but then the cold turned to numbness, dulling the pain. He'd need to wrap his hands before going out.

"*Did* you fry them in oil?" Bruce asked, sounding vaguely interested.

"Not that I recall."

"Perhaps it's another symptom of the illness that's slowly killing you."

Like he needed reminding. It would be a reasonable thought, though, had it not been for the fact that his shirt smelled like stale smoke. He wrinkled his nose, trying to remember if there'd been a bonfire at the party last night. There'd been a woman, he remembered that much. Had he insulted her into pushing him into the flames? Or a stovetop? He squeezed his eyes shut, trying to recall.

"I recommend locating a physician to assist with your injury," Bruce said.

"I'd prefer a recommendation for a good breakfast place. Know any?"

"I have not had time to catalog the city's eating establishments. I do not in fact know whether the city *has* eating establishments."

"Ah, well." Damian withdrew his hands from the fountain and gave them a shake. After a moment of consideration, he decided to forgo the wraps, instead pulling on his gloves. They chafed against the blisters, but would hopefully occasion less comment than bandages. "By the way, how did you get into the room?"

"I merely asked the sphere in the hall for access. At first it denied me, but I convinced it that I belong to you. Which was humiliating, by the way."

"You bear the burden well." Damian stepped up to the door, then paused. "You mean one of those orb things?"

"Yes. They refer to themselves as spheres. It is a general term, however. They have over five hundred individual classifications, including ears, irises, feet—"

"And let me guess, spleen."

"You are hilarious."

"I'll take that as a 'no.'" Damian examined the door, then cleared his throat. "Ah," he said. "I'd like to come out?"

The door slid open.

Unsurprisingly, Shannon was waiting for him in the hall. She looked up from her fliptab when his door opened, a twist of a smile on her lips. Had she been at the party last night? He hadn't seen her. "Finally figured out how to open the door, did you?" she said. "Hello, Bruce."

"Good morning, small-statured stowaway."

"Do you know where to find food?" Damian asked.

"Follow me."

His fear that they'd need to leave the building to find breakfast was short-lived. Shannon led him to the end of the hall and down a shallow staircase, where they emerged into yet another hall. A labyrinthian setup for a guest house, but fine. At least the carpets didn't carry the usual musty hotel smell. Not a single dot of mold between the bricks, either. He'd stayed in worse places.

How the woman had learned her way around so quickly, he didn't know. Wasn't sure he wanted to, really.

He'd expected the breakfast room to be as empty as the guest house; instead, he recognized Ahnien's voice drifting down the hall before Shannon had even reached the door. The empty halls made his words clear.

"We lost several grain warehouses to the fire," Ahnien was saying. "We're still assessing the damage. I hope we will not need to petition for aid."

"Souls forbid," another voice responded.

Damian paused, his fingertips throbbing. "What fire?"

Shannon turned back to look at him, eyebrows raised. "How drunk *were* you last night?"

"Very, doll. Very. Roll your eyes all you want, by the way. I'll just make a drinking game out of it. An orange-blossom whiskey shot for each. Any excuse to start early, you know."

"You would already have ingested three shots," Bruce said. "Make that four."

Shannon blinked at them. "There was a fire down by some warehouses last night during the party. It was bad. It lit up the whole sky, so I don't know what you were doing that you didn't see it." She held up a hand. "Actually, never mind. I saw the blonde. I don't want to know."

The startling thing was that Damian wasn't altogether sure himself. He'd been at the party, but he hadn't been drinking. Best to keep one's wits while visiting an alien planet. He remembered batting his eyelashes here and there, whispering in one ear or another. A tested way to learn more about where they'd landed without straight-up asking, if not an unpleasant one.

...and then he'd been rolling over in his hammock. He had no idea what had happened in between.

It was too much like the time skip in the alley to be a coincidence. Something was happening to him. He licked his lips, searching his brain for the moments between the curve of a pretty woman's neck and the fall from the hammock. There was nothing.

Shannon was watching him, like she expected an answer, so he turned on the best grin he could muster at the moment. Which, sadly, was probably no better than a fifth or even sixth best. "Actually," he said, "I finally found a good bro—"

"Never mind." She held up a hand. "Like I said, I don't want to know. You asked for food, here's food. I'm going to check on Zahlia."

Damian frowned. "A flower?"

"No." Shannon drew the word out into one long, impatient syllable. "She's Champion Sileux's wife. She was showing me around the city last night, and she practically threw herself into that fire they're talking about. I want to see if she's all right."

Damian paged through the list of names he'd been keeping in his head. His hands felt like they were on fire, especially where they brushed against his gloves. "Sileux? That's the cranky bumbling one?"

"Yeah. He's a genius, apparently. An epidemiologist."

"That sounds like a personal problem."

She smacked him on the shoulder. "He studies diseases, fool. She said there was some kind of a war. He was important in it."

Damian shuddered. He could imagine too well why someone who studied diseases would be important in a war.

"Go enjoy your breakfast," Shannon added, "and try not to get drunk before noon."

Damian's head throbbed in time with his fingertips. "No promises."

She shook her head and spun on her heel, tossing a wave back over her shoulder. The damn woman was already perfectly at home here, clicking along in her little heeled boots—where had she gotten *those*?—with her bright yellow shirt flowing around her. He watched her go, resisting the urge to run back to his room and dowse his hands in the fountain again. Or at least open these doors and sample some of the food from inside. He could smell eggs and toasted brown sugar.

Instead, he just watched her. A medical center or library might be helpful, but an epidemiologist? He could have all the answers. Every single one.

"You are about to do something stupid, are you not?" Bruce asked.

Damian sighed. Breakfast would have to wait. "Always. Stay here. And save me some toast, will you?"

"I cannot make any promises. I have no use for toast."

Damian could have sworn that he and Shannon had been in this city for precisely the same amount of time, yet the reporter navigated its streets like she'd been born to them. She was easy to follow; the streets weren't overly crowded, for one. Besides, she might as well have stuck a flag on the top of her head with a sign reading 'Not From Here.' She nodded to nearly every person who passed, earning startled looks that she either didn't notice or chose to ignore. And she walked with a bounce to her step that was definitely unique in this place.

He trailed her at a distance, though she'd no doubt spot him right away if she decided to glance behind her. He stuck out as much as she did. Even more, since her bright yellow shirt seemed to be the fashion de jour on Pheon, making his half-rusted aesthetic all the more noticeable.

But she didn't turn. She merely bounced ahead, like she might start skipping any second. He could smell the remains of last night's fire in the air, stale smoke and charred wood, and an extra tang of chemical flare. Perhaps that was why the people looked suspicious. Or perhaps that was merely their status quo.

When she reached the main canal, Shannon turned right and headed straight for the first door on the corner. The houses were as cloyingly bright as the clothing their residents wore. This door was purple; in that sunshine-yellow shirt, Shannon looked like a bee landing on a flower.

Damian retreated toward the opposite corner to watch while Shannon spoke to one of the floating orbs Bruce had referred to as spheres. After a moment, the door opened to reveal a pretty woman with golden hair that spilled down her back in long curls. Her green dress added a new brushstroke to the visual cacophony, and he could hardly look at the glittering row of bracelets she wore on both forearms. Eye-searing, indeed.

At first, the woman's body language was stiff, her nose tilted high enough that he questioned whether she could even see Shannon standing in front of her. After speaking with her for a minute, however, the woman's shoulders relaxed, and she unclenched her hands. She nodded, then followed Shannon down the steps and along the canal. Luck took them in the opposite direction of where Damian stood.

Clearly, Shannon was working her gossip-columnist skills in this world, befriending VIPs and whatnot. He had to admit, there appeared to be some merit to the approach.

Better to remain uninvolved, though perhaps that didn't apply to Shannon. She could stand in the light. She could bask in it. For Damian, that path had long been shut.

He waited on his corner, watching the house for a few minutes. There was no movement inside, no flutter of shades, but that didn't mean much. Sileux could be there sleeping, or focused on some task at his desk. The house could be staffed with cleaners, cooks, and sphere-maintenance technicians.

And speaking of the spheres, hadn't Bruce said that some of them functioned as 'irises'? Did that mean they were like eyes? The damn things were ever-present, hovering overhead, drifting above the slow-moving boats on the canal, and dropping in front of people when technological assistance was required. The people didn't appear to carry fliptabs or personal devices of any kind. They merely used these spheres when they needed something.

It would be better to return after dark, when at least he might have a hope of evading the spheres' notice. Assuming they were watching, which he chose to. But Damian's sore hands, and the lingering scent of smoke on his duster, said that he couldn't count on himself come nightfall.

Besides, the spheres could probably see in the dark. Another assumption, but Damian had not lived this long by ignoring the obvious.

Aware that his time was limited, and that the women would not be gone forever—particularly if Shannon really had hauled Zahlia from a burning building last night—he started across the street. Entering the house might be as simple as asking a sphere for permission; entering without his presence being logged and reported, that was another matter.

Shannon would probably tell him to knock on the door—or the sphere, as it was—and ask Sileux directly for help. If the man was anything like the scientists Damian knew in the Parse Galaxy, he'd revel in the chance to examine a new specimen.

Damian had had enough of poking and prodding. He needed answers.

In the end, it was a matter of exploring the sewer. As it so often was.

There was an access point hidden on the bank of the canal, though the crystalline nature of the water—not to mention the sweet smells of the city—promised it did not act as a drain. Damian waited until the canal was quiet, with no boats passing, then sliced open the grate and crawled inside. A good pirate always kept his tools close at hand.

From there, it was simply a matter of access hatches, over-sized pipes, and a very good sense of direction, and Damian found himself spilling out of another grate and into Champion Sileux's basement. Simple—and lucky—as that. Damian moved silently up the stairs, hoping he'd trod delicately enough through that pipe not to announce his presence by stench alone.

But there didn't appear to be anyone home to smell him; the house was silent. Damian moved through the ground floor, opening doors, until he came upon a promising one. Thank goodness these people used desks and bookshelves, rather than trying to work from hammocks. Really, he would have had to intervene in that.

Champion Sileux's desk was covered in paper. Such a strange thing. Paper was rare in Parse, with only the oldest texts and the most backup of backup manuals available in that form. Everything was on the fliptabs, if not the eye screens. Everything was accessible from... well, from anywhere.

When Damian picked up a sheet of the paper, however, it was stiff in his hand. It looked like paper, thin and... papery. But when he held it between his fingers, it didn't bend. Perhaps it wasn't paper at all.

More importantly, it was blank.

There were dozens of sheets on the desk just like it, and not a single one contained so much as a scratch of writing. He was careful to pick up each one separately, setting it back down precisely where it had been.

After a time—it might have been ten minutes or two hours—Damian heard voices approaching the front door. Shannon's voice was unmistakable; she sounded insistent, but he couldn't tell what she might be trying to convince the other woman of. If anything. Perhaps she was merely holding forth on his many flaws.

But no. That was an arrogant thought, even for him. Damian set down the final not-paper with a sigh, then slipped out of the room. He would need to return here. Now, it would be best to flee before his presence was detected.

CHAPTER 16

ON HER FIFTH morning waking up on Pheon, Shannon decided to treat this like a working vacation.

No more stressing. No more worrying. And no more waiting for Damian, who was once again missing from his room this morning. She didn't believe his brothel lies, not for a second. People didn't reprogram famously mysterious alien technology for the singular purpose of sampling exo-galactic sex. Not even Damian Riddle.

But clearly, Damian was on his own path. If he didn't want her help, she wasn't about to force it on him.

As she left the guest house and stepped out into the street, she supposed she should probably be feeling worried. Anxious to get home. But home didn't have any more to offer than Pheon and its Echao System. There was no one waiting for her, no one looking. She'd probably get back there eventually, and if she didn't? This place had food, friendly enough people, and sunshine every day. In fact, the only hint of rain so far had woken her in the night with gentle taps on the window that'd lasted an hour before fading away. This morning, the streets weren't even damp.

Most of all, this place had fresh stories to unearth.

Shannon made her way to Zahlia's house, taking her time and allowing herself to wind back and forth over the canal bridges at every opportunity. They were fashioned out of smooth stone, more like the inside of a bathtub than any canal she'd heard of in the Parse Galaxy. Though she supposed she'd mostly seen pictures of those, anyway. They always looked like too-straight rivers, with grassy banks and cargo ships making their dutiful way through the middle.

These canals might have been made for beauty alone. Bridges spanned them at intervals, and while there were some ships that looked to be carrying cargo, they resembled delivery vans more than freighters. Shannon wanted to hop onto one of their decks and ask the captain where they were headed. To the mountain range she could make out in the distance, perhaps? To other towns, cities? What was the city's main import? How did the grain reach the warehouses?

She hadn't wanted to interrogate Zahlia yesterday on their walk, not when the other woman had been so plainly shaken by the fire. Today, though, she intended to ask a few more questions.

Besides, she enjoyed the Echain woman's quiet presence. Despite her reckless dive into that fire, she was a calm, friendly companion. Shannon hoped they might even become friends after a time.

But when she approached Zahlia's door, a nearby sphere informed her that the other woman was out for the day. Shannon nodded, failing to hide her disappointment, and made her way along the canal in the same direction they'd walked yesterday.

Well. If Zahlia wasn't available, there were plenty of others. She'd tried smiling and nodding at them, but while they looked at her with curiosity, no one returned the gestures. That was to be expected; cultural differences and all.

After several such encounters, Shannon grew bolder, making

a point of meeting the gaze of the next person who passed. He was wearing a fire-orange hat that fell somewhere between a beret and a bowler, his brown hair flowing into a loosely tied tail at the back of his neck.

"Excuse me," she said, "I was just wondering if you could tell me—"

The man bowed slightly, shook his head, and hurried away without so much as pausing.

In a hurry, clearly. Late for work, or... whatever they did around here. The spheres appeared to do most of the jobs.

Undeterred, Shannon attempted to stop an older person in fuchsia shoes, then a parent holding the hand of a curly-headed child, and, finally, a trio of teenagers who stared at her with open interest.

No one said even a word to her. They merely returned her nods, somewhat clumsily, and quickened their steps.

Defeated at last, she sat down on the bank and pulled out her fliptab to snap a picture of the canal. Zahlia seemed willing enough to speak with her, and Ahnien, too. Why was everyone else avoiding her? Had they been instructed to do so? Or was she doing something to offend them? Perhaps if she asked one of the spheres for assistance, she could make sure she approached them appropriately.

"Homesick already?"

Shannon looked up, shielding her eyes so she could make out the person who'd spoken to her. It was the handsome council member from the first day, standing before him with his hands tucked in his pockets. Those crystal-blue eyes were practically sparkling as they met hers, a startlingly beautiful contrast to his dark hair.

"Champion Borona," she said.

He nodded in appreciation. "Excellent memory."

"Yes, well, it's easy to remember names when so few people

will actually agree to speak with you." Realizing that she sounded more than a little bit petulant, she tried to pair her words with a smile. Though she suspected that simply made her look pathetic.

He hummed, his voice smooth as butter. "Yes, well. You did arrive in a rather unconventional way." He offered her a hand. "Come. Let me show you around."

She took his hand, allowing him to pull her to her feet. His fingers were warm around hers. "I did get a short tour."

"Ah, but it was interrupted by disaster. Mine will be better." He leaned in closer, conspiratorial. "Pheon is best by daylight."

"I don't know, Champion. I saw the way the spheres sparkled at the party."

"Only the beginning, I assure you."

He led her to a spot along the canal where a collection of flat-bottomed boats waited, and they clambered inside to sit on a bench in the middle. She was about to ask about paddles and rowing when a swarm of spheres collected around them, pushing the boat into the water and remaining beneath it so they could usher the boat along the canal.

"Keeps them from tipping," Borona said, watching her with interest. "Do you not have spheres in your part of the galaxy?"

She shook her head, taking a few pictures. "I wonder that you need the water at all."

He chuckled. It was a pleasant, warm sort of sound. Shannon had very nearly forgotten what it was like to hang around with a pleasant person. "We'd need a lot more spheres, otherwise," he said.

She leaned over the edge of the boat to peer into the water. It was a milky sort of turquoise color, almost like the blue of the trade Currents. Not *quite* as blue, but close enough to raise a few goosebumps along her arms. It was more like amusement park water than anything she'd seen in a natural river. "Do people swim in it?"

"Oh, yes. There's a particularly good spot in the other direction. I can show you."

She could imagine it. Floating along the canal now, all of her questions about trade seemed... if not silly, then rather unimportant. As usual, she found herself wondering who the people were, what stories they would tell about their own world.

Trade was a piece of it, certainly. But she wanted to meet the traders themselves, the sailors, the shopkeepers, the cooks. The canal swimmers. She wanted to find the hidden kittens. She wanted to break through the facade of perfection, not to unearth dirt, but to find something... something real.

There were the questions surrounding the fire, of course, and the strange circumstances of the *Quandary*'s landing. Plenty of mysteries to solve. But who were the players here? What did they love? And what made them yearn?

The boat rounded a curve in the canal, giving them a straight-on view of the mountains in the distance. Jagged and frost-tipped, their exact situation relative to the city was difficult to judge; she didn't have the right perspective. At the center of the range—directly ahead, anyway—one peak jutted higher than the rest.

Borona was watching her with a slight smile on his face, though it wasn't a mocking one. Merely curious, perhaps. It looked good on him, a thought that made her flush slightly.

"Does the mountain have a name?" she asked.

He trailed a hand through the water, his long fingers dragging a trail of ripples alongside them. "Yes, of course. It's Locke's Peak."

"Who's Locke?"

"Someone out of legend."

Shannon added a mental note to locate that legend. And find out whether her translator would allow her to read it. "What's beyond the mountain?"

He chuckled again, his fingers still playing along the surface of the water. "You're good at digging, aren't you?"

"I'm a reporter." One who couldn't help but notice that he hadn't answered her question. She filed that away, too. What was beyond the mountain, and why didn't Borona want to tell her?

He frowned, but it was a playful one. A slight wrinkle to accompany his smile. She had the impression that he was flirting with her—and that alone might be reason enough for him to evade the question. "What is a reporter?" he asked.

She hesitated. "Someone who collects information and presents it for the public. They might investigate trade or crime. Or look into what the Fleet is doing."

"Ah, so you will tell your galaxy everything about us. And what is a Fleet?"

She found herself returning his smile, though she couldn't tell if he was teasing her. "Never mind," she said. "Maybe no one wants to talk to me because of all my questions."

Borona sat up, brushing his fingertips lightly on his shirt to dry them. "No, no. I promised to show you around. Forgive me. Ask whatever you like."

He seemed sincere enough, so she decided to take him at his word. If he grew tired of her questions, he could always find a way to ditch her later. She wouldn't even hold it against him. Mostly.

"What was with the funeral?" she asked. "I thought it might be a state funeral—like a Champion or someone—but then Zahlia told me when we arrived, it was for a shopkeeper's funeral. Not that a shopkeeper isn't worthy of a city-wide celebration, just... we don't do that at home. Anywhere. I don't see how you can have such an elaborate event for every single death."

Not that the population seemed enormous, but she had to imagine that there would be funerals constantly. And that event had been a lavish one, with the parade and the dancers, the apparent holiday that shuttered most activity for the day.

"Not every..." Borona hesitated, expression growing truly sober for the first time since they'd met today. He met her eyes, as if sizing her up. As if deciding whether to answer her question. "Some rely too much on old traditions. It doesn't make much sense."

"It's nice to celebrate a life."

He inclined his head. "Indeed, I don't disagree. But it's complicated. There are people who would like to change things. For the better, I hope."

Shannon didn't know this place well enough to ask why celebrating every life would *not* be for the better. Were the funerals a drain on their economy? Some form of religious oppression?

She suspected, however, that he was one of the people advocating for change. She wanted to form the words to ask why, to dig deeper, but this was apparently a subject of cultural and political importance. Not a topic to rush.

Perhaps she'd do well to ask where she could find a library. Or whether it would be appropriate to interrogate a sphere for more information. Surely a sphere wouldn't take offense at her questioning—though it might report every interaction to the council, and *they* might take offense.

"Now," Borona said as the boat approached an intersection of canals, "I think we should take this right turn here. There's a pastry shop along the Eastern shore that will make you weep with joy. Allow me to escort you there."

Shannon returned his smile, allowing the subject change. "I never say no to pastries."

She dipped her own fingers into the water as he instructed the spheres to change course. As she gazed into the water, she realized she could see Locke's peak reflected in it, the image shifting amid the ripples caused by the boat and her fingers.

Shannon looked up, turning to watch the mountain as the boat rotated ninety degrees to turn in the direction Borona had indicated. Her stomach fluttered with a sense of wrongness, and the certainty that the peaks should not be reflected from this angle. She might not be able to judge the distance, but she could tell that well enough. Her head tilted with a sense of vertigo, with the sense of witnessing something that was *off*. It felt like a mistake. Or a glitch.

She opened her mouth to ask about it, then realized that Borona was speaking. "...cupcakes with the most artfully fruity centers. You will have to tell me if there's anything like them in your part of the galaxy. I suspect not."

She nodded, forcing herself to utter something enthusiastic as she cast a quick glance back over her shoulder at the peak. But it was gone, vanished behind a row of short homes lined up along the canal. When she looked down, the effect in the water had also disappeared.

Borona made good on his promise, escorting her first to the pastry shop—which was as good as advertised, though she couldn't fully enjoy the buttery sweet taste of the cakes with the ghost of the mountain's reflection still singing in her head. They walked back toward the guest house through a thriving market strung with flags and hanging lights, the smell of roasting nuts and unfamiliar spices thick in the air, and they stopped for a richly flavored drink that tasted of mint and orange, with a thread of foreign sweetness mixed in. Music played in the background constantly, mainly plucked strings and high-pitched woodwinds, though she still could not quite tell where it was coming from.

The sights, the sounds, the smells, the tastes. It was all so vivid, so tangible. But as the day wore on, she began to wonder whether any of it was real.

CHAPTER 17

FOR ONCE, Damian didn't encounter Shannon lurking outside of his door when he left his room for the day. Wonders. They refused to cease.

Aside from the time skips and the throbbing blisters on his hands, Damian had been feeling mostly not terrible since arriving here. Though he supposed a fussier person might complain that time skips and mysterious blisters were more than enough to be getting on with, and shouldn't he lie down for a while?

But all in all, he'd felt... okay. At least compared to the past few months, when nearly every day had challenged his will to live. Every dip in the Current had sent him bouncing along a roulette wheel of consciousness, and pain had been a constant.

Yes, he still had poison lines etched through his chest, and yes, they still crawled up toward his neck. But they'd *been* on his face. It had to be a good sign that they were retreating.

Or perhaps it was wishful thinking on a topic he knew nothing about.

Leaving Bruce in the guest house to ponder the true nature of ennui, Damian made his way through the angular streets and down to Champion Sileux's home, letting himself in via the same convenient sewer panel he'd availed himself of yesterday. Hoping that Shannon was not here taking tea with her new best friend—it seemed like the kind of house where one would take tea, rather than just drinking it—he slipped into Sileux's office once again.

Yesterday, Damian had been too pressed for time to take a decent look around. He'd found an office-like space, and he'd started sifting through it. No time to see the sights.

Today as he slipped through the heavy door, he found himself struck by how... un-lab-like this place was. Shannon claimed this man studied disease? Well, Damian knew a lot of scientists in the Parse Galaxy—too many in fact—and every single one of them was determined to surround themselves with shiny tables and clinky glass beakers and fancy equipment that got your hands slapped if you tried to touch it.

In comparison, this room seemed old-fashioned to the extreme. No shiny tables or microscopes. It didn't even have any of those tech spheres floating around in it, though Sileux probably called some in to help him when he needed them; they appeared to belong to the city as a whole, rather than to individuals. Shannon would know.

Damian shook his head. Shannon would probably find the answer to his little dilemma in forty seconds. Of course, she'd get herself in trouble in the process, and he'd have to bail her out. Not worth it.

Damian returned to Sileux's desk and opened the top drawer. Like the desktop, it was stuffed with piles of that not-paper stuff. When he brushed his fingers across the surface, he found it rough and bumpy rather than smooth.

Interesting. But as every not-paper in this drawer was blank, it wasn't nearly interesting enough. Perhaps the bookshelves.

He was about to set the not-paper aside when a throat

cleared. Rather pointedly, it seemed, though that might have been his imagination. Always running away with him.

Damian looked up to see Champion Sileux standing in the doorway, looking as grizzled as always. His gray hair hung in frizzy puffs around his shoulders, the descending locks seemingly determined to make up for the receding hairline in the front. He held a single book in his hands.

And, strangely, he didn't look cranky. Which, before this moment, Damian had assumed to be the man's default state, and an absolute certainty when encountering an intruder in his home. Instead, Sileux merely looked befuddled. As if he were trying to remember whether he'd invited Damian over to rifle through his things, and it'd slipped his mind.

How in the name of everything cosmic had Damian failed to hear the man coming? He was losing his touch. Or perhaps it was the ringing in his ears. Perhaps he wasn't feeling quite as well today as he'd believed.

"I *thought* I'd left those pages a hair to the left." Sileux limped into the room, setting the book down on a round table in the corner. "You've been here before, I take it?"

Damian straightened, taking a long beat to replace the page before meeting Sileux's watery gaze. "Ah," he said, "is breaking and entering frowned upon here? Sorry. New here. I didn't realize."

Sileux pointed a shaky finger at him. "Funny, funny. You forget we're familiar with your part of the galaxy, hmm?"

"I'm not sure how familiar," Damian said, slipping his gloved fingertips into his pockets. "You seem to have dropped us some travel tech—thanks for that—and vanished. Mostly. Why not introduce yourself? Come by, say hello, make some friends?"

Sileux humphed. "Someone did try."

A fact of which Damian was well aware. He would not exist,

otherwise; he'd gotten his alien blood, Echain blood, from somewhere. And there had been that small matter of the planet-crushing dictator who'd taken up residence in the Bone System for a time. Though he was gone now.

But what did the Echains know about it? Damian leaned a hand on the desk, steadying himself. His ears were ringing more forcefully now.

"There was an attempt," Sileux said. "To usurp your galaxy. More than a century ago now, it was."

Damian leaned his thighs against the desk, hoping that would prevent him from swaying. "Popular goal, in the Parse Galaxy. A regular Tuesday. But the Currents have been there much longer than a century."

Sileux waved the comment away, like it was nothing more than a fly. "Yes, yes. Much longer ago. But that's another story."

Damian wanted to know it. More than that, though, he wanted to know whichever story would come closest to ending with: 'you have alien blood and somehow a disease that's killing you, and here's the solution to all that in a nice easy package so you can return to pirating and generally continuing to draw breath.'

He had no idea which question to ask first. So the best course, he decided, would be to simply choose one. *Any* one.

"All right," Damian said. "I'll bite. Who tried to take it over?"

Sileux humphed again. A tic, perhaps. "We've got a sister system. Drachao. Nearly identical to ours, and connected to us by a thread of what you call a Current. They acted... badly. There was a war."

The war that Shannon had referred to? Or another? Unless these people lived very long lives, which he had to admit as a possibility, Sileux would not have been around for that war. Maybe there'd been other skirmishes after the fact.

The guy was old, sure. But not *that* old.

"And that's why we can't have nice things?" Damian asked.

Like friendship between galactic sectors and tech sharing, and cures to mysterious alien diseases. For a start.

Sileux sighed, and Damian thought he detected sincere regret. "Indeed. Come, let me show you."

———

Sileux brought Damian back to his own ship.

Sort of. Damian recognized the building, at least; who wouldn't, when it was the single structure in the city with a rounded top? At least, that he'd encountered so far.

Though Sileux did opt to enter through the front door, rather than the ceiling. Though Damian still felt justified in his choice of escape route, given that there hadn't *been* a door that he could see when he and Shannon had arrived.

Now, all it took was a gentle request to a floating bubble that bobbed around the street outside. He supposed he could forgive himself for not thinking of that. Through an entry passageway and a second set of doors, and they were there. The floor was still covered in that thin layer of water, and his footsteps echoed into the space like he was walking through a cave with stone walls and vaulted ceilings. Though that was probably an acoustic trick, perhaps to do with the control panels that surrounded them to every side. Something about the sharp edges of those consoles, their diagonally tipped caps, made him feel like he'd stepped into a gift box. He knew instinctively that if the panels moved in closer, the sides would snap together.

The room looked the same as it had the other day, barring one crucial detail.

"Not to sound accusatory," Damian said, "but where's my ship?"

Sileux waved his hand, like the question wasn't important.

Just another fly to bat away. Strange; Damian hadn't seen any flies in the city. Or any insects at all, come to think of it. "Floor panels shift," Sileux said. "We keep this area clear."

"In case more visitors come crashing in?"

"Yes."

Damian folded his arms. The man sounded all too serious.

"Is there anything about this technology that strikes you as strange?" Sileux asked, gesturing toward the paneled consoles.

Yes, Damian thought. *Everything.* "I don't recall signing up for Pheon 101 class, professor," he said. "Why the quiz?"

Sileux laughed. Damian hadn't thought the man had it in him. "Humor me."

Fine. Damian turned a circle, scanning the consoles. "They don't appear to be operational," he said. "They look like a good hard poke would send them crashing to the floor."

Sileux scoffed. "A child would note that."

"Certainly. Children are brilliantly smart. Easily thirty times as observant as your average adult, I'd say."

Sileux wagged a finger at him. Damian had the distinct impression that the man was enjoying this lesson. "Even so, my thieving friend. Even so. Go deeper."

Damian raised an eyebrow, but Sileux didn't budge. How long had it been since someone had tried to teach him something? Not yank him from lab to lab, not lecture him on the properties of good behavior, not suck his blood into beakers for their experiments without asking his opinion on the matter, but actually *teach* him?

No one in the Parse Galaxy would dare. They were usually too busy trying to chase him away, for starters.

Damian turned a slow circle, pressing a finger to his bottom lip. Pebble-sized pockmarks marred the frames of several of the consoles, as if they'd been caught on the edge of a firefight. Some of the corners had taken on a hint of rust, though not as much as he might have expected in a room with a permanent layer of water on the floor. The yellow lights blinked, sickly. Like a fliptab on the fritz.

Like a fliptab. But these people didn't *have* fliptabs, or anything like them. Damian let his gaze drift toward the ceiling and up to the dome through which he and Shannon had escaped.

"No spheres," he said. "There are no spheres in this room."

"Correct." Sileux rested a hand on one of the frames with a reverence that Damian thought the man would have reserved for books and stern words. "The spheres will not come here."

"*Will* not? That makes it sound like they've got a choice."

"They do." Sileux patted the frame lovingly. "These are gateways. Wormhole-stabilizing ones, to be precise."

It was rare to feel the world literally tipping on its head. Metaphorically, sure. Damian made a point of tipping his metaphorical world on its head as often as possible. But for vertigo to strike because of a revelation like this, well. That was a rare sensation. One that he'd be sure to celebrate as soon as the need to brace himself on one of the portal frames passed. For now, the priority was to prevent his buckling knees from dropping him unceremoniously to the puddle-filled floor.

He held on carefully, though. Very carefully. Because if he understood what Sileux was telling him, this technology was precious indeed.

The Parse Galaxy didn't have wormholes. Yes, he had a friend who claimed to have unlocked the secret to creating them, but she'd stopped her work when her math told her she was destabilizing the universe.

More of a friend of a friend, really.

The point was, wormholes were impossible.

And yet... and yet, so was his miraculous landing here. There was no denying the fact that the *Quandary* had gone directly from the Current to the surface of this planet. No dip through space—Currents usually flowed along the outer edges of a star system—and no drop through a planetary atmosphere. If these were portals, that solved the mystery. His ship had come through a stabilized wormhole.

Damian felt the sudden urge to begin caressing the portals himself. "This is incredible."

"It would be," Sileux said gruffly. "If they worked."

Damian looked at him, trying to understand. "They do. We landed here."

"Yes. You did land here. That's why everyone's being so nice to you. Interrupting funerals for you. Dedicating parties to you that should be for the passed."

The man was frowning, still clearly upset about that. Damian still wanted to know more about those funerals, but they seemed... inconsequential, compared to what Sileux was saying. His mouth felt dry, and each swallow brought claws running down his throat. "And here I thought it was my winning person-ality," he said.

Sileux just stared at him, shaggy eyebrows raised.

Damian swallowed again. "I bent the Current to get here. Does that mean it was connected to these gates somehow?"

Sileux laced his hands together over his stomach. "It is connected, yes. Shall we run some tests?"

Damian's head pulsed with a sharp pain, his throat protesting every swallow. Not to mention the pins and needles running constantly across his chest, those poison lines. He'd had enough tests to last a lifetime, from people who were well-meaning friends. As trusted as anyone could be, in Damian's world.

He didn't want to tell Sileux any more than the man had already figured out. But he also didn't know how to proceed without him. Perhaps he should ask Shannon to accompany them. Or Bruce.

But no. He'd stay as close to working alone as he was able. It was crucial.

"All right," he said. "Let's run some tests."

CHAPTER 18

AFTER SPENDING the day with Champion Borona, during which Shannon had studied the water, the skies, the people, and even the food for any sign of the strangeness she'd noticed with the reflection in the canal, she went back to her room and settled on the floor with her back to the wall, where she spent the night paging through all the photos she'd taken on Pheon. The funeral parade, the council chambers, the guest room, the canals. The mountains. She zoomed in, examining every inch of every photo for another glitch, another sign that something was off in this world.

The mountains shouldn't have reflected in the water like that. It felt *wrong*, like a reflection of a reflection.

Even if she could shake the feeling, convince herself that she'd imagined it, she couldn't reconcile her experience with the people here. So many of them refused to exchange more than a hat tip or a bow. Nearly everyone she approached. Were they real, or were they part of some simulation—snippets of code working in the background? And if so, who had done this?

A good investigator didn't try to prove her theory. A good investigator took note, collected details, and then put the pieces together. But Shannon couldn't help feeling that everything here fit together too neatly. Too precisely.

When her pictures revealed nothing, she went through them again. By that time, night had blanketed the city in that eerie almost-darkness, and she rose to stand by the window, ignoring her sore muscles and searching for the source of the ghostly light. Another clue. But what did it mean?

One of the spheres cracked the window for her when she asked, allowing a breath of air to circulate into the room. It smelled like the canals, like the wet stone beside a waterfall. It smelled like sweet fruit and new-to-her spices.

When all else failed, she tried pinching herself. She didn't wake up in a game console or a water tank, though she did rather feel like she'd stepped into a fantastical drama vid of some kind. For a moment, she almost laughed at herself. Here she was, on an alien planet, spending the day gondola-ing around with an impossibly handsome man and sampling delicacies—and she was half convinced it was all a fabrication.

Maybe it wasn't a simulation at all. Maybe it was merely culture shock.

She let the thought wash over her. She acknowledged it. She filed it away.

And then she went out.

———

She didn't know what impulse pulled her toward the part of the city where the fire had occurred. An instinct, maybe. A gut feeling, the kind that led to breaking news stories. Shannon heard nothing more about the fire since it'd occurred; even Zahlia, who could have been killed in her reckless dive, had barely been hurt—and had brushed off any attempt Shannon made to discuss what had happened.

Zahlia ought to have been more injured than she was. Hell, *Shannon* probably ought to be more injured than she was.

Or maybe she was beginning to feel paranoid.

Still, a not-small part of her was braced to find the warehouses standing whole and undamaged. When she crested the low hill that looked down on them, however, the omnipresent yellow light let her see that this corner of the city had indeed sustained massive damage. Skeletons of buildings stretched toward the sky like a final gasp, their walls collapsed and broken, and the air contained a lingering bite of char. The fire had taken an entire block, and chunks of the surrounding ones.

She could also see, to her surprise, that she was not the only person headed toward the ruins.

Champions Ahnien and Borona were descending the hill, not twenty paces ahead of her. She recognized Ahnien's cap of gray hair, and Borona's wide-shouldered silhouette. If she'd gotten up here any quicker, she'd have run straight into them.

As it was, she stepped aside, attempting to channel Damian's sneaking skills as she hovered by the corner of the nearest home. Strange that this city appeared to have no trees. And inconvenient, when you wanted to hide.

A third Champion walked with Ahnien and Borona, one whose name she didn't recall. Perhaps it hadn't been mentioned. He was shorter than the other two men, and as she moved to follow, she could hear that he was speaking forcefully, waving his hands as he did. Borona kept turning his head to the side, making her jump, but he didn't look back; he appeared to be nervous that his colleague's diatribe would call attention. Every once in a while, Ahnien put in a word that prompted a new burst of anger from the shorter Champion.

And, because sometimes an absence could be a crucial detail, Shannon took note of the fact that there were no spheres in sight.

None hovering above. None waiting on corners or doorsteps. Not one, at least that she could see.

Shannon trailed the Champions as closely as she dared, straining to hear what they were arguing about. If it was an argument at all; it seemed to be.

The men headed into the warehouse section, where the smell of char hung heavier in the air. Together, they entered one of the burned-out buildings halfway down the destroyed block. Not the same one Zahlia had gone running into, though it might have been a twin to that one.

Picking her way over fallen beams and scattered bricks, Shannon followed, then paused to watch from a shadowed corner as Champion Borona dragged a large crate out from the side of the room. One side had collapsed, leaving awkward fragments of wood that the Champion attempted to use as handles.

"Destroyed," Ahnien said, peering inside. "All of it destroyed."

When Borona moved away from the box, its contents were all too clear. Twisted lengths of metal lay crushed and broken within the crate, surrounded by bits of shrapnel like discarded torkfruit shells. What was left of the crate was blackened and signed, with explosive patterns of char stamped into the wood.

Alien planet or not, Shannon knew weapons when she saw them. Grenades. Gunpowder. Explosives of one kind or another. They might have lost some food stores in the fire, but this warehouse hadn't been keeping them. No wonder it'd gone up like a cinder box.

Zahlia must have known it. Which made her all the more foolish for diving inside.

Borona dragged another box from the wall, and another. But the crates were little more than cinders, disintegrating at the slightest touch. For the most part, their contents were barely recognizable.

"What are we going to do?" Borona sounded sad, and there was an edge to his voice she hadn't heard before.

"Keep checking." Ahnien strode to the wall himself, dragging yet another crate forward. This one crumbled before he could get it halfway across the room, spilling its pitiful contents across the blasted floor. It was incredible that anything had survived at all. "There might be something to salvage."

"This sets us back months." That was the short Champion, the one whose name Shannon didn't know. He made no move to help with the boxes, merely standing in the center of the space and wringing his hands. "Years."

It set them back from what? Shannon felt herself leaning forward, straining to hear every word the men uttered. She felt like she'd entered a theater halfway through a play, with no idea how to catch up on the plot.

"And yet, we continue on," Ahnien said.

"Perhaps if we did not shut down the entire city for every funeral, this wouldn't have happened." That was Borona, the edge to his voice tipping into heat.

The short Champion wheeled around, raising his hands—to accompany his yelling, or maybe to strike at Borona—but a loud *crack!* resounded from above, and the Champions scattered as a beam came crashing down from the ceiling. Shannon clapped her hand over her mouth, stifling a scream as Borona dove out of the beam's path. It crashed to the floor with a crushing boom, scattering splinters of wood and ash.

Ahnien was the first to pick himself up out of the dust, hands shaking. Fair enough; Shannon's hands were shaking, too. She still had them clapped over her mouth. She absolutely could not afford to let them find her here. Not after what she'd learned about the weapons.

"Are you both well?" Ahnien asked.

"Well enough," Borona replied. The third Champion merely

coughed, but he was on his feet, too. The beam had missed them, if narrowly.

"Let us go," Ahnien said. "We'll report to the council. There's nothing to salvage, and this place is unsafe. We'll have to begin again."

Shannon let her shoulders sag in relief as the men left, passing within several feet of her hiding place. She didn't need to follow them back to the city. She'd let them get ahead, far ahead, and then she'd work her own way up the hill. If she stayed by the door, she could dart outside if another beam seemed ready to fall. Afraid the next falling beam might block her path, she kept her eyes on the ceiling. One crack, one creak, and she'd be out of here.

In the rafters, something *moved*.

Shannon squinted, searching the ashy air for the source of the movement. As she watched, a shadow melted into sight, picking its way along one of the remaining beams, and her chest went cold. What if that beam had not fallen by mistake?

She was moving before she could talk herself out of it, tiptoeing her way further into the room. A ladder stood against the far wall, and a quick yank told her it was still firmly attached. Enough to risk it, anyway. She climbed, taking her time and moving softly, trying very hard not to think about how precariously this building stood. Or the fact that she was very likely following someone who'd just attempted to murder three council members in front of her.

Shannon reached the top of the ladder and stepped onto a narrow catwalk. They must have used it to access wares in the middle of the building without disturbing the rest, which made sense. Particularly given that they'd been hiding weapons in here. No need to bump the explosives by accident.

The catwalk had a rail, but it slanted dangerously toward the floor, obviously broken by the fire. Ignoring the urge to hang on to something, anything, Shannon stepped tentatively out onto the walkway. It gave a violent shudder, and she paused.

But the shudder had nothing to do with the catwalk's precarious tether to the ceiling or walls or wherever it was attached; the shudder came from the person she'd seen from below. They were moving toward her, a shadow in the darkness.

Shannon fumbled her fliptab out of her pocket. This person had very likely dropped that beam on purpose; they might even have set the fires.

She could take their picture. She could report them to the council, or dig deeper into what was happening here. There was a pool of light drifting in from the ruined ceiling, illuminating a slice of the dusty walkway; in a moment, the shadowy person would step into it, and she'd be able to see who it was.

She waited, poised to throw herself down the ladder as soon as the attacker revealed themselves for a photo and fighting every urge in her gut that was telling her to run, *now*.

When the person stepped into the light, Shannon's fliptab dropped out of her fingers. It fell from the catwalk with a clatter and a smash that she hardly registered.

Because the intruder who'd dropped the beam was Damian.

CHAPTER 19

DAMIAN DIDN'T WANT to wake up. It was most unfair, in fact, that he could not spend five more minutes in his bed, nestled under the covers where it was warm and cozy.

But no. He wasn't in a bed. He wasn't even in the damn hammock.

He was looking into Shannon Forest's shocked face. Her eyes were like dark moons, her mouth open in a surprised O.

Also, they both appeared to be standing quite high above the ground.

Damian swayed, reaching for the rail beside him, but Shannon jerked forward and grabbed his arm, preventing him from leaning on it. Which, when he gave it a better look, was probably for the best. It didn't appear to be very stable.

His head felt like it was in the middle of being crushed in a particularly tight vise, his vision swimming. He could see Shannon. He could smell wet wood and char. He could hear the creak of the metal, feel its uneasy vibrations beneath his feet. Where the hell were they?

"Did you drop that beam?" Shannon's voice was hoarse, her expression one of absolute horror.

Damian swallowed. It hurt. "What beam?"

Shannon tightened her grip on his hand, dragging him forward along the catwalk, and it took every ounce of his concentration to place his feet correctly on the path. He couldn't quite see what was below, but catwalks meant heights, and heights meant the potential for broken limbs, smashed skulls, and other less than pleasant consequences.

He allowed her to drag him to a ladder, which felt more solid than the catwalk as he followed her down it.

As soon as he set foot on the ground, she recaptured his hand and began yanking him toward the door.

"There are pleasanter ways to wake a man up, you know," he said. As if she'd found him lounging on that precarious beam, rather than skulking along on top of it. He'd been standing there, damn it. How was that even possible? "I can give you some suggestions, if you—"

"Shut up." She stopped at the doorway, peering out toward the street. "They sent investigators. I really didn't think they'd be back tonight. We need to find another exit."

Damian scanned the area. There were dozens of spheres bobbing around outside, and he could see the shapes of several people directing them on where to go. Investigators, or a clean-up crew of some kind. What the hell had happened here?

His initial instinct was to push away, to stride off in the opposite direction. To take matters into his own hands. But he could not ignore the fact that he had no idea where he was or what had been happening. And that, somehow, Shannon did.

She might even know how he'd gotten here in the first place. Though judging by that adorable look of shock on her face, she hadn't been expecting to find him here at all.

Shannon dodged back into the burned-out warehouse, dragging him with her. She stepped over a fallen beam, stooped to pick up the fliptab she'd dropped—without letting go of his hand, by the way, which meant he was forced to stoop, too—then pulled him toward the far end of the room.

"If you wanted a date," he said, "you could have just asked. I'd have suggested a nicer place, however."

"You'll have plenty of time to talk later, believe me," she snapped. "For now, I suggest you shut up."

"That is not my forte, precious."

She jerked his hand harder, which he supposed he deserved. In a matter of a minute or so, she'd found a back door and was directing him through it, though none too gently.

"You're surprisingly good at sneaking," he said as they exited onto the street. "Are you sure you're a reporter?"

He half expected her to admonish him for talking. Instead, she said, "You'd be surprised how elusive celebrities can be."

"I thought you were a big war reporter now," he said. "No more celebrity gossip."

"I'd rather do the celebrity stuff." She pulled him up a short hill and into a non-burned part of the city. As soon as a tiny space between buildings presented itself, she dragged him inside it. There was barely room for both of them to stand there facing each other.

She let go of his hand, throwing it away almost angrily, then propped her fists on her hips to stare up at him. "Are you all right?" She held up a hand. "Actually, don't answer that. I still haven't decided whether I'm going to turn you in."

Damian had the unsettling impression that she was serious. Only he had no idea what she was talking about. His head was spinning madly, his memories a jumble. He'd gone to bed—hammock—and now he was here.

"Turn me in for what, doll? Excessive charm?"

She hit him on the chest. "This is not a joke. You dropped

that beam from the ceiling with three council members standing right below. It almost hit Champion Borona."

As far as he knew, he'd done no such thing. Not that it was a poor way to murder someone foolish enough to go wandering into a crumbling warehouse. But murder wasn't part of Damian's tool kit.

Still, he couldn't rule it out. Not when he had no idea how he'd arrived here in the first place. He suppressed a shiver, then decided to do what he did best: deflect.

"Ah," he said. "Borona. I see. He's the pretty one, yeah? I can see why his safety would concern you."

"Damian."

He fluttered his fingers, grasping for nonchalance. It felt slippery. Out of reach. "Don't worry, doll. I'm sure a tech bubble would've zoomed in and saved them at the last minute."

She gave him a strange look. "There were no spheres in the room, or on the entire block," she said. "Not until after. Even you should have noticed them."

He hadn't noticed that. But then, he hadn't noticed anything. It was all quite concerning, really.

He raised an eyebrow. "Even me? I'm very observant, I assure you. For example, I happened to observe a nosy reporter type poking around a burned-out warehouse in the middle of the night. Trailing after three council members who, I must note, appear to have been poking around in secret themselves. The plot thickens. And you're at the center of it, doll. How's that for observant?"

She continued to stare at him. "You're covering," she said. "What are you covering?"

He had absolutely no idea.

It wasn't that he'd never met someone who could see through him. His Fleet Commander friend did, well enough, and the strange collection of people that man now called his friends. Some of them. They knew his mask well enough, but there was nothing they could do to budge it out of place. And they lived with that. Why, he didn't know. They were fools, all of them.

Something about Shannon Forest made him feel like... like the mask wasn't there at all. Like it had no power in her presence.

"You've got me," he said finally. And he could have sworn the woman actually leaned in slightly. He almost felt bad. Almost. "I've got no idea how to get back to the guest house. Care to help a man out?"

She studied him for another minute, then shook her head. "If you'd added 'doll' or 'precious' to that, I'd have made you walk you around in circles all night."

"Oh, I know. I told you, I'm observant. I hope you appreciate the effort it took to refrain."

She sighed. "Come on."

Somehow, he also managed to refrain from asking whether she'd decided to turn him in.

When he made it back to his room, Bruce was powered down in the corner. Damian wanted to sink into the hammock—yes, even the hammock—but instead, he shed his coat and went over to tap the bot on the shoulder.

"Oh," Bruce said. "I was experiencing a resting hallucination involving an oil bath. I resent you for interrupting it."

"Apologies," Damian said. "Have you got a way to contact the ship? Without using the spheres?"

"Naturally," Bruce replied. He sounded affronted. "It was the seventh thing I did upon arriving here. First, I panicked. Second, I calmed myself. Third, I—"

"Don't need the full list," Damian said. "Just get in touch with Lex and Mojo, okay? Tell them we're coming to visit."

Bruce humphed, no doubt annoyed at being cut off. Damian would say he was persnickety for a bot, but since expanding the number of bots he knew personally, he suspected it might be a status quo kind of deal.

"And what should I tell them?" Bruce asked.

Fair question. "Tell them something's been borrowing my brain. And I need to figure out what the hell it is."

And then? They'd set a trap for it.

CHAPTER 20

IN THE MORNING, Shannon went to visit Champion Borona.

She'd considered stopping to check on Damian. But the odds of his being awake after the strangeness of last night were low, and even if he was, she wasn't sure she could take his particular brand of evasion this morning.

Borona had been evasive, too, but she still thought his was a shell she could crack. If only she could earn his trust. Besides, she did genuinely want to see if he was well after what had happened last night. Damian could tease her all he liked; it wouldn't change the fact that the man had been kind.

He'd pointed his house out to her during their tour, and she remembered the way well enough. It was painted a striking shade of red which, paired with its bright yellow shutters, called condiments to mind. Even on a street full of similarly bright-colored buildings, Borona's home stood out.

As she climbed the steps and sent a message through a waiting sphere, she didn't know whether to come clean about having followed him last night. A secret like that, once spilled, might have ripple effects she couldn't predict. If she wanted to learn to predict them, though, she'd need to dive in. To find out more. To dig up the truth. And, if she could, to help these people.

Borona himself opened the door for her. He smiled when he saw her, but the black circles stamped beneath his eyes said he'd slept little, if at all. His dark hair was disheveled, his complexion chalky in the morning light.

"Shannon Forest." He said her name like it was a surprise, though the sphere must have told him who was here to see him. "Please. Come in."

She followed him into a small sitting parlor, which was decorated in surprisingly calm tones of brown and blue. Borona retrieved a cloudy drink from a table with a base that was shaped like a bird, the surface balanced upon its beak. He held it up, as if offering her the same, but Shannon shook her head.

"Champion Borona," she began, but he raised a hand to cut her off.

"Please," he said. "It's too formal. We mustn't be so formal. Call me Jem. Please."

He was shaken, that much was clear; it felt like the charm and ease of the other day had been stripped away, leaving him raw. But whether it was because of the events she'd witnessed last night, or because of something else, she didn't know.

"You're distressed," she said, the secret of last night clenched tight in her throat. "Will you tell me why? I'd like to help, if I can."

Borona swallowed half his drink and set it back on the bird table. "Of course, and I thank you. You are…" He trailed off as he met her gaze. "Very kind."

"It's only right."

"Forgive me, but it's also rare. When directed at me, anyway. Violence is far more common, I'm afraid."

The crack of that falling beam reverberated in her memory as she watched him run a shaky hand through his hair now. There had been three council members in that warehouse last night, but Borona—Jem—seemed to believe the attack had been aimed at him.

Unless there'd been another attempt at violence that she hadn't witnessed.

He was watching her, his crystal eyes clouded with worry and, she thought, a bit too much to drink. Her throat dried as he took a step toward her, yet she found herself moving toward him, too. Like a magnet, like he'd caught her in his orbit. One she didn't mind entering. Her gaze drifted to his lips without her permission; they were full and inviting. Maybe Damian was right. Maybe she did care more about him than just...

He placed a hand on her waist, waiting for her nod before lowering his lips to meet hers. It was a sweet kiss, gentle. Hesitant, perhaps, but then they did hardly know one another. She could taste the lingering drink on his tongue, sharp but with a hint of sweetness. Like hazelnut perhaps, or sugared almonds. She pressed closer as he folded her close, reaching up to twine her arms around his neck. He smelled like sweet smoke; he felt warm, like home. A feeling she hadn't known in a very long time. He might well just be looking for a moment of comfort, nothing more. But she'd be lying if she pretended she couldn't use some comfort herself.

When he drew back, he offered her a smile. A real one, she thought, even with those smudges of darkness beneath his eyes.

"Please," she whispered. "Tell me what happened. Tell me how I can help."

He released her, then paced back to the table to retrieve his drink. "My views are not liked by everyone. By most people. I'm afraid this has made me a target. And last night... well. There was an incident."

She smoothed her expression as best she could, though she

felt like she was a heartbeat from coming undone. She could still feel his lips on hers, soft and strong.

She could still hear the crack of the beam before it fell.

If Damian really had been the one to drop it... why? What did he have against Champion Borona, or anyone here? She couldn't have been imagining the look of confusion on his face; he'd been as surprised to find himself there as she'd been to find him. She knew it.

At the same time, though, she had no idea why he'd come to this system in the first place. Why force the Current to spit them out of Parse? What was the fool man after? She knew half of what he said was nonsense, if not a full three quarters. Perhaps his confusion last night had merely been another layer of that mask he wore.

Her gut said it wasn't.

For now, she set Damian aside. He was a piece of the puzzle; this was another.

Borona was still standing there, his trembling hands gripping his glass so hard she feared it was about to shatter. She stepped forward, taking the glass gently from his hand and setting it on the table. She placed her hands on his shoulders.

"I need more information," she said. "I need to understand."

He licked his lips. It didn't seem possible, but he'd gone even paler; his lips were flirting with blue. "The technology here," he said. "It's different from yours."

"Different how?"

He opened his mouth, and a quizzical look flickered across his face. He raised a hand to his throat, swallowing hard. And then he fell to his knees, gasping.

Shannon dropped down beside him, shouting for help as she slung an arm around his shoulders, catching him before he could slam his head on the floor. A sphere materialized, flashing an alarm as it surveyed the scene. Distantly, some part of her noted that emergency lights blinked red in this world just as they did in hers. Champion Borona's lips were now fully blue, his mouth working soundlessly as she held him in her arms.

No. Jem. He'd asked her to call him Jem.

"Jem." She touched her fingers to his cheek, willing him to hear her. "Stay with me. Help is on the way."

A sphere descended on them—the same sphere or a different one, she didn't know—and began calmly scanning the Champion's body. Once it had finished, it soared toward his neck to administer a shot.

"Poison detected," the sphere said. "Please step away from the victim."

But the Champion was shaking his head, clasping tightly to her hand. She bent over him, touching her forehead to his. "He doesn't want me to leave him." She could hear the sob in her voice, but she didn't care. "I won't leave you."

"Acknowledged," the sphere replied.

She kept talking, though she was only vaguely aware of what she was saying. Comfort, little good it would do. She wondered, distantly, why her lips felt numb, and the inside of her throat. Like she'd been to the dentist for a filling. The thought felt far away, like a whisper.

"Bring help." She thought she might be screaming; she didn't care about that, either. "Bring help *now*."

"Help is on the way," the sphere replied. "However, you should prepare yourself—"

"No. I will not prepare myself. Get. *Help*."

Jem Borona spasmed, and then he lay still.

More spheres moved into the room, followed by people. But it didn't matter; Champion Borona lay dead in her arms.

Shannon swayed where she sat, dark shapes crowding into her vision, and she realized with a distant sense of horror that if the poison had been in his drink, then his kiss had exposed her to it, too.

"My lips are numb," she said.

The sphere descended toward her with a chirp of alarm. Before it could reach her, the world went black.

CHAPTER 21

DAMIAN HAD NEVER HAD any trouble assigning compliments to his own plans, and no trouble admiring the ingenious simplicity of this one. The fewer moving parts, the fewer things could go wrong. This plan was simple, yet elegant.

Unfortunately, it also relied heavily on Bruce.

The bot was currently sitting in one of the *Quandary*'s crew seats, its permanently upright posture increasing his air of disapproval. Though that might just have been the continuous volley of questions he'd been lobbing at Damian for the past hour.

"What if the thing that takes over your brain does not wake your brain up enough to fire signals?" Bruce asked. "Then I will not be alerted."

Damian braced his feet on the floor, using them to swivel his chair gently back and forth. Given enough time, and enough silence, he could fall asleep right here. It was no wonder, either, when his body kept insisting on walking around and committing crimes without his knowledge or permission. Honestly, he'd been missing out on the fun.

"There should be some kind of signal," Damian said. "My

limbs move, enough to walk me around like a remote-control drone. That has to mean my brain's involved somehow."

"You are giving your brain too much credit."

"Why not? It's a good brain. It's just a little bit hijacked at the moment."

Bruce didn't budge. "What if I receive signals that you have awoken, and when I arrive you are fist-deep in blood?"

"Then by all means, wake me up."

"What if I cannot wake you up? What if the thing that is doing this *is* you?"

A terrible thought. Damian rested his elbow on the arm of his own crew seat, his chin on the heel of his palm. "How could it be me if I don't know what it's doing?"

"Perhaps you are experiencing a personality split of some kind."

Damian wasn't about to rule out any possibilities. But he also wasn't going to interrupt the plan. He needed to find a way to trap this thing, or to pull it out of him. To discover what it was. "If Shannon could wake me," he said, "then I have faith that you can, too."

Bruce merely stared at him. "I do not like the responsibility."

"And yet, it is your lot. Lex, are you ready?"

The former nanny bot trundled over, popping open her storage hatch as she approached. "Would you like me to place the electrodes?"

"No need, doll. Can't mess up the hair." Damian took them out of her hands—claws, extensions, whatever they were—and pressed them neatly onto the skin above his ears.

"Lex would have placed them without messing up your hair!" Mojo said, scrambling out of the engineering hold and slamming the door behind it. Damian had no idea what the little bot had been doing down there. Probably playing hide and seek. "Lex is very good at placing electrodes and bandaids! She gives me bandaids every day, even though I don't have blood!"

Damian ignored Mojo's rambling. He tapped his ear, focusing on Bruce. "And you're not using any of those sphere things to catch the signal. Right?"

Bruce sniffed. "I am not an amateur."

"Bruce," Damian said, "I need to hear you say the signals are *not* connected through the spheres."

Bruce waited a long beat, as if to ensure that Damian knew he was being insulted. "The signals are not connected via any of the spheres."

"Good." Damian got up out of his chair and released the ladder he kept latched to the wall, propping it against his clock shelf. If he was going to hang out in here, he might as well do some winding.

"Now what?" Mojo asked. "Now what? Now what?"

"Now," Damian said, "we wait for the trap to spring."

CHAPTER 22

ZAHLIA'S ORDERS expressly forbid her from pursuing further information on the visitors. Command had made it absolutely clear that she was not to investigate them. That he had it well in hand.

For the first time in a long while, she found she didn't care what Command had to say, or what his orders might be. She found herself beginning to suspect—no, to *believe*—that Command knew far more about these visitors than he was telling her. He would say he owed her no explanations. Zahlia disagreed.

The visitors' spaceship had been shifted to the lower level of the temple building, which meant that someone had been in here working those mechanisms recently. The place smelled like rust and oil, like wet stone. She hated everything about it.

She descended the final step—the elevator required spheres, which would have given her away—and hid herself behind the door frame to study the ship. It was a strange vessel, with those claw-like extensions, its ramp lowered to kiss the stone floor. Like an open mouth. It brought scuttling creatures to mind. Sand-dwellers. Insects. She wondered if all the ships in their Parse Galaxy looked like this one.

From her hiding spot, Zahlia could see its owner moving about inside. She had not realized that Damian Riddle knew how to find his ship, though she supposed Shannon Forest was more than capable of locating it if she wished to. Still, Zahlia had expected to find the place deserted.

Never mind. She would wait.

Voices trailed through the space, echoing strangely off the empty stone walls and floor. Damian Riddle's voice was recognizable, but she didn't think she'd heard the others before. It was expected, of course, that a sphere would help operate a space vessel; perhaps Damian Riddle's ship contained something like this.

What strange names the visitors had. Riddle. Forest. Did every surname in their galaxy contain such meanings? Or was her translator merely grasping for the best approximation?

Zahlia was just beginning to consider sitting on the bottom step to wait—she *would* wait, however long it took—when a sphere zigzagged its way through one of the upper walls. There must be a sphere hatch up there, though she could not make it out from here. She stood, frowning. Spheres did not come to this space; they operated the perimeter elevators and the doors. Though perhaps that rule only applied to the floors above, where the gateways stood.

More concerning than the sphere's presence was the fact that it was glowing red, indicating an emergency.

The sphere cut a direct path for the open ramp, startling someone inside into a scream. Damian's voice spoke firmly, calming whoever it was, and Zahlia strained her ears to hear what the sphere had to report. But the voice was too quiet to make out from here. She wanted to stomp her foot in frustration, but she restrained herself. That was the kind of reckless action that had cost her the leadership, and she couldn't afford it.

She would prove herself. She *would*.

Whatever was in the sphere's report, it brought Damian Riddle running down the ramp less than a minute later. He made for the elevator rather than the stairs, thankfully, with the sphere hovering at his shoulder.

Zahlia waited.

The voices inside the ship had fallen silent. Perhaps Damian Riddle had taken them with him, or dismissed them for recharging. Perhaps.

Whether they remained or not, she couldn't afford to wait any longer. With a quick glance over her shoulder, Zahlia strode into the hangar.

At least this floor was dry. Easier to conceal her steps. She did not understand the constant pool of water on the floor above. She wasn't even convinced that the liquid was water at all. Did it help the gateways to operate somehow? Or was it part of the reason they no longer did?

She made her way across the floor and stepped up onto the ramp, listening. The room was silent.

And the ship's interior was as strange as its owner. It smelled of wood, oddly. Not the treated building wood of the city, but forest wood. Fresh wood. The kind she knew from back home, the kind that no longer existed on Pheon.

As she crested the ramp, she saw that Damian Riddle's ship was staffed by three strange... things. She did not know what they were. Statues, perhaps? One of them was molded in an approximation of a person, though only sort of; the head was a fat triangle, the legs spindly. There were knees, but they bent in the wrong direction, and the torso and arms were formed out of so many interlocking parts that it made her head hurt to consider how they worked.

The person-shaped statue was accompanied by a fat cone—this one was made of some kind of shiny, smooth material—and what appeared to be kin to a large, fluffy-tailed rat.

"Oh," the person-like thing said. "An intruder."

The rat thing spun in a circle, then began hopping up and down. "Alert! Alert! Alert!"

"Let's not jump to conclusions," the cone thing. "Damian might have sent her to greet us. Would you like some tea, my dear?"

Zahlia stared at them. "Are you beings?" she asked.

"That depends on how you define 'being,'" the person-thing said. "Can we think? Well, I can. Lex shows promise, upon occasion. Mojo, however, has always been a few circuits short of a full board."

"Thank you!" said the rat thing. Mojo?

Zahlia stepped deeper into the ship. "Damian did send me," she said slowly. "He was sorry he had to hurry away. I met him on his way out, and I promised him I would check on you."

It took a concerted effort not to add a question mark to the end of the sentence.

"That," the person-thing said, "does not sound like something Damian would do."

Zahlia turned a slow circle, taking in as many details as she could. There was a shelf above her head that contained a number of gadgets. "What do those do? Did they help bring you here?"

"No!" Mojo-the-rat-thing said. "We got here because Damian rerouted the Current. Right, Bruce?"

Zahlia dropped her gaze from the gadgets. "That is not possible."

"I do not trust you," the person-thing said. Bruce. "However, I am displeased at being commanded to remain on the ship. Therefore, I will talk to you, anyway. Furthermore, I will not lie. Yes, Damian did, in fact, reroute the Current to bring us here."

The cone thing, which had to be 'Lex,' made a clucking noise, but it did not admonish Bruce. Perhaps it had been feeling abandoned, too.

Zahlia shook her head. "It may be possible to reroute the Currents," she said. "But it is not possible to land here."

"And yet," Bruce said, "here we are."

Difficult to argue with such a fact.

Mojo let out a sob. It was still skittering around like a wild animal. "I want to go home," it said. "I miss my pet spiders."

Zahlia wandered toward the dashboard, taking in the depressed buttons on the controls. There had to be a way to crack it open, to get information. But how? This technology looked more like the gateways than anything else, and she was used to working with spheres.

If the red sphere had ventured here, perhaps she could convince another to do the same.

"Are there other beings like you in your part of the galaxy?" she asked.

Lex made a humming noise. "More than you would expect. We're called bots."

Zahlia shook her head. She didn't know the word. "Is that a race? A race made of... metal?"

"No, darling," the cone-thing said. "We are technology. Computers."

Strange. Very strange. It was natural that such beings, such technology, would have feelings and even personalities, as the spheres most certainly did. But it was not natural for spheres to exhibit such... independence.

As if summoned by her thoughts, a black sphere materialized in front of Zahlia without warning, like an eye made of darkness, and she startled as Command's voice boomed out of its shining walls. "Where have you been?" he demanded. "I've been trying to reach you for the better part of the hour."

At least the sphere had not been following her. "I've been busy."

"One of our operatives has been taken," Command said, and Zahlia cursed, heading for the exit.

"What about keeping us company?" Mojo called after her. "I want to play racerocks!"

"I don't think she was supposed to be here," Lex replied.

Zahlia ran for the stairwell. There probably wasn't any point in asking Command why he'd sent another operative, or why the person hadn't been directed to make contact with her. This was only her mission as long as Command said it was. "What happened?" she asked.

"He's been charged with Champion Borona's murder," Command said. "Apparently, they detected his arrival. They've been watching him."

Zahlia's tongue suddenly felt too big for her mouth, and she swallowed down a wad of fear. Champion Borona was dead? She shouldn't regret any Echain's pain, but he'd been... not unpleasant. Kind, even.

As she dashed up the stairs, she forced herself to focus on the moment. The accusation in Command's tone was unmistakable. "Am I to blame for this?" she asked. "I did not even know he was here."

It was not the question she should be asking. *Had* their operative murdered Borona? And if so... why? Murder was in the playbook, certainly. But she thought Command wanted to keep their interference below the surface. The Echains were not supposed to know they were here, working on the ground.

"He would not have *needed* to be there, had your performance been acceptable," Command said. "Had you been at your post, you would have known of this before I did. You could have reported it and received orders to intervene."

Her post. And what was that meant to be, exactly?

Wandering around Sileux's home. Supervising cleaner spheres. Reading books that had no point or purpose. Creating paintings of the city she despised. And waiting, always waiting for something to happen. Or waiting on orders to place ears in Ahnien's home, irises in the council chambers. They called on her but rarely; it was insulting.

Could Borona's death be the emergency that had sent Damian Riddle running from his ship? What did he care about Champion Borona, and why would they alert him of the man's demise?

The question made Zahlia's stomach flip with unease. Could Shannon Forest have been injured, too? Zahlia had observed the woman walking with Borona the other day, from a distance. Perhaps they'd been together again. Shannon Forest was interesting, and not unkind. Zahlia wouldn't want her to be injured.

"You need to free our spy before they get him to the prison," Command said, jolting her out of her thoughts. "They captured him one block from the scene of the crime. Borona's home. Fix your error, operative."

Zahlia ran.

When she reached the block, however, it was clear that it would be out of her power to free the captured operative. Red spheres swarmed the area, many of them swollen to near her size. She'd rarely seen them do that before. Unnerving. The throng was so thick that the spheres brushed her arms as she passed, which she was likely only allowed to do because of her husband's status.

Champion Ahnien was there, looking grave as he took a report from a sphere, and she recognized several members of the council staff pacing the block, each with a sphere hovering above their shoulder. The steps to Borona's home buzzed with activity as people hurried up and down, and she could see the flash of spheres moving about inside. Investigating, no doubt.

There would be no freeing their operative today if he was suspected of murder. Moreover, she suspected that Command knew it. That he had sent her here merely to punish her.

Because as the crowd parted, her gaze fell on the man being escorted—dragged, really—between Champions Marley and Cosir. His lip was bloodied, his eye swelling, and his head lolled as if he were only half conscious.

Zahlia couldn't help it. She lifted a hand to her mouth, covering a gasp. The operative accused of murdering Champion Borona? It was Ches.

CHAPTER 23

DAMIAN THOUGHT he would pay any price, any at all, if he could make it through the rest of his life without the need to meet an injured friend by their bedside. It was happening too often these days, far too often for his taste.

Not that Shannon was a friend. Damian didn't do friends, with a few unfortunate exceptions. She was an inconvenience, an annoyance, and a first-degree meddler.

Nevertheless, she was under his care. Sort of.

And he supposed he could admit that he'd developed a sliver of near fondness for her. Enough for him to hope she wouldn't die.

The emergency-activated sphere that had summoned him from the *Quandary* made straight for an especially flat building not far from the main boulevard. It appeared to contain just a single floor, though it stretched for more than half of the generously sized city block.

Alien world or not, he knew a hospital when he saw one. It might smell like mint and olives rather than antiseptic, and the halls might be curiously curved rather than cut at sterile angles, but there were there was no mistaking the businesslike strides of the staff, the carts piled with medicines, and the occasional bark of a cough down a corridor he could not see.

Also, there were beds here. Not a hammock in sight.

Shannon was sitting up when he entered her room. She looked small, propped up in the center of the bed like that. Smaller than usual, anyway. He didn't like it.

"I leave you alone for five minutes," he said, hiding his relief behind the sternest tone he could manage. Which wasn't all that stern, really. His sister would have done better. "What happened?"

She attempted a smile, but ruined it by allowing a tear to leak out of one eye. "No endearments?"

"The restraint might kill me."

He waited, aware that he was hovering halfway between the bed and the door. He could hear a fountain gurgling somewhere in here. What the hell was the obsession with running water?

"He's dead." Usually, her voice was loud. Musical. Today, it was barely more than a whisper. "Jem—Champion Borona. He died in my arms. Someone poisoned his drink."

That much, the sphere had informed him of. "And you were drinking with him?" Damian asked. If so, she was lucky to be alive. Even the magically ubiquitous spheres had been unable to save the Champion. Whatever poison the killer had used, it had acted fast.

Shannon dropped her gaze, tears falling freely now as she twisted the blanket in her hands. And with a sinking feeling he elected not to contemplate, he thought he understood. First name basis. Dying in her arms. Sharing drinks was not the only way to share poison.

Well. It wasn't as if Damian had bothered to offer her any companionship here, let alone comfort. Why shouldn't she make the best of the situation? Except for the fact, made all too obvious by today's events, that getting close to other people led to suffering in the end. It always did.

Which was why Damian was not a sit-at-the-bedside kind of person. He was an excellent avenge-the-fallen kind of person. Or, if he couldn't manage that, a tease-the-bastards-until-they're-too-confused-to-operate kind of person.

Unfortunately, he'd been spending all too much time with sit-at-the-bedside types lately. Which was probably why he didn't find it overly difficult to do it now. He eased himself down beside Shannon's feet, careful not to sit *on* her feet while she cried.

And, in a true test of will, he said nothing at all. Mostly because, for once in his life, he didn't know what *to* say. Everything last thing that came to mind was flippant.

Alien planets. They're the worst.

So you did *think he was pretty.*

Listen, doll, the universe is a tough place. It sucks, etc.

He didn't think she'd appreciate that. In fact, he thought he'd probably be the next to die, and at her hands, if he let himself utter anything like that. But he had to say *something.*

After a moment, he settled on, "You deserve better than this."

That was... not bad. A bit sugary, but acceptable. He found, to his surprise, that he meant it.

Shannon looked up, dark eyes shining, tears still tracking down her face. "That was almost an apology."

"Offensive. It absolutely was not."

"They captured someone," she said. "But I don't... I don't know why the murderer would have stuck around after administering the poison. Whoever they caught, I don't think he did it."

She'd nearly died, yet she was still investigating. He wanted to tell her to stop, that it wasn't worth it. But she was looking at him with a question in her eyes, and his throat constricted as he realized what she *wasn't* asking.

She'd found him in the rafters above a burned-out warehouse

last night, mere moments after a beam had cracked to the ground and almost killed Champion Borona.

It was understandable that she would suspect him. Or so he'd keep telling himself.

"I was awake and aware," he said. "I was on the *Quandary*. Ask Bruce."

Poison, of course, could be added to a bottle at any time. Hours before consumption. Days. Even weeks. Poison was a patient man's assassin. Therefore, Damian's whereabouts at the time of Borona's death counted for nothing.

He couldn't truthfully promise he hadn't done it. There was no way to know.

Next time, though. Next time, the trap he'd set with Bruce and Lex would spring shut. He might not be able to identify whoever was stealing his consciousness, but he could damn well stop them from committing more crimes.

She had to know that he couldn't guarantee his innocence, yet she only hesitated for a moment before nodding. "Do you think there'll be a funeral?"

"I don't know much about these people yet," he said, "but I do know that they *love* a funeral."

CHAPTER 24

SHANNON HADN'T PEGGED Damian as a visit-the-bedside type. In fact, if anyone had asked even a few hours ago, she'd have sworn he wouldn't have bothered to visit her at all.

Now, the man seemed determined to make up for repeatedly abandoning her during their time here, sticking to her side like he thought Jem's assassin would come after her again. But her poisoning had been an accident; not that she absolved anyone of the murder, but she'd clearly been an unintentional casualty.

Damian didn't seem to care. Whatever protective instinct had caused him to drag her out of the Catch Clan's party back on Bromar had kicked back in.

She expected him to object when she insisted on getting out of bed—she did prefer them to hammocks, as it turned out—but he kept his silence, likely aware that she wouldn't listen to a word he said. But neither could she stop him from shadowing her steps as she made for the council chambers where Ahnien had taken them on the first day. Damian didn't question her. He didn't tease her. He merely followed.

Whatever mission he was on here, he'd obviously set it aside for the time being. Not that she'd count on him to do so for very long. But if he wanted to keep her company, she wouldn't stop him.

The meeting was breaking up when they arrived in the large, open chamber. Champion Ahnien was speaking to a woman she didn't recognize, while the other council members filtered out in quiet pairs or trios. When Shannon and Damian entered, the woman excused herself, and Ahnien turned to greet them with a grave nod.

"I'm glad to see you on your feet," he said. His eyes were rimmed in red, and he kept drawing the back of his hand across his mouth as if to prevent some emotion from escaping. "I am sorry for what happened. Truly sorry."

Shannon glanced at Damian, who merely stood there with his hands in his pockets, gazing at the spheres overhead. She hoped he wouldn't start flicking them again.

"We were just wondering if we could assist with the funeral preparations," she said.

Ahnien dropped his gaze briefly. "The funeral is already underway."

His words were clipped, almost irritated, and Shannon frowned as he dragged his hand over his mouth again. "What, now? But... but don't those big affairs take a lot of planning?"

Damian was paying attention to the conversation now, too, his head cocked in interest. She didn't understand the man. She truly didn't. He made himself into a caricature, hiding his true nature behind layers of falsehoods until it was impossible to see who he really was. Was it the man who'd come to sit on her bed? The one who threw endearments at everyone, indiscriminately? The anti-heroic pirate of the comic books?

All of them, she suspected. And none.

"Jem Borona will not be getting a city funeral," Ahnien said finally.

Shannon settled her gaze back on him, failing to hide her surprise. "But if a shopkeeper—"

"He's not getting one." Ahnien started for the door. "Excuse me."

Tears pricked her eyes, and she blinked them away. Jem Borona had been a good man, a kind one. Welcoming to her, at least, when everyone else kept her at arm's length. He deserved a funeral. He deserved a sending. These people loved funerals, as Damian had said. Why would they not grant him one? She wanted to scream it, to run after Ahnien and shake him until he relented. But this wasn't her place, and she remained frozen, watching helplessly as the Champion made for the door.

"If we were to attend the funeral that *is* happening," Damian said, "where would we find it?"

Shannon blinked at him, but he didn't look her way. His expression was hard, unreadable. If the revelation about Jem's funeral arrangements surprised him, he didn't show it. He was asking on her behalf, though. That much was clear.

Ahnien paused, his head bent. Then he sighed. "By the main canal," he said. "The market intersection. I think you know it. But you'd do well to hurry."

"I don't know where—" Damian began, but Shannon laid a hand on his arm.

"I do," she said.

He met her gaze, eyebrows ticked up in question, then nodded as Ahnien hurried from the room as if afraid they might question him further. "All right," he said. "Let's go crash a funeral."

———

The strange reflections in the water were gone.

Because that, of course, was where the funeral was taking

place. At the intersection where Jem had turned their boat toward the market and the pastries, where the mountains had appeared in the water. Unnaturally. Impossibly.

Today, the water showed only the reflections of the canal banks, and the funeral pyre that floated between them. A small group of silver spheres circled the pyre as she and Damian approached, moving with stark efficiency as they morphed to lift and prepare and, eventually, to light. It would be like having a suite of pretty drones prepare one for death's embrace. Hardly the sendoff she'd have expected from this place. Quiet. Anonymous.

Jem's body, which she'd so recently cradled in her arms, was beautiful in death. Beautiful, but wrong. He'd been so full of movement and enthusiasm and warmth. Who could have killed him? And why?

She'd barely known him. Barely at all. But he'd been kind to her, and he'd loved his city. She thought he would have loved the beauty of this day, the clear skies, the crystalline waters. She almost expected him to round a corner and suggest they go for pastries, insisting with a laugh that the man on the pyre was too still to be him.

There was only one other person on the bank when they arrived. Champion Sileux, of all people. His wrinkled face was solemn, his hands clasped in front of him. Why was there no one else here?

"I don't understand," Shannon said, as she and Damian joined Sileux on the bank of the canal.

"I know," Damian said. "I thought they hated each other."

"I mean," Shannon said pointedly, "that he was a good man."

Damian shrugged. "Not mutually exclusive points, doll."

Oh, good. The endearments were back. He suppressed them for hospitals, but not for funerals. The man was a terror.

"He *was* a good man," Sileux echoed, and despite her admonishment to Damian, his words surprised her. It'd been hard to miss the tension, if not outright animosity, between the men.

"A fool," Sileux added, "but a good man."

Shannon had to force herself not to roll her eyes. That was more along the lines of what she would have expected.

The spheres danced around the pyre, each of them producing a flame. At least someone danced for him. Shannon brushed a tear off her cheek.

"I'll ask it, then," Damian said. "Why are we the only ones here? Why does a shopkeeper get a city-wide funeral when a council member rests in anonymity? Not that I advocate for idolizing politicians. Ugh."

It would be nice, in a way, that a shopkeeper could be celebrated above a public figure. If not for Ahnien's clear discomfort, she might have accepted it as custom. But this was clearly not the usual way.

Sileux said nothing.

"He said his views differed from others," Shannon said. "He said they made him a target."

Sileux snorted. "A fool who knew he was a fool. Didn't save him, did it?"

As one, the spheres dipped, touching their sparks to the pyre. Flames sprang among the wood, individual sparks melting into a single, crackling entity. Strange that she couldn't smell the smoke.

Shannon turned to Sileux. "How were his views different, Champion Sileux? What did he believe, that his life should end in such an anonymous way? That might have gotten him killed?"

Sileux was staring at the water, watching as the spheres began ushering the burning pyre down the canal. Shannon wondered if it would make it all the way to the mountain in the distance—Locke's Peak, Jem had called it—or if it would founder before that.

"Our technology is different from yours," the old man said finally.

Shannon swallowed, suppressing a shiver. Jem's last words had told her the very same thing.

Damian reached up to poke a sphere that had drifted close to his head. "Clearly."

"He told me that," Shannon said, ignoring Damian. "He used those exact words."

Sileux grunted. "Did he, now?"

Shannon lay a hand on the council member's arm, willing him to tell them more. "*How* is it different, Champion? Please, it might... I might be able to help figure out who killed him. But I need more information."

Sileux pressed his lips together, digging deeper wrinkles into his skin. After a moment, he sighed. "They're trying to keep this from you, you know," he said. "Ahnien and the others."

"You don't say," Damian murmured.

Shannon waited, afraid to say a word in case it should convince Sileux not to continue. Afraid to breathe, even.

"Our technology is different from yours," Sileux repeated, "because it is operated by human consciousness."

CHAPTER 25

ADMITTEDLY, Damian's mind had been a bit of a blur for the past few hours. He hadn't slept, instead spending the night with his bots trying to figure out what was taking over his consciousness at random but violent times. He hadn't had a chance to test the Bruce-to-Damian mind meld, patent pending, because the red sphere had appeared, hurrying him out of his ship to check on Shannon—who'd then insisted they come to this funeral. He supposed he might have walked away, but it felt wrong to leave her, so here he stood, before the depressing finality of a funeral pyre.

The fatigue was making his head ache. In a blissfully normal sort of way, rather than a dying-of-alien-illness sort of way, but still. He didn't favor it, particularly.

Added to all that, of course, was the creeping suspicion that he'd been the one to slip the poison into that bottle to murder Borona. And nearly Shannon, too.

Through the murk of the fatigue, Champion Sileux's revelation was just strange enough to catch his attention.

"Human consciousness," Shannon repeated. "Your technology operates on human *consciousness.*"

She looked as if she were about to whip out a fliptab to start dashing down notes. Damian didn't know if it'd broken after that fall from the warehouse rafters, but he knew her well enough by now to be sure that a broken fliptab would not prevent her from taking her notes. If she had to stab him and write her notes in his blood, she'd do it.

The funeral pyre was nearly out of sight, visible only by the curl of smoke that drifted up from the crumbling raft. Sileux was watching it, his watery eyes rimmed in red. He made no secret of his dislike for Borona, but he seemed to regret the man's death.

"After death," the Champion said, "our citizens donate their consciousnesses to the public good. They update the files, the library of downloads, as often as they like. Typically, it's done annually. Sometimes more, when one gets to my age."

He offered a weary smile at that, but Damian barely registered it. Human *consciousness*? It felt impossible. Unprecedented, certainly. How did one even *store* a consciousness? In a box? Difficult not to picture an oversized dresser full of pull-out drawers.

Sileux lifted a hand toward the sky. "Every sphere you see here, every ear, every elevator, every iris, every bone. They are all organized by our collective consciousness. The perfect meld of mind and machine."

It was impossible. *Impossible.*

And yet... yet it also fit with what Damian knew of the Currents. They made music of a kind, did they not? And he had a friend who claimed that pieces of them could whisper. He glanced toward the sky. "And the Currents?"

Sileux bobbed his head, his long gray hair brushing against the back of his shirt. "The Currents. The gateways too, once upon a time. All of it."

"Perhaps that's why they sing," Damian murmured.

Sileux frowned. "I had not heard that."

Shannon gave him a strange look, too. He'd forgotten, for a moment, that most people couldn't hear the song. He truly needed to get some sleep. Preferably somewhere other than a hammock. Perhaps if he feigned an injury, they'd allow him to sleep at the hospital.

He probably would not need to feign it.

"That's the reason for the big funerals," Shannon said.

Sileux touched his chin to his chest briefly, then lifted it again. "We thank and celebrate those who donate their intelligence, their gifts, to the public good."

Strange, Damian thought, that in a place with conscious technology, something—or someone—kept taking over *his* mind.

But Damian wasn't made of technology. He was flesh and blood. That, at least, he knew that for a certainty. Once, he might have said something of this sort could have taken over his tech inlays. But those were gone, ripped out by bloody Heloise and her merry band of villains, with only the scar tissue and stiff joints to show that they'd ever existed at all.

So how could an alien consciousness—a dead one, apparently —usurp a man's brain while he slept?

It couldn't. The answer was that it couldn't.

"So why isn't Jem being celebrated?" Shannon asked quietly.

Jem. Damian watched her without quite meaning to, wondering whether she'd slept with the man. Not that it was his business. She was the gossip reporter, not him. It was nothing to him, only that he felt bad, a little, for teasing her about the man's handsomeness. So she'd liked him. So they'd gotten close. It was nothing Damian hadn't done before himself.

It was easy to see the reporter in her. Her eyes were narrowed, focused entirely on Sileux, and Damian decided that she didn't need her fliptab or a notebook or a pen dipped in blood. She filed everything away in that lovely head of hers.

He'd do well to remember that, come to think of it.

Sileux kicked at the canal bank, a decidedly childish move for a man his age. Damian extended a hand toward the man in case he should lose his balance and tumble into the water. Sileux twisted his lips, as if his forthcoming words tasted sour. "Jem Borona did not consent to donate his consciousness. It was never uploaded. Therefore, his death is anonymous. Not to be celebrated."

Sileux looked up, meeting Shannon's sharp gaze. "He refused to contribute to the public good. That is why we did not get along. And after today, it will be as if he never existed."

"But he served as a council member," Shannon said. If her face showed none of her distress, the break in her voice revealed it like a wound.

"More than that, young lady," Sileux said. "Champions were heroes during the wars. One of the wars. Each one earned their place on the council through acts of great valor and sacrifice."

Damian noticed, idly, that Sileux referred to the council as though he were not part of it. Did he not consider himself one of those heroes?

"In death," Sileux went on, "none of that matters. You remain part of society through the gift of your talents, or you are deliberately forgotten. That is why no one else has come here. Borona knew this, yet he chose to remain stubborn. He would be surprised, if he'd chosen to live on, to find how *many* people attended his funeral. Not shocked at how few."

A harsh sentence. Damian watched the curl of smoke as it rode the canal in the direction of a distant mountain range. Soon, it would be out of sight altogether.

Honestly, he preferred this quiet affair to the gaudy rigamarole of the parades and parties. There was no contemplation in that. Celebrating a life was all well and good, but there ought to be time for tears as well. Even if they were only shed in the quiet of a man's private rooms.

But if the consciousness remained, had the person truly died at all? He let his gaze follow the nearest sphere as it floated along above their heads, its clear walls rendering it nearly invisible against the bright gray sky. In the midst of some task, perhaps, or waiting for a request. If a consciousness continued like this, existing in society only to serve—with the only other option to be forgotten altogether—could they still be said to live? Truly?

"And you agree with this?" Shannon asked. "You think it's right?"

Sileux kicked the bank again. "I do."

"And yet," Damian said, "you are here."

Sileux sighed, a trembling shudder of a sound. "So I am."

Damian's headache had kicked up again, back to full alien-illness throttle. He squeezed his eyes shut, then opened them again, just in time to see a last strand of smoke rising from the canal and disperse slowly into the atmosphere.

They stayed on the bank for a long time. And when they split apart, they did so in silence. Shannon took the opposite direction from Damian, and he understood; as she moved away, he made no attempt to follow.

CHAPTER 26

"HOW COULD you not know that they had constructed a prison?"

Command's voice was hot, disdain dripping from every word like poison. He clearly did not trust Zahlia to carry out this new mission herself; he'd instructed a stealth sphere to hover over her shoulder as she'd traced her way across the city rooftops. As if she couldn't be trusted.

Perhaps she couldn't, at that.

The sphere's presence meant that Command had been right there to hear her surprise when she jumped onto the final rooftop only to find that this particular block was not made up of homes at all. It was a front, a wall built to mimic a regular city block, homes and all.

Behind that front was a large rectangular courtyard, with prison cells lining each wall. Cages, more like. They were made of bars, with only a thin board on each to protect the prisoners from the nightly rain.

Zahlia crouched on the corner of the building, looking down into the courtyard and doing her best to tune out Command's string of curses. Which, of course, proved impossible.

"How could the Echains have a prison?" he went on. "How do they dare it? Who do they think to imprison there?"

She shook her head. "I don't know."

"Release your colleague," he said. "We will discuss the future of your mission later."

Without waiting for a response, the stealth sphere zoomed away, fading quickly out of sight. As if it had better things to do than supervise her.

Good. She didn't particularly wish to *be* supervised.

Zahlia remained where she was, watching the courtyard. A pair of guards had walked through here not ten minutes ago, and she intended to find out whether their rounds occurred at random or on a schedule that she could exploit. In the meantime, she scanned the cells, squinting for any sign of movement.

There was none. But when a pair of illuminated spheres bobbed by, no doubt irises sent to keep watch, Zahlia thought she could make out a pair of hands wrapped around the bars of one of the center cells. She couldn't see deeper into the cell than that, but something in her gut told her that those were Ches' hands. That her colleague, her friend, was imprisoned there.

But how to get him out, with spheres keeping watch as well as men? The guards—the human ones—returned after ten minutes, and then another ten, but the spheres kept up a near constant patrol.

Well. If Command questioned the future of her mission here, perhaps it was time to incinerate her own cover.

Zahlia withdrew a thick rope from her tool pouch and secured it around one of the spikes that decorated the wall beside her. The wall that was supposed to look like a roof. Perhaps Command was right to chastise her for not having noticed the spikes, the falseness, the fact that nothing ever occurred on this block. But it was a large city, and he kept her distracted with nonsense. Where were *his* irises, and the rest of his spies?

When the spheres returned, she would drop down on them from above. She would shatter them before they had time to react, and she would free Ches. If the guards interrupted, she would fight them. She waited, hands poised on the rope, playing it over in her mind.

More likely than not, this fight would end with Zahlia taking a cell of her own.

The spheres glided into view, and she tightened her grip on the rope.

Before she could act, a cell door to the left slid open and a shadow dashed out, rushing at the spheres. Quicker than she could gasp, the figure raised their hands and slammed the spheres together, hard. Their lights flickered as they cracked, and the person shoved them toward the ground. The spheres went dark as they shattered.

It was over in a heartbeat.

And it was a crime, too, of the worst sort. Though she'd been planning something similar herself—souls help her, she had—it turned her stomach to think of the revered consciousnesses that now lay damaged upon the stones. They might be revived if the damage was not too bad, but she didn't know how recently either of these had been backed up. They might not remember the last weeks or months. Even years. There were too many spheres to keep recent updates on them all.

The figure paused over the spheres, as if to ensure they were truly defeated. Whoever it was, they'd been hiding in the back of a cell. But how had they gotten inside in the first place?

The person headed straight for Ches' cell and opened the door. Ches collapsed into the courtyard, and the stranger bent over him.

Zahlia let herself drop. She didn't know this liberator, or what their intentions might be. They could be one of Ahnien's people, sent to murder Ches. They could be one of Command's, with the same goal.

If this shadow person thought they could kill Ches without a fight, they were wrong. Zahlia was well trained. But when her feet hit the pavement, the stranger merely straightened and ran for the exit. Without even glancing her way.

It was almost as if they'd known she was there. Like they'd been waiting for her.

Zahlia let them go. She ran for Ches, who was slowly picking himself up to sit. One eye was puffed shut, his lip cracked and bloody. Had the monsters not even given him something to drink after beating him near senseless? A lock of sandy hair fell into his good eye as he blinked up at her, confusion warring with hope in his dark eyes.

"Zahlia," he said. "Is this a dream?"

She blinked tears out of her eyes as she wrapped an arm around his waist, helping him to stand. "Come on," she said. "Let's get you out of here."

———

Zahlia had known of the safe house's existence, of course. She simply never had cause to use it. Whatever Command might pretend, she held her post well. For a year she'd worked toward obtaining it, positioning herself to wed the widowed Champion Sileux. And for five years since, she'd held that cover with distinction. She'd lived the life, painted the paintings, played the music. She'd become her cover, completely.

There had been no need for safe houses.

There was a need for it now. The house sat quietly at the edge of town, no doubt chosen to ease the path to escape. It was painted in a vibrant shade of blue, in keeping with the decor of the rest of the city—to do otherwise might call unwanted attention—but not bright enough to stand out. This section of the city was sparsely populated, though the council took pains to keep everything freshly painted. Nothing was derelict or broken down. Everything in its place.

The canal flowed quietly beside the house, dark and still. No boats passed at this hour, leaving only the crystal clarity of the reflected moon.

Zahlia brought Ches around the back of the house, to where a basement door waited. She unlocked it with a key she kept around her neck, breathing a sigh of relief when the door did in fact open, then helped him down the stairs. Situated as it was below the water level of the canal, it was the kind of room that would flood if the rains were ever allowed to fall in large amounts. They weren't, yet it made her nervous. Someone controlled these things. And someone could decide they needed changing.

She eased Ches in a chair beside a cement-gray wall, then flicked on a light in the corner, trying to find her bearings quickly. No spheres in here, not even stealth ones. It wouldn't be safe. But that meant there was no medical help, either.

The cabinet in the corner would be the most likely location for supplies, so she paced to it, throwing the doors open. As long as she kept moving, she wouldn't have to think about the meaning of all of this. Borona's death, Ches' arrest, and a stranger coming to release him before she could do so herself.

Twice now, someone had completed a mission on her behalf. Who was it? And why? Zahlia withdrew a basket of clean clothes and medicine from the cabinet, noting the supply of emergency rations and water on the bottom shelf. They might need those, before the end of the day.

She turned to find Ches watching her, the light reflecting in his eyes. She'd grown used to the atmospheric illumination of the city, and it was strange to have light coming from a single direction. It lit half of Ches' face like a caress, throwing the other half into shadow.

Zahlia knelt before him, pressing a cleaning cloth gently to his hurt lip. "Are you all right?" she asked.

"I was only in the cell for a few hours, Zahl. I'm fine." His words were muffled by the cloth, but his stubbornness was just as intact as it had been when they'd last met.

"This cut says otherwise," she said sternly.

"The cut merely says I shouldn't have taken a swing at the authorities."

Zahlia took his hand, pressing it against the cloth over his lip so she could apply a second one to his swollen eye. His fingers were cold, and she resisted the urge to wrap them in hers, to warm him. "I'm not sorry you did."

The corner of his mouth curved into a half smile, and she found herself returning it. Ridiculous as it was. They were cowering in a safe house, with him accused of a murder that he clearly hadn't committed. He was injured, and her cover might very well be destroyed. This was no time for smiles.

It didn't matter. When Ches smiled, Zahlia smiled back. Like they were connected by magnets, or an invisible elastic. Bound to each other. Even if they could never say so.

"Who was the person that saved you?" she asked.

Ches shook his head, then winced. "I don't know him. Tall. Reddish hair. Long jacket."

Shock prickled through her chest. "Damian Riddle," she breathed. "He's one of the visitors."

His brow twitched, as if he would have frowned had she not been preventing it with the cloth. "How could it be? He doesn't know of our conflict. And he's hardly been here long enough to take sides."

"Perhaps he knows more than we think."

But she understood what he meant. Damian Riddle and

Shannon Forest had only arrived what, seven days ago? It was time enough to find trouble, certainly. But was it time enough to fall into the mess of war and politics that made up Zahlia's life?

She didn't think it was. She dabbed at Ches' eye with the cloth, grimacing at the redness of the skin. Of all the ways she'd imagined their reunion, this had never been among them.

"Where were you?" he asked softly. "I expected to find you at your post. When you weren't there, I went in search of you."

He didn't need her to hold the cloth any longer. He could easily take over the job himself. Yet she continued to do it, anyway, as much for an excuse to remain close as anything else. "I was trying to get some information."

He swallowed. "What do you mean?"

"They're not telling us everything, Ches. You know they're not." He glanced around, eyes scanning the room behind her, and she shivered. If Command heard her utter those words... "There are no ears here," she said, more confidently than she felt.

"There could always be ears," he whispered. "You of all people should know it."

She did know it. But to place ears here would be to make the safe house vulnerable. And if the Echains had placed them, this place was no longer safe at all. What did it say that she was as concerned about spies from her own side—more, even—than she was about spies from theirs?

Zahlia dropped her hand. "I should get us something to eat."

He caught her wrist before she could back away, and she found herself pausing. All too willing—eager, even—to rest in his nearness for as long as she could. "Thank you," he said. "For saving me."

She swallowed back a protest that it seemed as though Damian Riddle had been the one to save him. How many times had she imagined this moment? How long had his voice kept her tethered to herself, making her laugh, making her feel less alone?

Even if it had only ever been an illusion, Ches had been her comfort.

He was watching her now, his fingers warm on her wrist, his breath close enough to mingle with hers. Zahlia ached to lean in, to close this space between them. To allow herself to love him, the way she had not been allowed.

But the space between them... it was more than just air. It was duty, and it was necessity. It was Sileux. Most of all, it was Command.

If Command were to find out, he would not just punish Zahlia. He would make sure Ches suffered as well.

She drew back, pulling her hand gently out of his grasp. "It's almost dawn," she said. "Try to rest. At nightfall, we'll get you out of the city."

CHAPTER 27

THE MUSIC WAS TERRIBLE. Too much percussion, for starters —Damian couldn't hear a damn thing over the constant hammering of the drums, the murky *bong* of the bass. He tried to yell at the band to please try for a better balance, but when he opened his mouth, no words would come.

Odd.

When he opened his eyes, someone was pounding on his door.

As much as he disliked the hammock, he distinctly remembered having tucked himself *into* it before falling asleep. And yet here he was, waking up with his chin buried in the carpet.

He'd have blamed the hammock for it, if he could. But his chin was buried in carpet all the way across the room from it. Unlikely that he'd have tumbled so far, and without waking. He rolled over, taking in the color of light in the window. Daytime, he thought, even if the homogenous nature of the light made it difficult to tell the time. Mid morning, at least. Maybe later.

There were no messages from Bruce attempting to wake him.

All together, the facts made it abundantly clear. His body-stealing thief had taken him for a spin again. Without his knowledge, never mind his consent.

The trap hadn't worked.

And now someone was pounding on his door.

He staggered to his feet, taking a minute to get his balance. "For the love of everything sordid, I'm coming," he said. "Please calm down."

His head hurt like hell, and the pounding did not abate. If anything, it merely grew more insistent.

When he instructed the sphere to please and thank you open the door, Shannon stormed straight inside. No good morning, no sorry to wake you. Not that he expected those kinds of niceties from her at this point. Her dark hair was a mess of frizz, her eyes faintly bloodshot, as if she hadn't slept much, either.

Well, his *brain* had slept. It was only his body that hadn't.

"Do come in," he said, shutting the door behind her.

Shannon whirled around, her eyes wide and wild, hands balled into fists at her sides. He didn't think she intended to hit him, but that was never a guarantee—particularly since he didn't fully know what he'd been up to in the last several hours—so he took a step away from her, just in case.

"There's something wrong," she said.

Images flickered through his mind—prison bars? A cage of some kind?—and Damian blinked hard, trying to will them away. That was new. A blocked memory? Or a forgotten dream?

He could delve into the mystery in a minute. As soon as he'd dealt with whatever Shannon was freaking out about.

Because there was really no other phrase to describe her emotional state right now. She was shaking, her whole body quivering as she stood there staring at him like she'd just announced something he didn't know. Yes, there was something wrong. There were many things wrong. He needed more information on which particular bit of wrongness had brought her storming into his room at... whatever time it was.

Before he could ask for that information, she frowned at him Like the 'something wrong' was his face, or at least his fault.

"What happened to you?" she asked.

He opened his mouth, then closed it, wishing Bruce were here. Maybe the bot would know what she meant. Though it was fifty-fifty on whether he'd share it, if he did. "What?"

She pointed to his head, and he lifted a hand, wincing as he brushed a tender new bruise across his cheekbone. "Oh, you know," he said, "it turns out this place does not have the best brothels."

"Damian. This is serious."

He dropped his hand, filing the bruise as another accusation for his thief. "I'm categorically unable to be serious. You see, I was already serious once this year. That was today, incidentally. Or yesterday. Uncertain. Either way, it was the funeral. The seriousness nearly killed me, so my quota is full until next year."

Her expression darkened, enough to make him take another half step back. If she did that again, he'd be sitting in the fountain. And it still might be preferable to facing her.

"Listen," she said, negating his retreat by taking a step forward. "I think we might be in a simulation."

Damian blinked. If Bruce were here, he could confirm that she had in fact said what Damian thought she'd said. "A simulation," he repeated. "Like a VR game?"

She nodded. "I'm not sure we ever left the *Quandary*. We might even still be in the Parse Galaxy."

What, sitting in game modules? Or strapped into some kind of a pod? No, that didn't make sense. He didn't know how she'd reached this conclusion, though no doubt she'd tell him—and in detail—but he did know it wasn't possible. Even the VR games weren't *that* good.

Despite yesterday's seriousness, with the funeral and everything, he felt like they'd been getting along fairly well. Like they'd understood each other, or gotten halfway there at least. Like they were allies in gathering information about human-consciousnesses-run technology and all that.

He didn't want to ruin the rapport, mostly because he didn't feel like getting yelled at. She was upset by Borona's death, understandably. Could he blame her for wanting to believe there was a reset button hidden somewhere that she could press to bring the man back?

"Look," he said slowly, "we just had a hell of a day. A week, really, or thereabouts. It stands to reason that there might be some..." How was he supposed to finish that sentence without making her angry? Confusion? Insanity? Coping mechanisms? "Trauma," he said finally.

She folded her arms across her chest, her frown deepening. "You think I'm making things up."

He raised his hands. He was going for placating, but surrender would work just as well. "No, I think you're imagining something that—"

"Imagining *is* making things up, jackass."

"And here I thought you objected to endearments."

She drew in a deep breath, letting it out slowly. "When Jem showed me around the city, I noticed something strange about the canal. The mountains in the distance shouldn't have been reflected in the water from that angle, but they were. And then yesterday at the funeral, they were gone." She bit her lip, frowning at the floor. "And the pyre. It should have had a smell. But it didn't."

It hadn't, come to that. He *knew* she'd been noticing things. "We don't know everything about alien wood," he said, stifling the urge to turn that into a joke that would definitely earn him a slap. "Or trees. We don't know about their traditions. We don't know what smells and what—"

"Have you ever seen a fire that didn't smell like a fire?"

"Sounds like a riddle, doll. Typically my favorite, as we know, but—"

"Damian."

He dropped his hands. His head was aching. The bruise, the alien disease, sleeping on the floor. It was all starting to wear on him, truth be told. Shannon was staring at him with this pleading look on her face, like she needed help and he was the one who could provide it.

But she needed to know that she'd come to the wrong person. He couldn't help her; he couldn't even help himself. And bedside manner was very much the opposite of his forte.

Forget Bruce. He wished Lex was here.

"You understand how this sounds, doll." He tried to temper his tone, to make himself sound calm. Gentle. Reasonable, since someone in the room had to be.

"You think I'm insane."

Well, not quite that. "You're trying to tell me you think we're what—inside our ship? Trapped in the Current? And that we never arrived here at all. That these people and their world don't exist. Or they do, that they're keeping our brains in some kind of video game. Do you know how that sounds?"

She glared at him, but she didn't say anything. He didn't know whether that meant she was planning her next attack or that he was actually getting through to her. Knowing Shannon, it was probably some obscurely random third option that he never would have considered.

"Look," he said, "I don't think you're insane. I think you're grieving."

She took a step closer, shaking a finger at him. An attack,

then. "What were you doing in that warehouse? Why are your boots muddy?

He looked down. Huh. His boots *were* muddy. Fascinating.

"Do you want to know what I think?" she asked.

"I sense I don't have a choice."

"I think you don't know what you were doing in the warehouse, or why your boots are muddy. I think you've been blacking out."

He appreciated her attention to detail. He did wish, though, that she hadn't opted to attend to *his* details. "Think what you like," he said.

Another step closer. "Why won't you let me help you?"

Damian retreated, remembering at the last minute to skirt around the fountain. Why he was afraid of the woman, he couldn't quite say. He could hold her off with one arm, a palm to the forehead. She was small enough.

And yet, he suspected that would be the last move he ever made.

She started to take another step, but he held up his hand again, this time to warn her away. "I work alone, doll," he said. "Always have. Always will."

She scoffed. "What about the crew you keep bragging about running with before this?"

"Hardened criminals. The galaxy's worst. Not friends. Not my crew. A job's a job."

Oh, how they'd laugh at him if they heard that. But then, they probably all thought he was dead. Better that way.

Shannon stared at him for a long moment, fire burning in those dark eyes. She noticed things, plenty of things, but his mystery belonged to him. The damn woman was already fifty times more involved than he'd wanted anyone to be. This was why he ran with bots. In his presence, someone always got hurt. Always.

She could dig into anything she wanted, try to prove her crazy simulation theory—yes, it *was* crazy—but she could damn well do it without him.

"Fine," she said. "I'll figure it out myself."

"It's a good life skill," he said.

Somehow, she managed to slam the door behind her.

As soon as she was gone, Damian brushed off his boots. And then he headed out to visit Champion Sileux.

———

"And your companion knows nothing about this?" Sileux's brows were raised as far as Damian imagined they could go. If his hairline wasn't so distant, they'd be tangled with it. "Why have you not involved her? She seems a good ally."

Damian was fully aware of the irony involved in going directly to Sileux for help mere minutes after announcing to Shannon that he worked alone. But he could no longer pretend that he could figure out the consciousness issue on his own. Or the disease issue, for that matter, which had been the entire reason for coming here in the first place. They were probably related, at that. Perhaps it was a virus taking over his brain.

He couldn't know. And he couldn't figure it out on his own.

Sileux stood behind his desk, fingertips pressed into the surface beside those piles of not-paper that Damian had so ineffectually investigated.

"She can't help me," Damian said finally.

Best to keep her out of this. Let her explore. Let her follow her theories, write her stories. Let her stay as far out of his orbit of danger as possible.

"Very well," Sileux said. "Did these memory lapses affect you at all before you left the Parse Galaxy, as you call it?"

Damian paced to the window, barely seeing the traffic on the boulevard, the boats on the canal beyond. "I don't think so, I..." He trailed off. But there had been something, hadn't there? A ship that didn't belong to him—a pod. And the reason he'd left that crew in the first place.

He ran a hand through his hair, trying to shake the sensation of disorientation. "Yes, actually," he said, turning back to face Sileux. "It did affect me there."

"Fascinating." Damian lifted an eyebrow, and the old man smiled, apologetic. "I am sorry. My enthusiasm gets the best of me. You tried to set a trap for it, you say? All right. Let's see what we can do."

CHAPTER 28

IT DIDN'T MATTER what Damian thought.

Shannon crashed out into the city, hardly noticing the people who scattered to avoid her. She might as well have a storm cloud above her head, complete with errant lightning strikes ready to take out anyone who stepped into her path. They were all heading for their homes, hurrying along with heads bent, yet they easily scampered away from her as she drew near, like they could anticipate her movements.

The feeling of wrongness was insistent. A flood of adrenaline. An ache in her throat. A clenching of her stomach, and her heart. Did these people exist at all? Or would they vanish like mist if she tried to touch them?

If Damian refused to help her, then she'd damn well figure it out herself. Just like she always did.

Obviously, she was grieving. Water was wet, the stars were infinite, and Shannon Forest was grieving a man she'd barely known. She'd been poisoned herself—no more than ten percent, at most—but that had no bearing on the fact that there was something *wrong* with this place.

If Damian couldn't see it, if he didn't care to dig deeper into where he'd been disappearing and why, there was no way to force him. But it was all connected. She knew that it was.

With tears blurring her intentions—as well as her vision—she didn't quite realize where she was headed until she found herself at the intersection of canals where Jem's funeral had taken place, where he'd turned their boat toward the pastries and the market. In the distance, the last few bars of sunlight skipped off of Locke's Peak like a farewell kiss to the day. What was out there, beyond the mountains? Why did no one speak of it?

And why did she keep ending up here, of all places? The city was full of canals, bursting with them. Not to mention plenty of parts she hadn't yet seen. She could have turned down any number of unexplored streets. Had she even meant to come here? The feeling of wrongness pulled at her gut, insistent.

Turning her back on the cursed intersection, she crossed the nearest bridge. Damian could stay in this city and rot for all she cared.

Shannon was going to find out what lay beyond it.

She crossed the bridge without a glance at the water, keeping to the narrow walk along the bank of the canal. If this city wouldn't reveal its secrets, then she'd leave it. She'd find the edge of the simulation, the secret to waking herself up. Whatever was happening here, she'd crack the truth. She had a vague notion that it had to do with those mountains. So she'd go that way.

And when she got home, she'd have one hell of a story to tell.

The next bridge arched gently above the river, giving her a view of the block ahead. The final block of the city, or so it seemed; the neat rows of houses came to an abrupt halt at the crest of the hill. She paused, examining the route ahead. Though she couldn't see what lay beyond, the canal did seem to continue forward. Maybe it fed into a natural river of some kind. Or maybe it continued through the countryside, helping to irrigate crops.

If there *were* any crops.

Shannon started forward, then paused as a shadow moved out from between the last two houses. Unlike the hurrying, forward-looking people back by the guest house, this person glanced over their shoulder, darting a last furtive look at the house she'd just left.

It was Zahlia.

Shannon opened her mouth to hail her friend, to say hello or even, perhaps, to ask for help. But the words died in her throat when Zahlia's clothing registered. She wore *black*. Black pants, not like her flowing half skirts, but cut to hug her body. Shannon hadn't thought anyone in this city even owned black clothes. Clearly, Zahlia didn't want to be seen.

Shannon crouched beside the rail of the bridge to avoid notice, though if Zahlia hadn't seen her standing there, she was probably somehow in shadow. Twilight was coming on quickly, but the city's eerie everywhere-lights hadn't yet faded on; this might well be the darkest part of the day. And it probably would not last very long.

Zahlia paused, waiting. And then a man limped out of the house to join her on the street. Zahlia said something to him, and he lifted the hood of his cloak, hiding his face deep in shadow. As soon as he'd done so, Zahlia put a hand on his arm, and the two began hurrying toward the end of the block. The end of the city, as far as Shannon could tell.

Was the man a friend? A lover? Whoever he was, it was clear that Zahlia was smuggling him... somewhere. Back to his home? If so, why not simply part ways now? Why head out of the city?

Maybe they were leaving together. To go where?

Shannon followed the couple, hoping they wouldn't elect to glance back. But they seemed confident in their solitude—there weren't even any spheres out here, strangely—and completely focused on each other. Their heads were bent close, and she could imagine them whispering.

She shouldn't interrupt. It was Zahlia's business. But she'd been going this way, anyway, and she couldn't ignore the fact that the journalist in her wanted to know. She'd never report it—despite her reputation, she'd actually kept plenty of career-ending secrets for the Parse Galaxy's Most Famous—but she wanted to *know*.

Zahlia and her friend reached the end of the block and hurried around the corner to the right. Shannon followed.

The city ended abruptly in a final intersection of canals. The one that ran horizontal to where she stood looked like it might cut around the perimeter of the city. The canal she'd been following, the one that led toward Locke's Peake, continued forward by way of a tall, thin waterfall.

Even here, standing above it, the water fell silently. Shannon shivered. What waterfall was *silent*?

What funeral pyre burned without smell?

Zahlia and her friend crossed a narrow bridge, heading for the opposite bank. And for what looked, from here, like a hill that rolled down alongside the waterfall, ending in a wide, green plateau. The hill was steep enough to demand watching each step with care, but just gentle enough to allow a safe descent.

The plateau extended all the way to the peak. The mountains looked closer from here, almost distorted. Strange.

Zahlia and her friend crossed the bridge, and then they stopped. They exchanged a few words, and Zahlia withdrew a small, dark orb from the folds of her cloak. It looked like the opposite of the spheres that dominated the city, a black eye compared with those crystalline bubbles. Bending her head low, Zahlia pressed it *into* the air. The sphere disappeared.

And then the air *opened*.

The air wasn't air at all. It was a door, and Zahlia slipped through it, her friend right behind.

Shannon ran, throwing herself forward to catch the door

before it could close. She paused for the briefest moment, her fingertips wrapped around its glass-thin edge, inspecting the crack, the invisible hinges. The door—the wall—shone as bright as a mirror. Or, perhaps a better analogy would be to say it shone like the surface of a clear, still pond that was cast in shade. The barrier between air and water was unmistakable, but the view to the bottom superseded any reflections from above.

A window. It was a window. But why?

She ought to pause here. She ought to stick a pebble in the door to hold it open and run to find Damian.

Shannon didn't even glance back as she opened the door and stepped through.

Shock made her let go of the door. It closed silently behind her, but she couldn't find the space to worry. She could only stare.

The lush hills promised by the vista from the bridge were gone. Instead, a wasteland of blackened boulders filled the space between the city at her back and the mountains in the distance. Which did exist, not with white caps or golden light illuminating their sides, but as jagged silhouettes against a red-orange sky. Her first breath brought the taste of ash, and she froze before she could finish the inhale, afraid it might be poison. But the door had closed; there was no way back.

Tentatively, she drew in a breath. When she didn't fall over, she tried another. Zahlia and her companion had not donned masks before exiting the city; Shannon had to believe that she could breathe the air as well as they. Though when she scanned the rocky landscape for them, they'd disappeared.

It wasn't as if she had an alternative.

About halfway between the city behind her and the mountains in the distance, a huge cylindrical column rose out of the land like a beacon. It glowed with orange and yellow light, as if to reflect the burning tones of the planet's surface. A collection of platform stations clustered around it like watch-keepers.

Watching the city, no doubt. What else was there? Nothing moved on the hills, or down on the plain. There were only rocks and those jagged mountains. And that column, which had to be the size of the city behind her. At least.

No wonder the waterfall had made no sound. It didn't exist.

Still taking shallow breaths, Shannon twisted to look at the city behind her. The door wasn't a mirror, and it wasn't a window. It was—it had to be—some kind of screen. She could see inside, to where the canals flowed past rows of brightly colored homes. But the people in the city couldn't see out.

They must know they were trapped, though. Ahnien did, and Jem certainly had. No wonder no one else had wanted to speak with her; they'd probably been instructed to avoid it. But why could Zahlia get out, when it seemed they could not? Who was she?

Shannon took a careful step away from the wall—screen—craning her neck to see how far it extended. It curved at the top; she could just make out a smear of burnt-sienna clouds lingering in the sky above.

This wasn't a simulation at all. It was a dome.

It was a *sphere*. A huge one, perhaps extending underground. In fact, unless the people in the city had no urge whatsoever to escape—not humanity's default, in any case Shannon had ever seen—it was very likely that this was a full sphere and that it did in fact extend that far, to prevent its inhabitants from digging their way out. Keeping them captive.

No wonder the council had been so interested in the *Quandary*'s landing. It shouldn't have been possible.

"I've been eager to meet you."

Shannon turned so fast she nearly lost her balance, and the man who'd spoken shot out a hand to steady her. He was tall and reed-thin, his black hair streaked with blue. He wore a vest plated in some kind of bronze-tinted metal, his arms covered with black sleeves. A spiral symbol on his chest contained a trio of dots that might have represented a star system. Or a disease.

Also, he was surrounded by soldiers. Apparently, there *was* more to the plains than just rocks and mountains. A hundred crevices to hide in. A thousand.

"Where am I?" she asked.

"Come," he said. "Let me show you to our camp."

Though his tone was pleasant, and the corners of his mouth lifted in a smile, Shannon could tell it was not a request.

She went.

CHAPTER 29

WHEN DAMIAN THOUGHT of his childhood, he thought of it in shards. Fragments. Scattered pieces of lives he might have led.

A year in a fancy Halorin System city. Six months in the Fringe. Two on Anro Moon. And, once, an idyllic three years with the Interplanetary Dwellers: three years in which his father had been married, ish, to a woman Damian hadn't hated. Whose daughter had become a sister, and still tried to be, when he let her. Their home had been a distant station, always on the drift, always between systems.

He walked those halls now, his sister's name catching in his throat. He should call out to her, let her know he was back. She would be worried, wouldn't she? He thought so, but he couldn't quite recall why.

But some instinct insisted that he didn't dare speak, didn't dare call out. His inlays glowed in his arms, fully intact, connecting him to every circuit in the station, every command console, every wire. He could reach out and open a door without speaking. He could call a pod to him or change the station's layout with a thought. The electricity pulsed in his veins, while his sister's voice tutored him to take it slowly, slowly, it was so easy to be overwhelmed.

When he looked down, the inlays glowed beneath a coating of blood.

Damian awoke mid-axe-stroke, his muscles straining, poised to take the next swing. Behind his eyelids, the dream still swam.

It took a moment to understand that this wasn't *part* of the dream. His fingers were really wrapped around the hilt of the tool. He was here, on Pheon.

And he appeared to be breaking into a building.

Damian dropped the axe, letting it clatter heavily to the ground. His hands ached, the still-healing blisters protesting the strain of working an axe, of all things. What was he, a lumberjack? The damn consciousness thief hadn't even bothered to protect his hands with gloves. The pest clearly had no nerve endings.

Sileux's trap had worked. Whatever he'd done, whatever tweaks he'd made to Damian's electrodes, it had interrupted the thief in the midst of its plans.

"Whatever you are," Damian said, "you've lost. I won't carry out your little missions any longer."

Something *pushed* at his mind, a gentle pressure. He frowned, trying to mimic the feeling, to push back. How did one *push* with one's brain? Seemed utterly impossible. But he tried, anyway. Impossible was a relative term, more these days than ever.

A breath, and another, and the sensation faded to a dull awareness. Not so impossible after all, then. He closed the feeling away as best he could before taking a moment to look around.

He was standing on the top step of the most eye-wrenchingly red house he'd ever seen. Even among the bright colors of this city, it stood out like a sore. Or a flower that *really* wanted to be pollinated. Especially with those yellow doors and shutters.

Damian peered over the wrought iron rail, squinting at the window to try for a glimpse inside the house. All he could see was a sitting room of some kind, the shadows of chairs, and a table that appeared to be shaped like a bird. "What were you trying to do here?" he murmured.

The thief, locked away in his mind, said nothing.

A red-tinted sphere dropped in front of Damian's face, barring the little he could see of the room. "Remain where you are," it said. "Do not move."

It was what Damian would have said to someone with a stinging insect on their neck, or a snake sizing up their rear end. He didn't move.

And then he was surrounded by an army of red spheres as Champion Ahnien came dashing around the corner and up the steps, all too recognizable in the reflection of the window. Despite the sphere's instructions to stay still, Damian risked turning around to face him.

Ahnien himself was surrounded by a posse of men who might've been Champions or police officers, or perhaps soldiers. They placed themselves between Damian and Ahnien, like they feared he might take a shot at their leader. But Damian didn't have any weapons; he was caught, and he didn't even know what his crime was.

"You," Ahnien said. "I didn't want to believe it. Not after that display in the council chambers, and your demand to attend the funeral."

Damian didn't have to feign his confusion. He shook his head, and the trapped thief in the back of his mind tested the wall with a push, a press. "Believe what?" he asked.

Ahnien was trembling with anger, his cheeks flushed. "You freed the murderer from prison."

What, Borona's murderer? Damian opened his mouth to

deny it, then stopped. He *couldn't* deny it, not truthfully. He might well have done exactly that. There was no way to know.

"You were in league with the murderer," Ahnien said. "And now you return to the scene. For what purpose?"

Ah. This was Champion Borona's house, then. Sileux had said that the man was supposed to be forgotten, so perhaps that was why Ahnien wouldn't speak his name—though he still seemed keen enough to find the man's murderer.

But how had Ahnien known to find him here? Had the spheres been watching? If so, they ought to know well enough that he was no murderer. Though if spheres were run by human consciousness, they could very well have their own agendas, could they not? Human consciousness was nothing if not opinionated.

Of course, Damian's bots were opinionated, too, and they were not run by human consciousness. Difficult to work out where the line might be. Fascinating. He hoped he'd live long enough to study that.

"Where is your companion?" Ahnien demanded, taking another step toward him. "Is she involved?"

Damian gave his head another shake. He didn't know where Shannon had gone after their argument. Far away from here, he hoped.

"Arrest him," Ahnien turned back toward the street, and his companions took his retreat as instructions. Two of them surged forward, grabbing Damian by the arms, though it was hardly necessary. He could fight these two off, perhaps, but not with dozens of spheres looking angrily down at him like they were ready to start throwing lasers his way. Not with two more thickly muscled soldier types waiting below.

As they wrestled him down the stairs—again, the force was hardly necessary—Damian's eyes fell on Champion Sileux. The old man was waiting at the bottom of the steps, his expression hard. Unyielding. He met Damian's gaze with sparkling dark eyes, and Damian understood what people meant when they said their blood had run cold. His felt like winter on Olton Moon.

So that was how Ahnien had known. Whatever trap Sileux had set up for the consciousness thief, it had alerted not only him but the council as well.

Huh, he thought. *I've been betrayed.*

CHAPTER 30

SHANNON FOLLOWED the dark-haired man along a path that twisted back and forth between rows of chunky boulders. Though it was only just large enough to navigate single file, she caught movement each time they passed even a narrow crack between the rocks. Guards, watching from between the rocks. She was aware that she was being escorted, the soldiers having arranged themselves in front of and behind her, but no one had tried to touch her. Thankfully.

They switched back a few times along the path before a strip of boulder-free land opened up before them. Shannon couldn't keep her mouth from falling open; how in the worlds had she missed *this*? It was practically a city in itself, with neat rows of tents and wooden shelters, well-worn paths, and cook fires with flames but no smoke. Like Jem's pyre, none of them had any smell. It was too close to Damian's 'alien wood might have weird properties' theory.

Well. He'd never need to know he'd been right. Assuming these people ever let her see him again.

Soldiers came and went through the camp, exchanging words with other soldiers before heading out—on duty perhaps—or settling themselves to eat beside one of the strange fires. Spheres wove through and over the camp, but like Zahlia's, they were black rather than clear-sided. Perhaps that was why she hadn't spotted them from above. Or perhaps they simply didn't rise high enough.

Shannon supposed she could be excused for not having noticed the camp. Not that they'd bothered to hide it; these people didn't seem like the hiding type. It was just that the landscape was arranged so that it obscured the view.

Still. It was so close. As the bird flew, they were probably half a mile from where she'd been standing just outside the city walls. Perhaps even closer. How was it that fire could have no smoke? No smell?

Nearby, the orange column burned into the atmosphere. Her mind searched for a description, each attempt coming up short. A huge, molten tree trunk. A misshapen hunk of glass, still hot from the forge. A gravity-defying weed. Now that she was closer, she could see movement within its core as doughnut-shaped platforms drifted up and away from Pheon's surface. An... elevator?

As they entered the camp, Zahlia came running out of a nearby structure. Her movements were those of a soldier, economical and quick. Her expression was one of unrestrained concern, her mask of calm propriety all but erased. She'd knotted her long hair into a messy bun at the back of her head. And then there was the black, which still clothed her from head to foot. Most of the soldiers wore interlocking armor, like the dark-haired man who'd escorted Shannon to the camp; Zahlia did not.

Shannon would have liked to meet someone in her life, just one person, who *didn't* wear a mask.

"What happened?" Zahlia asked.

The dark-haired man gave Zahlia a scathing look. "This woman followed you out of the city, is what happened. She is one of the visitors, yes?"

He phrased it as a question, but it was clear that he already knew the answer.

Zahlia met his gaze for a long moment. "What are you doing on the ground, Command?"

"Cleaning up your messes, it seems."

Zahlia stepped around the man—Command? Was that a name, or a title? The latter, most likely—and lay a hand on Shannon's arm, withdrawing it when Shannon flinched. She couldn't help it; how could she trust people who appeared to be imprisoning an entire city?

"You're not a prisoner," Zahlia said.

Shannon glanced at the armed soldiers, the tightly contained fury of their dark-haired leader. "It doesn't feel that way."

Zahlia cringed, and Shannon risked a step toward her. "They've been keeping this from us. The dome. All of it. *You've* been keeping it from us."

Zahlia beckoned for her to come further into the camp, pointedly ignoring Command, who raised his eyebrows. Whether in offense or surprise, Shannon didn't know. She'd have to observe him longer to wager a guess.

Maybe Zahlia was the leader here, and he had to let her do what she wanted. But Shannon didn't think so.

Still, she followed the other woman deeper into the camp. It was probably a good thing that Damian hadn't come along; he'd be spouting all kinds of nonsense, and probably getting himself shot in the process.

"You're not Echains, are you?" Shannon asked. "You're from the other system. You're the conquerors."

Zahlia grimaced, shaking her head. "Whoever told the story, they told it backwards. *They* are the ones who tried to take over your Parse Galaxy. Not us. This dome is their punishment, their prison, and we are their watchers. They believe that you can provide the means for their escape. They would not tell you the truth."

Because Shannon and Damian had come through those gateways. Wormholes? It was *impossible*. Except now she was looking at this domed city, and the truth of the highly patrolled skies above it. The *Quandary* could not have landed here the usual way. One way or another, it had arrived through those... gateways.

But that didn't mean the Echains were the ones with grand plans to conquer the Parse Galaxy. Zahlia hadn't told the truth, either. Her people could just as well be the ones to watch. "You'll understand if I find it a little hard to believe," Shannon said.

"I am sorry I misled you," Zahlia said. "I had my orders."

Orders. They existed across the universe, apparently.

"You are very eager to tell our story to a stranger." Shannon hadn't realized that Command was ghosting their steps, but she probably shouldn't have been surprised to find him sauntering along behind them. A scar slashed his right cheek on a diagonal, so light that it was barely visible.

Zahlia rounded on him, her face a mask of barely contained fury. Whatever else was happening, she hated this man. And she hated him openly. "Let us take her to the station," she said. "She can help us."

"She can end us," Command replied. He studied Shannon, his eyes unreadable. "But perhaps it would be well. To get her as far from the surface as possible. Then you may tell her what you like."

Shannon didn't love the sound of that, but really, what choice did she have? When Zahlia led the way, she followed.

———

The column *was* an elevator.

There were no space elevators in the Parse Galaxy, except in old stories and drama vids. She'd watched one as a child, which had been not-so-cleverly titled "Spellavator." If memory served, it'd required witches to keep it running.

Because that was how out-of-reach the technology was, in Parse. Leaving an atmosphere required thrust, more of it than a gently rising platform could provide. It was a problem that hadn't been cracked.

No one much bothered with it, anyway, except for the sake of narrative or thought experiments. Their ships came and went with little trouble, and with the Currents sweeping through the sector, travel was easy. What good would an elevator do? It would probably be slower.

Or maybe that was just what people said about technology they hadn't managed to crack.

"Do not be anxious." Zahlia had remained by Shannon's side, as if concerned that letting her out of sight for a moment might end in disaster. That only increased the feeling of being a prisoner—especially after Zahlia's friend, whose name was Ches, came to mirror Zahlia's position on Shannon's other side—but Shannon merely told herself that the interesting story was here. If she needed to be a prisoner for a few hours, so be it. She'd find a way out.

"I'm not anxious," Shannon replied. "Just taking notes in my head."

It *was* nerve wracking to rise like this, but she had no desire to let any of the Drachains know that. Besides, the view made up for it. Not that it was beautiful; it was unnerving at best, frightening at worst. A world stripped of green and blue, left only with shades of charcoal and mud. The dome glittered in the distance, like a diamond set within a broken crown. From here, she couldn't make out the city beneath it. The dome merely sat like a misplaced bubble, one that refused to pop.

Unnerving. Frightening. And *interesting*. That was the key. That was what kept her going.

"We had to defeat them." Zahlia's voice was soft, and Command growled from behind them when she spoke—Shannon kept trying to forget he was there—but Zahlia merely shot him a look of annoyance. "Who will she tell from here?"

He scowled. "Fine. Continue."

Again, Shannon wondered who was in charge. She sensed a power struggle. But Zahlia had been masquerading as Sileux's wife—did *he* know about that?—while Command had been out here... commanding. It seemed clear enough.

"The only way to defeat the Echains was to prevent them from using their gateways to access your part of the galaxy," Zahlia continued. "We only defeated them after we discarded the key to the gateway by tossing it through. Skirmishes still arise, but they *are* defeated. We locked the key on the other side, where it was hidden. It trapped a few Echains there, and we're aware of the trouble they caused. But it was better than the alternative."

"Invasion," Shannon said.

Zahlia inclined her head.

Questions. So many of them. To begin with, why did these Drachains care whether their twin system invaded some far-off sector of the galaxy? Why was it worth a *war*? And if the Echains were so well in hand, why slip spies among them? Why did they need to sabotage warehouses full of weapons? Which, it was clear now, they must have done.

The questions swirled through Shannon's mind like wisps, slowly circling a theory, perhaps even a conclusion. Or maybe several of them.

"So I did mess up Damian's calculations," Shannon said slowly. "He was trying to end up in your system. Not theirs."

"A betrayal," Command said. "That he would dare return here."

"He doesn't know," Zahlia shot back.

"His mother's failure, not ours."

Shannon frowned. They'd ascended into the upper atmosphere now, where the black of space suddenly stretched out before them. She hadn't realized how much she'd missed the sight of it. The strange light of the city had obscured the stars, and probably for good reason. It would make the dome too obvious.

Or perhaps it was merely another part of the punishment.

To Shannon's knowledge, Damian hadn't ever visited this part of the galaxy before. He'd been performing the calculations for the first time; he'd said so himself. And though he said plenty of ridiculous, far-fetched things, he'd said that particular far-fetched thing in a moment of annoyed accusation. Her gut told her it was the truth.

Sometimes, when facts spun on their heads, her gut was all she had left.

What, she wondered, had caused Damian to believe he could bend the Currents in the first place? She'd dismissed it as mere hubris at first, or evidence of his ridiculousness. She hadn't given it much thought beyond that. What had he said at Sileux's funeral? That the Currents *sang*. He was connected to them, somehow. And he'd known, or some part of him had, where he was headed. Half calculations, and half instinct.

"You think Damian's the key," Shannon said slowly. "Don't you?"

Zahlia studied her for a long moment. But in the end, it was Command who answered. "We know that he is," he said. "And there's only one way to ensure the Echains do not regain their access to the gateways. We need to find him. And he needs to die."

CHAPTER 31

THE PRISON FELT FAMILIAR, though Damian was certain he'd never seen it before. In fact, before the moment those men had shoved him between the flimsy-looking walls and into the court-yard of cages, he'd have sworn those flimsy walls were actual buildings. And also, that these people couldn't possibly have anything so garish as a prison in their sparkling city.

How wrong of him. How very wrong.

He'd seen plenty of jail cells in his time, from inside more often than out. Spare ones. Lush ones. Even a menagerie cage, in which he'd been the main attraction. And though this particular cell was nothing special, he knew he'd never set foot inside it before.

But then, that was the entire problem. Because as long as the rogue *thing* kept taking over his mind, he couldn't be certain of *anything*. It was still there, thumping at the wall he'd erected in his brain, like a toddler kicking a door in protest of time out. And these people did seem pretty well convinced that he'd helped someone else escape from here.

So maybe he *had* seen it. Or maybe it was one of Sileux's lies. Difficult to say.

And Shannon wanted to know why he accepted no help. Please.

He hoped that she was all right. Her friend Zahlia was married to Champion Sileux. Would she shelter Shannon, or betray her as Sileux had done? Damian usually erred on the side of betrayal. When he didn't, well, his current circumstances were a case in point.

Perhaps since Shannon had nearly been poisoned, Ahnien and the other council members would believe her innocence.

There was nothing he could do about it from this cell, either way.

A pair of guards passed through the courtyard every ten minutes, give or take, and Damian spent the intervening time considering what to say to them on their next pass. Now, as light spilled out of their little guardhouse and into the courtyard, announcing their imminent arrival—finally, a place where that omnipresent illumination had dimmed—he paced to the bars and wrapped his fingers around them.

The guards appeared, their attention locked on his cell. Either this place had no other customers, or he was today's main event.

"Excuse me," Damian said, "I'm looking for the nearest tavern? A place with good strong pours, mind. No watering down the drinks. Do you know anything?"

One of the guards smacked his hands.

It was the closest thing to an answer that he'd received thus far. Progress. "Terrible service," he called after them. "One star. And I'd like to speak with a manager."

The guards merely strode away.

...and Damian's vision *scattered*.

When he opened his eyes, he was sitting in the back corner of the cell, and the guards were entering the courtyard again. He blinked. The pressure in his mind was like a wave battering a sea wall, insistent. Uncontrollable.

Ten minutes. He'd lost ten minutes.

"Nothing to say this time?" one of the guards said.

Damian sniffed. "If I'd known it was that easy to get you to speak, I'd have not said something much sooner."

They disappeared again.

Damian flattened a hand against the ground—dirt here, rather than the glassy stone of the city streets—and pushed himself to his feet. "Now," he said, "whatever you are, whoever you are, I'm going to need you to stop. I can feel you pecking at that wall. If you want me to do something, just tell me."

Movement flickered in the corner of his eye. But when he turned his head, there was nothing in the cell. He blinked.

When he opened his eyes, the guards were passing once again, and his finger hurt like the devil. The nail was split halfway into the quick, the skin bloodied and drying.

Something pushed his chin *down*. The same something, he suspected, that had scratched a bloody message into the dirt.

If you weren't so dense, the message read, *I could tell you*.

Damian got to his feet, swaying only slightly. "Oh, good," he said. "You're a smart ass. You couldn't have gone with something more concise, like *Listen* or *Take Heed*. You just had to insult me."

The world stuttered.

When he woke, his hands were on the bars again. Only this time, he was crouched at the bottom of them, feeling at the spot where they met the stone below.

He wasn't sure whether to be glad or disconcerted that he was starting to get *used* to this. "Fine," he said. "You want to tell me something. Then tell me something."

He prodded at the bars, running his fingers along the fixtures.

The cell floor might be made of dirt, but the bars were secured deep into a row of stone.

All but one. When he poked it, the stone *rippled*. And then, before he could absorb that little detail, the stone poured itself into the cell. Like it had just been hanging out there, pretending to be a rock and waiting for him to activate it.

It was a sphere, of course, though this one was black as the vacuum instead of clear like the rest of them. Now that he'd freed it, the thing spun a circle around his head as if checking his identity, then zoomed toward the lock and squeezed inside.

Damian waited. Nothing happened. But when he gave the door a tentative push, it cracked open. The mind-stealer *could* be helpful, then. Finally.

He waited for the guards' next pass before slipping out of the cell, making his way for the door at a run, and darted quietly out into the street. Either they hadn't bothered to station any guards there, or there were other spheres working on his behalf.

As far as escapes went, it was probably a record.

"Not so dense after all," he said.

When he woke again, he was standing in front of his ship.

The *Quandary* was still on the lower level of the gateway building, where the floor was dry, the walls stretching just high enough to accommodate the ship's height. The gateways were absent, no doubt working—or not working, as it was—somewhere up above.

Whatever this consciousness-stealer was, at least it appeared to have the same goal as he did. For the moment. Damian started for the ship. He could leave the planet, *had* to leave it as soon as possible, if not by gateway, then by the usual atmosphere-slash-space route. Assuming he could find his way out of this glorified parking garage.

He should probably pick up Shannon before they did that, though.

Mojo came rushing down the gangplank as Damian stepped up onto it, the little bot's claws tapping as it ran. Usually it would be yammering on about missing him or worrying or wanting to know how to win some game. Bruce must've decided to silence it.

"Hey, Mojo," Damian said, still disoriented. He had the urge to hide the fact that he hadn't meant to come here at all, even from the bots. How many times had that thing taken over his brain back in the cell? Four? Five? He was starting to get confused. "I think we should find—"

The bot skittered straight up to him and poked him in the leg with a needle.

Damian swore, swiping for Mojo, but the bot was too fast. It ran up his leg, then used his jacket to scrabble up to his shoulder, no doubt scratching any number of holes in the leather on its way up. Mojo knew the coat was off limits. And if there was one thing Mojo held sacred, it was following the rules.

"Hello, Damian," Mojo said. Except that it wasn't Mojo's voice at all. It was deeper—not so difficult, since Mojo was permanently squeaky—and it spoke with the hint of an accent that Damian didn't recognize. "I think it's time we had a chat."

CHAPTER 32

"YOU DIDN'T HAVE to lock her up."

Command's face was like a rock. Zahlia had always thought so. An ugly, humorless, crag of a rock, as cruel as Pheon's surface after the war, as inflexible as the mountain range that glared down upon their enemies.

Even rocks could be worn away in time.

The soldiers had been waiting for them when the elevator docked at the main station. They'd hauled Shannon Forest away, and none of Zahlia's pleas could deter them. Command had simply watched, his hands pressed behind his back. Placid as a poisonous sea.

She knew that her distress was obvious. Her hands shook as she stood before him now, in the suite he'd claimed as his office on the main station that watched over Pheon. A broad stretch of windows looked out toward the surface, as if he planned to personally observe everything that dared to twitch on the planet below.

Command stood before the windows, calmly looking into a sphere at his eye level. As if her presence had been noticed and deemed unimportant. "I would not have had to," he said, "if you had kept more of our secrets to yourself."

"She can help us."

"She is his ally. She will protest his death. It's a complication we cannot risk."

Zahlia scoffed. "His ally? They hardly tolerate one another. But frankly, I do not see why he needs to die, either."

Command looked up from the sphere, aiming his unwavering gaze at her. Cruel, yes. And unyielding. "That, Zahlia, is why I lead. And you do not."

She couldn't hide her flinch. He wasn't wrong. He'd been chosen over her own supposedly radical views—for which she'd been exiled, in reality if not in name. But that had been before Damian Riddle and Shannon Forest came crashing into their sector of the galaxy without warning. Contact had already been made. Surely the man could recognize reason when he heard it.

"We are locking away an entire section of the galaxy," she said. "We could establish contact with them. We could share resources. We could—"

"Extinguish ourselves," he interrupted. "Extinguish *them*. No, Zahlia. Contact is not an option."

"Ches agrees with me." The words fell out of her mouth before she could stop them. "Where is he?"

She didn't want Command to know they'd discussed it. She didn't want him to know they were anything more than colleagues.

Not that they *were* anything more. Friends, perhaps. That she could allow.

But Command trusted Ches. More, clearly, than he did Zahlia. Ches might not have the man's ear, exactly, but he had spent more time at Command's side. Perhaps Command would listen to him.

In the chaos of Shannon's arrest, however, Ches had disappeared. He wasn't here to speak the words himself—nor had he been in the barracks or the sick bay when Zahlia had gone looking for him.

"Ches," Command spat, "is on his way back to Drachao."

Zahlia stared. As long as she'd been on Pheon, Ches had been stationed here on the station. His voice was a constant, a tether in the dark. It wasn't that shuttles between the systems were uncommon; they were connected by a thread of what Damian and Shannon called a Current, making travel easy.

It was simply that Ches hadn't left. Ever.

Command flicked the sphere aside, and it retreated toward the wall, hanging in wait as he made his way around the table to face her. He wasn't a bulky man, but his reed-thin form hid knots of wiry muscle. He was strong, and he was tall. Intimidating, when he wanted to be, and he knew how to leverage that. He kept coming, stopping only once he was well within the bounds of Zahlia's personal space.

She held her ground.

"I did not think it would be necessary to remind you," he said, "but you *have* a husband. And you will return to him."

She tilted her chin up, hiding her fear behind a glare. "And if I refuse?"

He turned away. "Drachao is not too far to exact punishment. All it will take is one command, one order, and you truly will be alone. Do you understand what I'm saying?"

She swallowed, nodding. Command would kill Ches, or lock him up, because of Zahlia's failures. She didn't doubt it. "I understand."

"Then you are dismissed, soldier. Prepare to return to the surface within the hour. By now, I expect you will have been missed."

Nodding in what she hoped he would interpret as terrified agreement, Zahlia fled.

CHAPTER 33

DAMIAN BLINKED AT HIS SHOULDER. "MOJO?"

"Not remotely." The voice sounded amused. Mojo never sounded amused; Mojo sounded excited, hyper, or giddy.

Bruce rose from where he'd been sitting at the side console, joints clicking ominously. "What did you do to it?"

At first, Damian thought Bruce was accusing *him* of altering Mojo. But the bot's eyes were laser-focused on Damian's shoulder, on the creature itself. Damian had experienced plenty of moments to be thankful for the fact that Bruce did not have *actual* lasers, or weapons of any kind, installed in his head; this was most definitely one of those times.

Before this moment, Damian wouldn't have expected Bruce to care about Mojo's fate. He'd have expected Bruce to sit down, invite the intruder onto his lap, and start asking it questions about how it had done what it had done and whether, pretty please, the change would be permanent.

Instead, Bruce stood terrifyingly still, waiting for a response. He had to know that any violence would potentially hurt Mojo, too. It might *only* hurt Mojo, in fact. Because though the pressure had eased in the back of Damian's mind, he could still feel it, drifting around back there like a specter.

It was still there, in his blood. Or his brain. Both, probably. And yet it was also... outside. In Mojo, apparently.

The thing that wasn't Mojo let out a huffing sort of chuckle. "Your fearful little bot is still here. It's merely suppressed."

"Your particular talent," Damian commented.

Bruce didn't move. "I wish to speak to it."

The bot made a sighing sort of sound. After a moment, it skittered over Damian's back to his other shoulder, then hopped excitedly onto his head. Definitely more Mojo-like, though Damian wasn't sure until it squeaked, "I have a friend! A real one! It's playing hide and seek with me, inside my processors!"

Bruce tilted his head slightly to look at Lex, who'd been hovering in silence beside the dashboard. "It's Mojo," she confirmed.

How she knew that, Damian couldn't say for sure. But she seemed certain, and since she hadn't pricked him with any consciousness-transferring needles, she was probably as trustworthy as anyone else in the room.

"That thing is not your friend," Bruce said. "Expel it at once."

Mojo spun a pirouette on Damian's shoulder, and he winced, suppressing the urge to bat it away. "You can't make me!" it said. "I like my new friend!"

Bruce twitched, as if to take another step toward it, but Damian held up a hand, hoping that for once, his directions would be heeded.

Mojo stilled, which Mojo rarely did. "Happy?" it asked, again in the smoother voice.

"Perfectly," Damian replied before Bruce could interrupt. "You must be the alien consciousness that's been hijacking my body. Forgive me for saying it's not particularly nice to meet you."

The thing that wasn't Mojo took a flying leap from Damian's

shoulder, then took up a perch on the shelf beside one of his clocks. A boring, cube-shaped one. He wasn't sure why he'd even kept it, really. A momentary fancy.

Blinking hard against the ringing in his ears, Damian let himself collapse in his pilot's chair. If he was going to speak with a dead alien consciousness, or whatever this thing was, he would at least be comfortable while he did it. He only wished there were some snacks.

"I am not so alien," not-Mojo said. "The Parse Galaxy was founded by Echains and Drachains who disagreed with our tradition of dedicating consciousness after death. You and I have the same roots, Damian Riddle."

Founded? Like an entire section of the galaxy was a university or, worse, a charity organization? The Parse Galaxy's origins dated back thousands of years. Ilya System had been first, and they'd expanded to the rest of the Centers. The colonization of the rest of the galaxy—the sector—followed shortly afterward. It was well documented; even Damian's oft-interrupted schooling had taught him that much.

Of course, all documentation ended somewhere, and certain scholars did still love to dig up bones and argue about when and how humans had first materialized. Or whatever the current theory was.

Not-Mojo sat patiently on the shelf, awaiting his response.

"Did they name the Parse Galaxy, too?" Damian asked. "Because I always thought the name was very stupid."

"Ill thought out, would be a nicer term," Lex put in. She still stood beside Bruce, both bots watching the conversation unfold with that eerie stillness. Lex didn't have weapons installed, either, but she *could* run over your toes something terrible.

"We believe it may be a time-garbled version of the word 'parcel,'" not-Mojo said. "There was a contingent who thought it was based on parsecs, to indicate the distance between our part of the galaxy and yours. But that was pure speculation."

Sure, pure speculation. How distasteful of them to presume.

"Maybe," Damian said, "it was just supposed to mean a part of something larger."

Not-Mojo hopped up onto the cube-shaped clock. Damian would have preferred it not do that, but at least it was just the cube. No need to disturb the birds, or the working hov-train. He wouldn't put it past this annoying little thing to start knocking the clocks down purely out of spite, and he didn't have it in him to perform any miraculous catches at the moment.

"So they were detractors," Damian said. "Seeking refuge from persecution, I imagine?"

Champion Borona had not seemed all that persecuted, being a council member and all. But then, there *was* the matter of his funeral. Perhaps he'd have been persecuted thousands of years ago. Now, he was just... punished in death, as it were.

How had the man come to be a detractor in the first place? Maybe they hadn't all left. Or maybe some had changed their minds with time. Very likely, it was a little of both. They were talking about handfuls of millennia here. The very fact that this consciousness-blended tech had existed that long... it nearly defied imagination.

"They were fools," not-Mojo spat.

Still a touchy subject. Noted. "So the detractors didn't object to the Currents?" Damian prodded. "Because Parse has those, and we use them rather enthusiastically."

Not-Mojo hopped from the cube to the cuckoo clock. "The Currents, as you call them, came later."

"A timeline would be helpful," Damian said.

"Be careful of the owl clock," Lex said, her voice just placid enough to hide a layer of disapproval. "It's his favorite."

It certainly wasn't. Damian's favorite was the spaceship, and Lex knew it.

Not-Mojo squeezed behind the owl clock and gave it a good shove. It dropped off the shelf, and though Lex rushed to catch it, she wasn't fast enough. It hit the floor and cracked open, the sides shattering into splinters.

"Sadist," Damian said. He wished he could close his eyes and sleep in the chair. This discussion was wearing on him. And while he was making wishes, he might as well add one for the thing to get away from his damn clocks. Bad enough that it had to invade his brain. Now it was messing with his property, too. So the owl hadn't been his favorite. He still *liked* it. "And here I've been thinking my blood was alien."

He'd certainly been told so, and by scientists much smarter than himself. Not that he'd have ever admitted that to them.

"Certain changes may have occurred over the millennia," not-Mojo allowed. "We have not had ample opportunity to study such effects, though your blood would give us a chance to do so."

"Not happening," Damian said. He'd had enough pins and needles stuck into him to last a lifetime.

Not-Mojo made a clicking noise. "We shall see. But the main differences in your blood are due more to the alien technology seeded within it. A key."

Damian spun the chair, pressing a finger to his bottom lip as the bot rotated out of his field of vision, then back into it. "My blood is a key."

It certainly didn't feel like a key. It felt like a poison. A dribble of which had been extracted from his body so it could inhabit Mojo and speak with him directly.

The universe was a strange place indeed.

"You're the consciousness of a dead alien," Damian said. His thoughts felt murky. Or perhaps tumbled would be a better word for it. Like they'd spent all day banging the sides of a dryer and had emerged full of wrinkles. If he could only find the right iron, the pieces would fit together.

"Not so alien," not-Mojo corrected. "And I am a blend of many."

"The consciousness of dead... ancestors, then. The dead ancestors run the tech, the tech is in my blood, and my blood is a key."

The bot waited, patient. Like a tutor, in expectation of their student's likely errant response. It reminded him uncomfortably of Sileux.

Damian had all the facts. Now he just needed to put them together.

He snapped his fingers, dropping his feet to stop the chair from spinning. "The gateways. I'm the key to the portals. That's how we got here. That's why everyone's obsessed with me."

"Please," not-Mojo said. "*I* am the key to the gateways. You are merely the host."

Not-Mojo poised itself to leap across the shelf, making a direct arc for the spaceship clock. More quickly than Damian would have imagined possible, Bruce stepped forward and extended an arm, capturing the pest in one of his dextrous hands. The little bot struggled, but Bruce held on, peering at it like it was a rodent that needed exterminating.

"And how," Bruce said, "did *you* get into the captain's blood in the first place?"

"Excellent question, Bruce," Damian said. "I'd like to know the answer as well."

Not-Mojo stopped struggling abruptly and leaned a small claw on Bruce's silvery fingers. "Your mother hosted the key. She passed it on to you."

Damian's mouth went sour. "And here I thought she hadn't bothered with a parting gift."

"She did not realize she'd passed the key to you. She still does not."

Damian pressed his lips together, unwilling to reveal his feelings on the matter by blurting out the first response that came to mind. Every variation of which inevitably boiled down to, 'fuck her.'

Though judging by not-Mojo's dive for the spaceship clock, the pest knew a lot more about Damian than he would have wished. It *had* been parasiting around inside his cells. Still was, in fact. It no doubt knew exactly how he felt about his missing mother.

"Is she here?" That was Lex; Damian didn't care one way or the other.

For the first time in this entire conversation-slash-lesson, not-Mojo hesitated. "I do not know."

"That sounds about right," Damian muttered.

He could understand why his mother would have abandoned Archimedes Sol. That had never been in question. The man was a thug, a con, a thief. A murderer. The list went on. Essentially, he was a bad guy, in every sense of the term. Damian hadn't quite realized it as a kid, much as he'd resented the way his father had dragged him from system to system, home to home, ripping him away as soon as he'd begun to settle in and make friends. When he'd gotten older, though, it'd become painfully obvious.

But no revelation about his father could explain why his mother hadn't taken Damian with her when she'd left. In fact, the worse the revelation about his father's deeds, the more baffling—and horrible—her abandonment had seemed.

Not-Mojo gave up the calm act and squirmed in Bruce's grip. Had it been a real squirrel, it would have tried to bite Bruce on the hand. And gotten a broken tooth for its trouble, but still. It would have tried.

"None of this matters," the little bot accused as it fought, while Bruce merely watched its efforts, implacable. "You are a terrible host. Dense and unobservant. I've been trying to contact you."

Damian propped his hands behind his head. He didn't favor being lectured by a dead consciousness, whether alien or ancestor. "I did notice that, actually."

"Not quickly enough. Your refusal to acknowledge my presence has been killing you."

"I noticed that, too. Forgive me for not putting the pieces together fast enough for your liking, but I had the misfortune of not being conscious when you took over my body to do ruthless deeds. Did you kill Champion Borona, by the way?"

"I did *not*. I wished to unearth evidence of who had."

Hm. Probably Sileux, then.

Not-Mojo pinched its limbs together, making itself small enough to squeeze through Bruce's grip before the bigger bot could notice. It dropped to the floor and darted across the space, spider-quick, to scramble onto the dashboard console.

Bruce started after it, but Damian shook his head.

And again, Bruce actually paused. Obeying orders. Maybe there was hope for him after all.

Though Damian immediately regretted giving this particular order when not-Mojo hopped from the console to his shoulder and gave his ear a tweak. "If I'm ruthless, it's only because I'm trying to save *your* sector of the galaxy. You landed among the conquerors, *not* the watchers. Which was impossibly stupid, by the way. But it did give me the opportunity to do some infiltrating on the watchers' behalf."

So Shannon's presence had affected the calculations after all. That, or his calculations had been off in the first place. Always a possibility.

"So that's why Sileux attacked me," Damian said. "Makes sense, actually. Bit confusing, but I think I'm getting it."

The bot tweaked his ear again, which seemed entirely unnecessary. "Here's what's not confusing. Your reporter girlfriend is a prisoner on one of the watchers' space stations. They keep Pheon under guard. And if you don't rescue her, she's going to die."

"She is not his girlfriend," Bruce said. "She does not like him."

True. That was true.

"Okay, now I *am* confused," Damian said. "I thought you said you were with the good guys."

For the first time since the start of this odd conversation, the little bot hesitated. "It's... complicated."

Damian sighed. "It always is. All right." He swiveled his chair back toward the console, with not-Mojo's weight still pressing on his shoulder. "How do we get out of here?"

"It's going to be tricky," not-Mojo said. "Seeing as the city is trapped under a dome."

"You don't say." Damian should probably be surprised, but he'd apparently hit his quota for shock. Shannon had been right about part of it; there *was* something wrong with this place. "All right, not-Mojo. Show us the way."

CHAPTER 34

THE DRACHAINS HAD SEALED Shannon in a cube. That was the only way to describe it; the room was a box, with a gray metal floor, a gray metal ceiling, and four gray metal walls to match. No carpets. No furniture. No grates or bars.

Had Shannon been introduced to these two places—the city on the surface and the space station watching from above—and asked to guess which was home to the would-be conquerors, she'd have said it was the station. For certain. She hadn't seen much of it, but what she had was stark and military. Lots of ships. Guns. Soldiers.

And they weren't like Parse Galaxy Fleet soldiers. Those were annoying, but more likely to grant you a speeding ticket and a lecture than haul you off to a cell. Certainly not without a trial. They were self righteous that way.

These soldiers wore the same interlocking armor as their commander. They walked with rod-straight spines and down-turned mouths. They didn't speak.

Resisting the urge to curl up in the corner and weep, Shannon paced the perimeter of the cell, running a hand along the wall. This room might not have any weaknesses. It might be a fortress; it might have a failsafe where the slightest attempt to manipulate it would detach it from the rest of the station and shoot her out into the black.

But she'd be damned if she stopped trying to survive. So she paced. And she inspected. And she searched for any sign of weakness.

Her legs were aching by the time the door swung open.

Shannon could not have said where the door even *was*. She should have made note of where they'd entered, should have dropped a hair to mark the wall or something, but she hadn't. So it was a surprise when a slit revealed itself in the nearest one. Not unlike the way the wall of the city's dome had cracked open.

Shannon faced the door, hands fisted at her sides. She was ready for whatever came through that door.

Not ready to be killed, maybe. But ready to fight, if that was what she needed to do.

It was Zahlia who entered. A day ago, that would have been a relief; now, she knew the woman was just as likely to slit her throat as anyone else in this awful place.

"Are you here to kill me?" Shannon asked.

With a furtive look over her shoulder, Zahlia hurried into the cell, grabbed Shannon by the arm, then wrenched her into the hall before she could ask another question. "Quiet," she said. "I'm getting you out of here."

Unexpected, but she'd take it. "Not going to argue with that."

They ran. Zahlia released Shannon's arm to withdraw a weapon from her belt, a bulbous, radish-like thing that had to be some kind of grenade. Which would help them exactly once, if it didn't crack the station open and blow them out into space.

But the other woman was clearly a soldier. Shannon decided not to question it.

Zahlia led them into a corridor lined with windows that looked out on the swell of the burned-out planet below. It was a miracle that there was air down there to breathe outside of the dome.

Above Pheon's atmosphere, a chain of stations kept a silent watch on the surface. There were so many of them. If anything moved down there, they would know. What kind of conflict had she and Damian stepped into?

She hoped he was alive down there. And not stepping into any *more* trouble, at least until she could go back and help him.

For now, she needed to help herself. As they rounded the next corner, shots pinged against the window at their backs, and Zahlia grabbed Shannon's arm again, guiding her around the corner and out of sight. She held the radish-like weapon at her shoulder, aiming the leaf-end back toward the attackers.

A wave of energy pulsed through the hall, and Shannon clapped her hands to her ears as it thrummed into her eardrums, vibrating the roots of her molars, the core of her collarbone. When she risked a glance around the corner, the soldiers were down, writhing on the floor. A couple of them had blood leaking out of their ears; those ones lay still.

Not a grenade, then.

"Where are we trying to go?" Shannon asked, breathing hard. She had the impression that the oxygen levels were lower up here. Or maybe the gravity was higher. Something was challenging her ability to keep moving, anyway.

"The fighter bays," Zahlia replied, aiming another shot at their attackers. "We need a ship. Run to the end of the hall and turn left. Take the stairs down. I'll cover you from behind."

Shannon stared at her. "That didn't take them out?"

Zahlia's expression was grim. "Only a dozen."

How many *were* there? "But what if—"

Zahlia gave her a shove. "Go."

Shannon went. She felt the next energy blast more than she

heard it, the shock of it vibrating through her feet. Zahlia seemed to be the only one using such a weapon

Trying not to think about what would happen if Shannon encountered soldiers, unarmed as she was, she dashed to the end of the hall and took the left as Zahlia had described, which did indeed lead to a staircase that might have been transplanted into any working space station in the Parse Galaxy.

Some hysterical, panicked part of her brain wanted to laugh at the thought. This part of the galaxy might use hammocks instead of beds and shoot each other with deadly radishes, but at least the stairwells looked the same.

Footsteps rattled along the grated stairs behind her, and Shannon hoped it was Zahlia. There was no time to turn back and check. She ran, heart hammering, lungs screaming for more air.

The stairs opened out into a bay, where a shining row of black fighter ships waited, ready to face some unknown threat. What, though? It wasn't as if the Echains had fighter ships down there. The ships were small, tube-like vessels, with fat spheres welded to each side—they called Zahlia's radish to mind—and no wings, and they were arranged before a massive sweep of a window. At least, Shannon hoped it was a window; there didn't appear to be a barrier between the bay and open space, but her brain said there had to be one. It looked so clear that she felt like she could step forward and reach past it to touch the vacuum. Pheon's crescent swept by outside, giving the bay a reflected orange hue, and she could see the archipelago of stations that were lined up to keep their constant watch. Clear as crystal.

But she was breathing. Her lungs hadn't exploded or frozen. So it *had* to be a window.

Zahlia dashed in behind her, turning a circle to cover them from behind, but they'd somehow managed to get ahead. She nodded to the nearest plane, and they hurried in through the back, which stood open. No doubt to allow pilots easy access in case of a sudden attack. Though, again, who could attack them, Shannon didn't know.

Of course, she *was* still new here.

The cockpit, if it could be called that, consisted of two bucket seats with crisscrossing straps. And, of course, a massive sphere. It took up the center of the space, and Shannon's head spun for a second as she tried to reconcile the absence of any recognizable dashboard or control panel. The sphere *was* the control panel.

Zahlia threw herself into one of the seats, touching the sphere with a fingertip. "Thin the barrier," she commanded. "We need a quick exit."

Shannon wasn't sure what that meant, but she found she wanted to know more. Was the barrier the window? Could the ships come and go without depressurizing the bay? The Parse Galaxy did have something like that, though it was expensive technology and somewhat rare. It definitely couldn't boast the same invisibility, either.

The sphere blinked white, then black again. "Denied," it said. "You are in violation of Drachain civil law. Your weapons will be disabled. Please await arrest."

Its tone was simultaneously polite and accusing.

"We just want to escape," Zahlia said, pleading. "If you thin the barrier, it will be like we were never here."

"And I just want an assignment on the surface," the sphere snapped. "Yet here we are."

Shannon opened her mouth, then closed it. The technology had a preference. Well, of course it did. It was powered by human consciousness, wasn't it?

Zahlia got up and stepped toward the door, peering out of the back of the ship. "I should have anticipated this."

"Indeed, you should have," the sphere agreed, calling after her. "We know a traitor when we see one."

Zahlia growled. She was looking around, as if trying to form her next plan, and Shannon wondered suddenly what had happened to her friend. Ches. She'd smuggled him out of the city, and they'd seemed... well, close. He'd stayed by her side on the elevator. Where was he?

Perhaps he hadn't agreed to help Shannon escape. Perhaps he'd turned against her.

"I don't know where to go next," Zahlia whispered. "The elevator. Maybe..."

She trailed off, shaking her head. They were trapped, with no allies to fly to their aid. This time, Zahlia would be locked up right along with Shannon. No doubt there.

And then, from behind them, the sphere said, "Barrier thinned."

Its voice was quiet as a whisper now, but the words were clear enough. Zahlia whipped around, surprise widening her eyes. But before she could re-enter the fighter, a new ship soared into the bay, knocking aside a pair of the fighters as it came to rest between them. Shannon had never seen a more beautiful sight than those crab-like claws, and the ship that rested upon them.

"That is a strange vessel," Zahlia said.

Shannon could have wept with relief at the sight of it. "That's because it's Damian's."

The gangplank fell open, and Damian came striding down it before the ship had fully settled on the ground. Mojo was perched on his shoulder, looking uncharacteristically still.

Shannon could have hugged him. She was still mad at him, but she couldn't hide the relief that opened her lungs and let her breathe again. Not just because he'd come for her, but because he was safe as well. She'd feared he might be dead.

He walked straight up to her. "I've negotiated one additional moment of seriousness with the powers that be." His expression was pinched with something that might have been concern. "Are you all right?"

She nodded. "Not a scratch."

He brushed the back of his hand across his forehead. "Thank goodness. I'd have had to pay a fine if I'd been forced to visit another bedside."

"You're not normal."

"Don't I know it."

Zahlia was staring at him. "How did you do that? The barrier wouldn't open for us."

Damian stepped away from Shannon and winked at her. *Winked*. "That's the problem with sentient technology," he said. "It literally has a mind of its own. But *my* pet sentient technology happens to go way back with the sentient technology that runs that barrier. They struck a deal."

Shannon had no idea what he was talking about. But then, that was true of at least half the things that came out of the man's mouth.

"Please stop saying sentient technology like it only applies to them," Bruce complained from the top of the ramp. "I am right here. And I consider myself to be sentient."

"Of course you are, darling," Damian soothed. He gestured toward the ship. "Hop in, loves. We've got a sentient wormhole to crash."

CHAPTER 35

IN DAMIAN'S OPINION, the *Quandary* had been overcrowded with just one extra human on board, and Shannon didn't take up very much space at all. He hadn't wanted her there, but it was tough to hold against her when she'd only been on the ship for about five minutes. That he'd known about.

With Sileux's wife on board, the place was positively cramped. Bruce had given up his seat by the righthand console with only a grumble of drama at Damian's reasoning, which revolved around the fact that the bot could lock himself to the floor and the humans could not. Now, Shannon sat in the chair to Damian's left, while Zahlia had taken the one on his right.

Perhaps if he removed the extra seats entirely, it'd send the right message to the trickster that ran this universe to *stop sending people to his ship*. And his life, for that matter.

With his luck, removing the seats would only result in him sitting on the floor himself.

Damian ran his fingers over the dash and pushed the ship out of the bay, reveling in the rippling flow of the barrier as it rearranged its atoms just enough to let them exit without depressurizing the space. As the *Quandary* shot away from the station, Damian didn't think he'd ever been happier to be flying his own ship again.

"No offense," he said, glancing at Zahlia, "but I'm confused about who the good guys are here."

Zahlia sat rod-straight in her seat, her gaze skimming along the dashboard as if it were the strangest thing she'd ever seen. To someone used to interacting with endless spheres, Damian supposed, it probably was. She was barely recognizable as Sileux's wife, her blonde hair tied back at the nape of her neck, her flowing dresses replaced with what was clearly a soldier's garb.

And Shannon claimed he wasn't observant.

"People say that about you, you know," Shannon commented.

Damian raised an eyebrow at her. "Number one, you didn't know who I was when we first met, so you have no idea what people say."

She opened her mouth, then closed it. Satisfying, to shock this particular woman into silence. She always had something to say. Yes, she'd tried to pretend she'd stowed away on his ship so she could interview him. Had that been the case, though, she'd have descended on him the second he appeared in that Catch Clan hellhole. She was a terrible liar.

"You didn't think I'd realized that," he added. "I know. It wounds me, but I'm getting over it. Number two, I'm not confusing at all. I'm pure evil."

Shannon rolled her eyes, and some part of him relaxed just a hair. That part of him hadn't completely believed that she was well, but if she could roll her eyes at him, she couldn't be too bad off. How the hell had she found her way up to this station, anyway? Not that he'd expected her to stop digging herself into holes after their argument. He'd assumed, and he thought it was fair enough, that she was still poking around the city and getting into the usual kind of trouble as she tried to prove her simulation theory.

She'd certainly dug her way to the truth, hadn't she?

It was more than he'd managed. He should have listened to her in the first place.

"It is hard to see properly from this vantage," Bruce said, with a pointed look at the seat Zahlia had taken from him, "but I believe there are enemies on our tail."

Damian checked the proximity sensors, which were just now registering the threat. Bruce always had been extra sensitive to danger. "Thank you, Bruce," Damian said, instructing the dash to initiate evasive patterns. "Way to go the extra parsec."

Bruce sniffed.

Not-Mojo gave him another tweak on the ear. "I can open the dome for you."

Obviously, since it'd done so to let them escape in the first place. "Or," Damian said, "we could jaunt over to the Current, and you can show me how to use it to access the gateways so we can flit down to the surface, quick as you like."

"The gateways are not active," the bot said. "You have to go there."

"We *came* through them. How can they not be active?"

"You have enemies here, Damian Riddle. Or had you forgotten?"

No. No, he hadn't.

"Champion Sileux drained the water," not-Mojo added. "It must be replaced before you can jump."

Annoying, but the solution was simple enough. The *Quandary* tilted, and Zahlia gripped the arms of her chair, knuckles whitening as Damian urged the ship toward Pheon's atmosphere. He wondered how often she'd been on a spaceship;

with that elevator column dominating the sky, ships must be a rarity. Of course, she'd gotten from her system to this one somehow, so she had some experience at least.

The ship was rumbling all around them, the dash registering a smattering of laser fire to the stern, but the shields were working just fine. Bruce initiated firing patterns without being asked—miracles abounded—allowing Damian to focus on pushing the *Quandary* into Pheon's atmosphere, the thrill of the ride coursing through his veins. He was feeling better, somehow.

"Not to intrude," Shannon said, "but that bot clearly isn't Mojo. So what the hell is it?"

The woman had spent so little time in their presence, and still she recognized that. She even knew Mojo's name. Impressive. He needed to get her back to the Parse Galaxy and her reporting, where she could do some good. There *was* still a war going on there. Unless his friends—acquaintances, rather—had somehow managed to prevent it.

"I've forgotten my manners." Damian hooked a finger in not-Mojo's direction. "This is my alien consciousness parasite. I named it Larry."

"No," not-Mojo said.

Damian gave it a pat on the head. "I need to call you *something*, cupcake."

"A parasite," Zahlia breathed. "It is not done."

"Actually," Shannon said, sounding thoughtful, "that explains a lot."

Damian decided not to take offense at that.

Not-Mojo straightened on Damian's shoulder, like a tiny and *very* miffed Fleet officer. "I am a conglomerate of a thousand individual souls. A name is trivial."

Damian grinned. Sometimes, it was just too easy. "Trivial it is, then."

"*No.*"

"Triv, would you mind opening the dome for us so we don't get squashed?"

Bruce cleared his throat. "I don't think you should antagonize it."

"No worries, Bruce. Triv doesn't want to die, either. Do you?"

Apparently, Triv didn't. As the *Quandary* careened toward the dome, the reflection shifted. There was no other way to describe it; first, Damian was looking at a glassy reflection of his own descending ship as it catapulted toward a city that was barely visible through the dome. His stomach had the lurching impression that he was about to crash into himself, which would have been unpleasant, to say the least.

And then the city crystallized, the ship's reflection disappearing just in time to let them drop through the barrier toward the city. It had been a long time since he'd flown in atmo, and it was difficult to stifle the urge to turn a few flips just to feel it in his gut. People on the streets stopped to point as the ship skimmed the rooftops, spheres scattering out of its way like frightened birds. This was a sight they hadn't seen before, that was for sure.

"Bring us home, Triv," Damian said.

Trivial growled. Miraculously, though, it did what he asked, helping to navigate the ship back to the main boulevard and toward the domed roof of the gateway building.

"Now," Damian said, as they swooped toward it, "what's our play, exactly?"

"Simple," Triv said. "We activate the Parse Galaxy's portals so you won't need to snap the Currents around. If our predecessors did their work, there should be a room like this somewhere in your sector of the galaxy."

Huh. That was new information. "And how do we do that?" Damian asked. "A password? A gift? A pretty, pretty please?"

"No," Triv replied, its tone making it clear that Damian was a fool, and that it planned to ignore that fact. "You replace the water. And then you walk straight through it."

CHAPTER 36

SHANNON GRIPPED the arms of her chair as Damian hovered the *Quandary* above the domed building, waiting for his parasitical bot-pet—she could see why it'd been necessary to give the thing a name—to open the ceiling so they could drop through. It certainly seemed like it should be easy enough to twist it open, widen the gap she and Damian had pulled themselves through when they'd arrived here. Just find the correct button. Right?

But as the ship descended, the roof didn't budge. Maybe it only *looked* like it should twist open. But if that were the case, how would they get ships here to pass through the working gateways?

"Any time now, peanut," Damian said.

"I cannot." Triv sounded frustrated, like it wished it had teeth just so it could grind them. "The temple roof won't open."

Damian tsked. "Bad history with its minders?"

"No," Triv replied. "I believe you've been taught that spheres do not guard the temple."

Shannon couldn't help a spark of sympathy for the thing. It *had* been living inside Damian's mind. She wasn't sure she wanted to know all the things it had seen.

"Right," Damian said. "My apologies. But, and I hope this isn't insensitive of me to mention, *you* seem to have no such hesitations."

"I am not a sphere."

"But you're not *not* a sphere, either."

"I don't—"

"Never mind. We don't have time." Damian pressed some buttons on that strange dashboard of his, and the ship made a tilting swoop toward the main thoroughfare. People scattered out of the way as he set it down in the center of the street. "We'll have to use the front door."

He lifted himself out of the chair, leaning heavily on the arm as he rose. He looked... tired, though he was hiding it behind a pasted-on grin and a quirked eyebrow. When his shirt shifted, Shannon caught sight of one of those strange thorn-like tattoos sticking up out of his collar. She tilted her head, trying to see them better, but Damian was already moving toward the exit.

"What are we after here, Triv?"

"A ride home," the bot replied.

Damian paused, resting one hand on the frame that separated the main part of his ship from the gangplank. "I can't go home," he said softly. "You know that."

Shannon frowned. Why not?

The statement, however, did not appear to be news to Trivial. "A test, then," it said. "If you prove you are the key to the gateway, you will have the leverage you need. You can use it to obtain the information you seek."

Damian was still hanging onto the doorway, the tips of his fingers pressed tight against it. "Unless the Drachains decide to kill me."

"Only some of them want to do that," Zahlia protested.

"Some is still too many." A muscle in the back of Damian's

jaw twitched. "Fine. A test. Leverage. The stuff on the floor is just water, right? Not secret gel or slime or chemicals?"

"Just water," Trivial confirmed. The bot was still sitting on Damian's shoulder, its small claws digging into his jacket. Damian didn't even seem to mind.

To Shannon's surprise, Bruce unlatched himself from the wall and joined Damian as he made his way down the gangplank. She stood, too, following them out of the ship. She was *not* going to stay in here and miss the action.

"Zahlia and I can get the water," she said. "From the canal."

Damian looked back over his shoulder, surprise raising his eyebrows just a hair. He might like to work alone, but he didn't have to be so shocked at her willingness to help. Honestly. If he fought her on it, she'd smack him on the head.

He probably sensed that, because he nodded. "Thank you."

Shannon took off at a run, hoping Zahlia would follow even though she'd volunteered the other woman for the job. She still didn't know what Zahlia's end game was, or why she was helping them. She might go alert her husband to their presence. She might call her Drachain friends for backup—or simply decide this wasn't her fight and disappear into hiding.

But Zahlia fell in to run beside her, and Shannon let herself exhale in relief. She could do this without Zahlia, but the job would be easier with her.

"How do we carry the water if the spheres won't go into the building?" Shannon asked. She'd seen them dowsing the flames at the warehouse blaze, so they seemed the most obvious option. Shannon couldn't help wondering if they'd even agree to obey her at this point. How did they work? Did someone control the access?

She had the dizzying feeling that she'd spent the last week asking all the wrong questions.

"They don't need to go into the building." Zahlia pointed

toward the twisted opening in the temple roof where Shannon and Damian had first emerged into the city. "We can drop the water from above."

"Will they even do what we ask?" Shannon asked.

"We will find out."

Shannon wasn't sure she liked that answer, but she didn't have any other ideas, either. Together, they ran.

CHAPTER 37

DAMIAN HADN'T PAID much attention to the front entrance of the gateway building—the temple, they called it—when he and Sileux had come here before. When he'd come to find the *Quandary*, he'd cut directly to the right, where elevators and staircases provided access to the lower floors. He'd been too distracted to heed his surroundings.

Now he stepped into the curving hallway and looked around. Five paces separated the outer doors from the inner ones, which led to the gateway room, making him feel rather like he was standing inside of an onion. Or between layers of a nesting doll. The colors here were all bland neutrals, a stark contrast to the riot of colors outside.

It was almost a relief to find Champion Sileux guarding the inner doors. First, because the silence of this place was eerie and unpleasant, his own bootsteps echoing like a threat as he approached the entrance to the gateway room. Second, because Damian had expected the entire council to be waiting for him, and Sileux appeared to be very much alone.

Except, of course, for the posse of red-tinted spheres that

surrounded him. They made him look like a wizard out of a story. And not a benevolent one.

"Have you been waiting here since I escaped?" Damian asked. "I hope you had a crossword puzzle or something."

Sileux didn't smile. The corners of his mouth dragged toward his chin, in fact, giving the impression of a disappointed rabbit. He didn't speak, merely watched as Damian stepped closer. The spheres didn't so much as quiver, but Damian had no illusions about them; these were attack spheres.

Actually, no. He'd prefer to think of them as attack bubbles. Words had power, after all.

"What, no explanations?" Damian pushed. "No treatises on why you betrayed me, and what you plan to do next?"

Bruce shifted. "That would be a foolish course of action."

But it was oh, so common. "My enemies like to describe in detail why they hate me," Damian explained. "It's an unfortunate downfall. For them. I've no trouble taking full advantage."

Sileux cleared his throat with a rasping cough. "I have no personal grudge against you. But you ought to have known better than to trust."

Yes. Yes, he ought to have.

Sileux flicked his wrist, and the spheres peeled away from the door, flying at Damian's face—and his arms, his legs, his chest; all of him, really—in one synchronized movement. Like an aesthetically pleasing volley of missiles.

He ducked out of the way, but the murderous bubbles merely swerved to follow. One of them brushed his wrist, sending a jolt of pain through his arm, and it was all he could do to somersault out of their way to evade them. He had no weapons in his pockets, not even a measly shooter. If a shooter would even do anything to stop the damn things.

In a minute, they'd have him. What they'd do with him, he

didn't know, but he'd very much like to postpone the discovery process.

And then Bruce stepped between Damian and the oncoming spheres. Three of them cracked into his torso, but he didn't seem to notice as he shot his arms out and began batting at the spheres, knocking whole handfuls of the things down and away. They smashed into the floors and walls, splintering and shattering as they hit the stones. He looked like he was playing a deadly game of dodgeball, except that he was *trying* to get hit. They didn't appear to hurt him at all.

But there were too many spheres for Bruce to handle alone. The first attack thinned the group considerably, but the rest of them swerved to avoid the bot's attacks even as he changed tactics, shooting out one foot to kick at the nearest batch. His foot slammed into one, lobbing it into the far wall and forcing Sileux to duck. The rest, however, kept coming.

Damian decided to make a run for it. Not out the doors—he'd come too far for that—but around the circle, like a quick jog along the track. Maybe he could draw some of them away, throw his jacket over them and trap them, or kick them like Bruce had done. They stung, sure, but if he kept moving, then he wouldn't get overwhelmed.

He made it halfway around the circle before a dozen spheres met him head on. He waved, then turned back, surprising a second volley of spheres that were closing in on him from the other side. He threw himself to the ground before they could descend on him, sending them cracking into the other group.

Huh. That'd been mostly an accident. He'd definitely pretend it was intentional if he lived to retell the story.

When he got back to the gateway room doors, a bunch of spheres had collected around Bruce's feet, locking the bot to the ground. He was still flailing, but the spheres had learned to avoid him. Damian took shelter behind him, positioning his back to the bot so that he could see any oncoming attack. Bruce had thinned the horde, but there was still an occasional dive bomb.

"Now what?" Bruce asked.

They needed to get past those doors, that was what. As he understood it, the remaining spheres wouldn't follow them beyond that point. Sileux might—the old man was cowering in the doorway—but Damian flattered himself that he could take the old man, even without his weapons.

"I was thinking dinner, dancing, a quick stroll in the park." Damian jumped, trying to grab a sphere as it rocketed toward his face. It hit his hand, hard, but he wrapped his fingers around it, drawing the thing close. He hugged it to his chest, ignoring its struggles and the zaps of electric pain it sent roaring across his skin. "This is rather an irregular situation, don't you think?"

"Hardly. It is a routine Tuesday on your crew."

"Bruce. You're understanding sarcasm."

"I am being serious. The spheres are biting my feet. Do something."

There wasn't much to do. He didn't want to say it, but he thought they might be just a little bit screwed.

The outer doors parted in a rush, and Champion Ahnien burst into the hall, accompanied by several other council members. Ahnien held a vaguely gun-shaped thing in one hand, and a fresh platoon of spheres drifted menacingly around his head. At least these ones were clear; the red tint of Sileux's mean spheres was giving Damian a headache.

Definitely screwed, he thought.

But instead of pointing his weapon at Damian, Ahnien aimed it at Sileux. His face was flushed, his eyes flashing with anger, but his hands were steady. "Go," he said.

Damian didn't know how or why Ahnien appeared to be on his side, but he didn't need the man to tell him twice. He tugged Bruce away from the grabbing spheres—it felt like popping a stuck shoe out of a pile of mud—and together they rushed through the gateway doors, shutting them fast.

Damian squeezed through the closest two panels and stumbled into the ring of ancient tech, still failing to understand how this rusted junk could usher him back to the Parse Galaxy. The panels merely looked like dead consoles. No openings. No windows.

When he and Shannon had come here, each console had sported a line of blinking yellow lights. Now, the lights were dark. Why were the lights dark?

"I hesitate to point this out," Bruce said, "but the floor is still dry."

So it was. Perhaps that was the reason for the dead lights. "It's hardly a surprise," Damian replied. "I didn't see Shannon out there hauling water past the murder bubbles."

What would happen if Damian tried to walk through the gateway when the floor was dry? Would his entire body dehydrate, or go up in flames? Perhaps the wormhole wouldn't work at all. Or perhaps the stabilizers would fail, and, as his scientist acquaintance insisted, he would implode the universe. No big deal.

Something exploded against the door, and Damian whirled around, but it remained shut fast. It sounded like a battle out there. Was Sileux escaping? Had he gained allies?

Time, it seemed, was running out.

And then a trickle of water hit him right in the middle of the forehead.

"Bullseye."

Damian looked up to see Shannon grinning down at him from the gap in the ceiling, and he couldn't help it. He grinned right back at her. Though he also took a step back as a waterfall poured through the opening in the ceiling, filling the room with the sound of water splashing against stone. For once, he didn't mind the sound. Didn't mind it at all.

On the tech consoles, the lights flickered on, as ugly and yellow as he remembered.

"Now what?" Damian muttered.

"Now you go through the gateway, I believe," Bruce said.

How did one walk through pure titanium? Or aluminum, or whatever alien alloy they'd used to make these things?

Damian stepped forward, trying not to look as tentative as he felt, and lay a hand against the console.

And the barrier dissolved, allowing his fingertips to pass straight through it and into a cool sort of nothingness. With his hand still inside the console, Damian glanced up at the ceiling, but Shannon was no longer silhouetted in the circle. Where had she gone?

Didn't matter. He was stepping through, and he wasn't bringing her with him. Not until he'd guaranteed it was safe.

Tiny claws splashed across the floor behind them, and then Triv was scrambling up Damian's coat and onto his head. Damian found he didn't want to withdraw his attention from the gateway barrier for long enough to look at the pest. "You missed the battle, pal," he said.

Triv sniffed. "I am too important to risk."

Typical. "Bruce," Damian said, "would you care to join us?"

"Absolutely not," the bot replied.

When Damian stepped through, Bruce followed on his heels.

CHAPTER 38

SHANNON WAS TOO LATE.

She made it past the confusing jumble of council members and cracked spheres and into the gateway room just as Damian disappeared through the portal with Bruce at his side. She ran, her footsteps sloshing in the water, but by the time she made it to the portal, it was once again made of smooth metal.

She'd thought that he would wait for her.

Yes, he'd said it was a test. He'd said he couldn't stay there. But they'd come here together, hadn't they? It seemed right that they would test the portal together, too.

"He'll be back," Zahlia said, squeezing through a gap between the consoles to join Shannon in the middle of the circle. "You should come and rest. We can monitor the room."

Shannon shook her head. The minute she left this room, she'd have to start sorting through her place here. Champion Ahnien had been outside cleaning up a mess of an attack, and Champion Sileux was apparently behind bars. She didn't know who to believe, what to believe. She didn't know who to trust.

Not that she trusted Damian, exactly. Except that she knew

he meant her no harm. Perhaps that was enough for trust, in this place.

"I'll wait," she said.

An hour passed, and the portals remained disengaged. Quiet.

Another hour. Zahlia went away, returning with a chair and a hot drink. Shannon accepted the chair, but she let the drink cool in her hands without taking a sip. Zahlia stayed for a time, then went away again.

In the fifth hour, Lex wheeled into the room, and they waited together in silence. Shannon's brain buzzed with fatigue, the adrenaline long since drained from her system, leaving her to stare numbly at the gateways.

In the sixth hour, she said, "He abandoned me."

Lex didn't deny it. She just unfolded an arm out of her secret hatch and used it to pat Shannon on the leg. Shannon had never imagined that metal and plastic could be so very comforting.

Abandoned. It was reason enough to leave. Still, she stayed.

And then, in the eighth hour, a rush of heat dragged Shannon from a dreamless sleep. She opened her eyes, leaping out of her chair when sparks poured out of the console, her half-sleeping mind wondering how she might use the water on the floor to dowse a fire.

The gateway twisted open.

Shannon dashed forward, barely making it to the console in time to catch Damian as he fell out of it, with Bruce a step behind. Triv clung to the bigger bot's head, or maybe it was Mojo again; she couldn't tell.

Damian collapsed in her arms, and for a horrifying, chest-clenching moment, she thought he was going to die in them just like Jem had. She eased him to the ground, feeling for the rise and fall of his chest before daring to study his face. He was awake, blinking and looking around, but he was also bleeding; his lip was sliced through, and something had shorn through the sleeve of his jacket, leaving an angry slash that was quickly welling with blood.

"Don't worry, doll," he said. "I just stepped into a little bit of a battle by accident. I'm all right."

Was he, really? Lex was calling for help, bending over the wound on his arm. It seemed shallow enough, but he could be injured elsewhere, too.

Or maybe he'd been injured when he arrived here. Maybe he'd been in danger all along. Shannon ran her fingers under his collar, pushing the edges of his shirt aside to expose the thorn-like web of tattoos on his chest. They covered his collarbone, and the base of his neck, in a thick network of raised lines.

They weren't tattoos at all.

His skin was warm beneath her fingers, and Damian closed his eyes briefly as she touched him, his throat working soundlessly.

"Why can't you go home?" she asked softly.

"Oh, that." He touched a finger to his lip, then gave it a puzzled look, as if surprised to find he was bleeding. "It's a bit of an inconvenience, really. But Triv is slowly poisoning me."

She looked at the bot, which was still clinging to Bruce. "Poisoning you?"

He licked his lip, then cringed, as if forgetting it was covered in blood. "Not on purpose, though. I think... I believe I may need your help to stop it."

———

Thanks for reading!

Book 2, SHADOW FORCE, will be out in May 2024.

**

Who's on the 'hardened crew' Damian keeps mentioning?

Damian's story takes place within a larger universe of sci-fi adventure. He also shows up to cause trouble in the *Parse Galaxy* series :) Visit books2read.com/chaos-zone to learn more!

ALSO BY KATE SHEERAN SWED

BOOKS IN THE PARSIVERSE

The Parse Galaxy

(*Adult - Space Opera*)

Outlaw Rising (A Parse Galaxy Novella)

Chaos Zone

Bounty War

Traitor Game

Exile Sky

Battle Fringe

Empire Claim

Current Drift

Fallout Strike - Coming January 16th, 2023!

The Star Current Saga

(*Adult - Space Opera*)

Claim the Void

Shadow Force - Coming May 14, 2024!

The League of Independent Operatives

(*Adult - Superhero*)

Alter Ego

Anti-Hero

Mastermind

Nemesis

Defender

For the most up-to-date information on my books, visit KateSheeranSwed.com.

ABOUT THE AUTHOR

Kate Sheeran Swed loves hot chocolate, plastic dinosaurs, and airplane tickets. She has trekked along the Inca Trail to Macchu Picchu, hiked on the Mýrdalsjökull glacier in Iceland, and climbed the ruins of Masada to watch the sunrise over the Dead Sea. Kate currently lives in New York's capital region with her husband and two kids, plus a pair of cats who were named after movie dogs (Benji and Beethoven). She holds an MFA in Fiction from Pacific University.

You can find more of Kate's work, and pick up a free novella, at katesheeranswed.com.

facebook.com/katesheeranswed

instagram.com/katesheeranswed

youtube.com/@katesheeranswed